I0762124

DEVIL'S COAST

DEVIL'S COAST

A NOVEL

COLIN CAMPBELL

First published by Level Best Books 2025

Author Photo Credit: Colin Campbell

First edition

ISBN (paperback): 978-1-68512-902-6
ISBN (hardcover): 978-1-68512-901-9

Cover art by Level Best Designs

This book was professionally typeset on Reedsy.
Find out more at reedsy.com

For Joyce Peluso
Who continues to read me,
no matter what I throw at her

Praise for the Books by Colin Campbell

"Very real. And very good."—Lee Child

"There's nothing soft about Campbell's writing. If you enjoy your crime fiction hard-boiled, the Jim Grant series is a must read."—Bruce Robert Coffin, author of the Detective Byron series

"A cop with a sharp eye, keen mind, and a lion's heart."—Reed Farrel Coleman

"Campbell writes smart, rollercoaster tales with unstoppable forward momentum and thrilling authenticity."—Nick Petrie

"Grim and gritty and packed with action."—*Kirkus Review*

"The pages fly like the bullets, fistfights and one-liners that make this one of my favourite books of the year. Top stuff!"—Matt Hilton

"An excellent story well told. A mixture of *The Choirboys* meets Harry Bosch."—Michael Jecks

"Sets up immediately and maintains a breakneck pace throughout. Its smart structure and unrelenting suspense will please Lee Child fans."—*Library Journal Review*

"This is police procedural close-up and personal. A strong debut with enough gritty realism to make your eyes water, and a few savage laughs along the way."—Reginald Hill

"Fantastic story, fantastic characters—fantastic everything."—Chris Mooney, International Bestselling author of the Darby McCormick series

I

SEXY BITCH AND THE GOOD LOOKING MAN

"You cannot avoid the inevitable my friend."
— Eduardo Perez

Chapter One

"LOOK ON THE BRIGHT side. Fat people don't get kidnapped."

"What? Like they too big to carry off?"

"Yeah. If they've got a choice, kidnappers always go for the thin one."

Eduardo wasn't convinced. "Other side of that. If plane crashes and they have to go cannibal. Fat kid is first to go."

Ben was beginning to wish he'd never mentioned it. "I didn't say you were fat. Just carrying a few extra pounds."

Eduardo sucked his cheeks in. "I'm just short for my weight."

Ben let out a sigh. "It's not weight, it's fitness. Almost needed an ambulance at the top of the hill last week."

Eduardo huffed his disdain. "Shouldn't have built resort on hillside, then."

Ben gave him a steady look. "We're in Spain. It's all hillside."

Benjamin J Green was always amazed how naïve Eduardo Perez was about the resorts along the Costa del Sol. Considering he was Spanish you'd have thought he'd realise that this section of the coast was all steepness and hill climbs. Laguna Park was no exception. Just because it was an upmarket resort, competing with the Don Carlos Leisure Club on the next hill, didn't make the hills any less steep or the resort any easier to navigate. Especially if you were carrying a few extra pounds. The only part that was on the level was the outdoor swimming pool at the bottom of the slope.

Ben squinted as the sun rippled off the water and tapped his watch. "You'd better get ready for the darts competition."

Eduardo pushed off from the side of the lifeguard's chair and leaned against the ladder. "Rota says it's your turn."

Ben shook his head. "Rota's wrong. I covered for you last week, when you were getting over that hot date."

A look of serene reminiscence came over Eduardo's face. "Ah, la bella." He gave Ben a stern look. "She didn't think I was carrying extra pounds."

Ben returned the look. "That's because she had glasses like jam jar bottoms and a father who wouldn't let her out of his sight. She'd have fallen for a gorilla, given half a chance. I call that shooting fish in a barrel."

Eduardo looked puzzled. "I don't understand this, fish barrel shooting."

Ben smiled. "It means you couldn't miss."

Eduardo stretched his neck and flexed his shoulders. "Do not forget my friend. Our job is to provide for the guests' every need." He nodded towards the acres of tanned flesh surrounding the pool. "And you haven't provided for any of them."

Ben wouldn't be swayed. "My job is to keep the kids occupied while their parents enjoy the sun. That means teaching them tennis and darts and crazy golf."

It was Eduardo's turn to smile. "And a little bit of crazy for the mothers."

Ben wagged a finger. "I'll leave the crazy to you. I'm going up top." He turned before Eduardo could think of a parting shot and began the long climb towards the main reception.

* * *

LAGUNA PARK WAS A terraced resort 5 miles east of Marbella on the south coast of Spain. It climbed the hill between Nikki Beach Marbella and Playa Cabopino and was in direct competition with the more upmarket Don Carlos Leisure Club in the next urbanization. Don Carlos was more of a hotel complex with its tall central building standing out against the skyline. It wore its Five Star status across the top of the hotel like a taunt to its upstart neighbour.

The neighbour was more spread out, covering more ground than the twelve-storey hotel and offering more accommodation. That accommodation comprised of Spanish style villas and similarly designed apartments fanning out on either side of the sloping central walkway in terraces that started at the swimming pool and ended at the main reception block at the top of the hill. The villas and apartments were tastefully designed to blend with the local architecture, featuring distressed roof tiles, orange walls, and shapely balustrades. The ground floor had family patios, and the bedrooms had balconies overlooking the sea. The only drawback was that the south-facing resort didn't have the beautiful sunsets that the west coast enjoyed. And the slope.

Ben slogged his way up the central walkway, pacing himself so he didn't get out of breath and pausing to take a swig from the bottle of water he carried with him everywhere. He was halfway up when he noticed a family wheeling suitcases down the hill from reception, a mother and father and two young children. The suitcases were threatening to run away from them. The children *were* running away from them. One of them, a young girl, made a break for it, and the father reached out to grab her sleeve. He lunged to his left and caught her by the arm, sounding remarkably calm. "Hold up there, Little Pony."

The calmness evaporated when he realised that holding a suitcase in each hand and grabbing his daughter revealed a weakness in his strategy. He didn't have enough hands. One of the suitcases broke free and picked up speed down the slope. "Oh shit."

The daughter gasped in giggly shock. "Daddy."

The son saw an opportunity. "Lightning McQueen."

The mother saw Benjamin Green. "Watch out."

Ben saw the suitcase racing towards him and screwed the lid on his bottle of water. Ever since the advent of four-wheel suitcases, runaway luggage had become more of an issue, and building the resort on a hillside exacerbated the problem. Ben had seen this before. He waited until the suitcase was almost upon him, then raised one leg and stopped it with his foot. The flexed knee absorbed the impact. The son looked deflated, but the rest of the family was relieved. Ben wheeled the suitcase onto level ground in the nearest crosswalk. The father tried his Spanish but didn't come close to thanking him. Ben held up a hand.

"That's okay. What apartment you in?"

The mother looked at the number on the key. "F 13. Unlucky for some."

Ben stepped aside to reveal the crosswalk sign. Terrace F. "This is the Costa del Sol. There's no such thing as bad luck." He waved towards the left-hand terrace. "Third one along. Let me give you a hand."

Out of the corner of his eye, he saw the resort manager, Max Overend, watching from the reception balcony. Overend gave the faintest of nods, but he wasn't smiling. Ben turned away and started wheeling the suitcase towards F 13, thinking that what he'd just said wasn't entirely true. No matter where you were, there was always room for bad luck.

* * *

GIVING THEM A HAND didn't extend much beyond showing the family where their apartment was and helping them carry the suitcase up the three steps to the patio. The children were excited. The parents were stressed. Ben knew that would ease once they settled into the apartment. The sunshine coast had a way of relaxing even the most stressed of travellers, and the sun was already working its magic. The parents offered Ben a drink for his troubles before realizing they hadn't bought any supplies yet. They gave an apologetic laugh, and Ben waved his bottle of water. "No problem. But thanks anyway."

He stayed on the patio until the family had their luggage inside. He was about to leave when he noticed the husband take a thick envelope out of his flight bag and wedge it under the settee cushions. He recognised the travel money wallet and wondered how much they'd brought with them for the envelope to be so thick. A lot, would be his guess. Too much for a week so they were probably here for two. Even so, that was a lot of money to be carrying around so the husband was hiding it under the cushion. Ben made a mental note of where the money was hidden for when the family went to the Supermercado Laguna.

The sun was hot on the patio, reflecting off the tiled floor and orange walls.

It was another glorious day in paradise. Ben closed his eyes and turned his face up to the sun. The glare burned through his eyelids, painting the world orange and pink. He could see the spots and veins that lined the eyelids as he unscrewed the bottle with his eyes closed. There were many things it felt like he could do with his eyes closed, such as case a joint, identify a mark in a crowd, and open locked doors of any description. That's what being a master thief taught you. What it didn't teach you was how to live with the consequences.

He took a swig of water, then opened his eyes. Instead of going down the steps, he went back to the patio door and pointed at the settee. "You don't want to keep your money there." He tapped the sliding door. "Locks aren't very secure." He waved at the stairs to the bedrooms. "There's a safe in the wardrobe. Or they'll keep it for you at reception."

The father thanked him again, and Ben took one last drink, but the bottle was empty. He puffed out his cheeks. Running on empty was the story of his life. He went down the stairs and dropped it in a waste bin on his way back to the central walkway. Max Overend was waiting for him when he came out of Terrace F. "That was very touching."

Ben didn't ask how he knew.

Overend gave Ben a steady look. "Don't forget it's thieving that got you here." He lowered his voice. "And it's me knowing that makes you stay."

Chapter Two

BENJAMIN GREEN CONSIDERED why he was working as entertainment coordinator and tennis coach over a glass of fresh orange at the street café out front of Laguna Park. The cafe was an extension of the Supermercado and was in the shade at this time of day. Sitting in shadow felt like the right place to be while he contemplated his past and wondered about his future. His past was hidden more securely than the money wallet in F13, but not securely enough. His future felt like it was on hold, tied in by that very lack of security.

Ben took a drink of orange, the cool fresh taste reflecting all that was good about working at a tourist resort in the height of the summer. Sun, sea, and sex. The sex part was mainly for Eduardo, but Ben wasn't exactly celibate. There was a pretty waitress in nearby Elviria, but nothing serious. This was the Costa del Sol; nothing was serious. Apart from the reason he was here in the first place.

Ben downed the rest of his orange and considered getting another. He shook his head and pushed the glass away instead. The shake of the head wasn't about the fresh orange; it was about the past that was never all the way in the past.

* * *

THE TWO BODYGUARDS keeping watch in the hotel corridor should have warned him what kind of man he was stealing from, but at thirty-five years old, Ben was at the top of his game, and having to avoid a couple of heavies was less of an obstacle than bypassing the alarm. Hotel security was more about keeping trouble out of the rooms and away from the bar, not making the rooms impregnable. The alarm system was just a buzzer on the door. Nobody burgled the guest suites from the outside on the tenth floor. Ben burgled room 1042 from the eleventh floor.

The sky had slipped from twilight blue to full night black, but the horizon glowed orange from the city centre streetlights. Leeds was the fifth largest city in the UK and the biggest in West Yorkshire. Most of the buildings retained the carved stone and decorative features of a bygone era, but the riverside developments were all shiny metal and stained glass. The hotels were no different, except they were along the canal basin, not the River Aire. They looked modern and impressive but, in fact, were made from the same materials as the council flats and tower blocks. That meant the balcony windows could be opened with a screwdriver and a wire coat hanger.

Ben looked over the balcony rail of the room he'd paid cash for under a false name. It was a long way down, but he didn't need to worry about more than one floor. He checked that the backpack was secure and glanced at the neighbouring buildings. Most were apartments or offices. Nobody was looking this way.

A police siren sounded in the distance, and blue lights flashed somewhere across town. A train from London pulled into platform 10 at the Leeds City Railway Station. The siren went quiet. The train didn't make any noise as it slowed and stopped. A gentle breeze rattled the flagpole on the office building opposite, and a pigeon cooed in a hidden alcove. Night sounds in the city. Background music as Ben swung his legs over the railing and lowered himself to the balcony below. He concentrated on his handholds and footing, not the drop. After three short movements, he dropped onto the balcony, flexed knees softening the landing and rubber soles dampening the sound.

He remained crouched below the railing as he listened for movement inside the room. The curtains were open, and there was a desk lamp on in the corner, but the room was empty. He knew that because he'd seen the guest leave in a taxi twenty minutes ago, but he waited anyway. Once he was satisfied, he knelt beside the sliding door and swung the backpack off his shoulder. He laid out his tools and prepared to force the lock. Before he started, he tried the handle. The door slid open. It wasn't locked. That should have been his second warning.

He repacked his tools and entered the room. Room 1042 was one of the hotel's executive suites with a lounge area, mini bar, and separate bedroom. There was an en-suite shower and toilet in the bedroom and a larger bathroom near the main door. He quickly checked the bedside tables on either side of the bed and the desk drawer beside the balcony window. He wasn't expecting anything of value, but it was always best to check. The prize would be in the safe, and the safe was in a wardrobe next to the mini bar.

Ben wheeled the desk chair over to the wardrobe and sat down. The safe was standard hotel issue with a digital keypad and a solid chrome handle. He laid the backpack on the floor but didn't take his tools out. He didn't need them. Instead, he took a piece of paper from his pocket and read the code he'd bought when he booked the room upstairs. Sometimes, knowing who to bribe was more important than having burgling skills. He typed in the code, and the keypad beeped, blinked twice, then unlocked.

Ben let out a sigh and sat back in the chair. The safe was empty, apart from a single item on the top shelf. There was no jewellery and no envelope of money. He was leaning forward to examine the item when he heard the toilet flush and the bathroom door open. A voice with a Spanish accent spoke in his ear. "Wake up, sleeping beauty."

* * *

"IT'S TOO EARLY for siesta."

Ben opened his eyes as Eduardo pulled up a chair and sat down. The Spaniard put a glass of fresh orange and a can of Coca-Cola on the table, but Ben's mind was still in the hotel room. It took him a moment to come back to Laguna Park. When he did, he took a drink of orange and gave Eduardo a sideways glance. "I wasn't sleeping, just collecting my thoughts."

"Well, here's a thought. Nearly big injury again."

Ben put the glass down. "Darts?"

Eduardo nodded. "Missed the board and the backstop. Almost hit family walking down to lower deck."

Ben shifted in his seat. "Still in the far corner near the table tennis table?"

"Bad place. You need talk with manager."

Ben shrugged. "Why me? You tell him."

Eduardo tugged the ring pull, and his Cola hissed. "Because he seems have more interest in you. He listen what you say."

Ben snorted a laugh. "Any interest he's got in me doesn't extend to the darts competition."

Eduardo let the bubbles subside then took a drink. "If we stab a guest he be very interested in lawsuit against Laguna Park. We need to move the darts."

Ben took another drink and nodded his agreement. "I'll talk to him. Stabbing guests isn't in the brochure."

Eduardo drank too fast and the bubbles made him hiccup. He took a moment to settle, then smiled at Ben. "On bright side. Good news. Hen party gets here tomorrow. All women. Plenty to choose from."

Ben lowered his head, then glanced up as if looking over the top of imaginary sunglasses. "You choose. I'll stick to Elviria."

Eduardo wagged a finger. "Check contract. You're supposed to entertain more than Elviria waitress."

Ben shook his head. "You entertain. I exceed my contract more than you know."

The main entrance of Laguna Park reception opened, and Max Overend stood in the doorway. He waved at Ben. "Got a job for you tonight. Come by the office later." He went back in without waiting for a reply.

Ben's shoulders sagged, and he looked at Eduardo. "See what I mean?"

Chapter Three

THE JOB TONIGHT was not in Ben's contract but he was bound by a stronger incentive, self-preservation. He went to the resort manager's office once he'd finished the afternoon table tennis session. Table tennis wasn't as dangerous as the darts competition, but the kids seemed to like whacking the balls more than getting them in. This wasn't Wimbledon on a table it was baseball. There were Ping-Pong balls everywhere. Three ended up down the hill on the lower deck and there were half a dozen floating in the paddling pool. It took him half an hour to pack the bats and collect the balls, leaving the net on the table for private use.

He stood next to the main pool with the box under one arm, leaning against the lifeguard's chair and soaking up the sun. The sun loungers were just as full as this morning, but the guests had changed, the early risers having moved on to other activities, and the afternoon crowd having taken over.

There was still lots of naked flesh. Ben still ignored it. Eduardo leaned over from his seat at the top of the ladder, this being his hour as lifeguard and pool attendant. "You cannot avoid the inevitable, my friend."

Ben looked up at him. "I can avoid whatever I want."

Eduardo smiled. "Like they said in *Jurassic Park*. Life finds a way."

"Not everybody's life." Ben pushed off from the ladder and headed to the storage cupboard. Only one of those statements was true. This was definitely not everybody's life, but he couldn't avoid whatever he wanted. He put the table tennis kit away and started the long climb up the central walkway.

* * *

"NO."

"What do you mean, no?"

"I mean, I'm done stealing for you."

Max Overend stood up from behind the desk that he felt made him look like some kind of movie mogul, and leaned forward, both hands planted firmly on the green leather inlay. "You most certainly are not done."

Ben remained seated in front of the desk. He was used to people looking down on him. It had been happening his whole life. He'd be lying if he said it didn't bother him, but he'd managed to turn it around. People up top looking down had further to fall, and if you're at the bottom the only way is up.

Overend straightened up and examined the man sitting before him. His eyes seemed to bore into Ben, as if they could see what made him tick. He nodded once. "You think you've reached the bottom?"

Ben flinched at the twinning of his thoughts.

Overend pointed at the floor. "There is always further. And if you say no to me again, you'll see just how low you can go." He took a step to one side but kept the desk between them. "You think because you started as Robin Hood, you're not a thief like the rest of us?" He gave a sad little half smile. "Well, console yourself that you're only robbing the rich." He shrugged. "Just not giving it to the poor."

Ben didn't nod or shake his head. He kept his face blank. "Isn't there a saying about shitting on your own doorstep?"

Overend's face was anything but blank. He was positively beaming. "There's also a saying about, do bears shit in the woods? Well, you're going to shit in the woods." He moved to the window and looked at the five-star hotel on the next ridge. "And anyway, Don Carlos isn't on the doorstep."

* * *

IT WAS THE ROBIN HOOD jibe that hurt the most. No matter how Ben had turned out, and there was no denying he'd turned out to be a very capable thief, it hadn't always been that way. In the Green family, it was his brother Christian who had been the burglar and their domineering matriarch who had encouraged him. If being a single mother was a handicap, Amanda Green turned it into a club to beat the world with. The scarred weight of that club was Christian Green, five years Ben's senior. The soft underbelly was Benjamin Green, a boy with no father to guide him and a rotgut mother to drag him down. It was amazing that he turned into Robin Hood to his brother's Sheriff of Nottingham.

Bottom line was, his brother was a nasty thief.

But he was still his brother.

There was a brief moment in time when the two brothers were inseparable. Less than a year, more than six months. Something like that. Christian showed Ben how to hotwire a car, open locked doors, and climb a wall without a drainpipe. He taught him to land and roll from a high drop and how to make sure nobody could see you unless you wanted to be seen. Burglars never want to be seen, so Ben learned how to become invisible. The trouble was, he was always invisible to his mother, and that's when he started to rebel.

How it worked was like this. Christian was the burgling breadwinner. He would come home after a night breaking and entering like Santa bearing gifts. Some of those gifts were high-end expensive items, jewellery and cash. The stolen goods reeked of wealth and privilege. Nobody got hurt, and there wasn't anything that the insurance wouldn't cover. Their mother drilled that into them; "What's theirs is ours. No harm, no foul." Except as time went on some of the items were more careworn and less high-end. They didn't reek of wealth and privilege; they smelled of ordinary people scrabbling to make a living.

That's when Ben put his brother's teachings into practice. He would shadow him on his night excursions and see which houses he burgled. If it was a working-class home, Ben would go back the following night, break-in, and return the stolen goods. It began to give him a buzz. It felt better than stealing. After a while he started to test himself by breaking into the wealthy houses and returning their property as well. There was a begrudging respect from his brother. There was only anger and venom from their mother.

Ben went from being invisible to being the family pariah. Amanda Green disowned him, and his brother had to keep his distance. That was difficult since they were still living under the same roof. The atmosphere became poisonous. The soul curdled and died. Ben lived the life of a leper, shunned by his mother and untouched by the family he craved.

Then, his brother got caught and went to prison, and Ben became the burgling breadwinner. Somewhere over the years, the poison spread through his system, and he stopped being Robin Hood, becoming the thief he was always destined to be. The only thing he changed was the target demographic. No working-class people anymore, only the wealthy. When his brother died in prison, it signalled the end of the family. He stopped stealing for his mother, but he didn't stop stealing. He was too good at it, and he never got caught. Not by the police. Being caught by somebody else was why he was going to burgle the Don Carlos Leisure Club tonight. He told himself he was simply doing what bears do. Shitting in the woods.

Chapter Four

THE MAIN DRAWBACK of burgling a twelve-storey hotel in the summer is that you've got to break in while it's still daylight. If you wait until dark then the guests are back in their rooms or getting close to coming home. Unless they're all-night party people, they get in by eleven o'clock and lights out by midnight. The Don Carlos Leisure Club didn't cater for all-night party people, so Ben would have to break into the penthouse suite while they were out to dinner. Therefore, it would still be evening going on twilight. Leaving it until dark wouldn't give him enough time.

Ben couldn't help remembering his brother's training. Christian had been an accomplished burglar, teaching Ben everything he needed to know about locks, alarms, and security cameras. When it came to breaking and entering, Ben took the less-is-more approach. Yes, you could take a bag of tools and drill your way through any door or window, but most windows were vulnerable to a well-placed fulcrum, and doors were only as secure as their weakest point. Ben knew all about weakest points. Unless you were breaking into Fort Knox or The Bank of England, Ben could gain entry to most houses, apartments, or hotels. Hotels were the easiest. Whether it was the penthouse suite or not.

Ben paused under the trees along Avenida Marbella Arbolada and looked up at the side view of the five-star hotel. Don Carlos was written in big letters across the top with five silver stars lined up beneath them. The sun had set hours ago but the sky was still blue and cloudless. He checked his watch to make sure the target was deep into his dinner reservation in

Elviria, then examined the approach and climb.

Edificio Don Carlos was the central hub of a leisure complex that covered less ground than Laguna Park but packed plenty into the smaller footprint. There was an indoor spa and swimming pool next to the conference centre, and covered parking across the road to keep the sun from baking your car. The Oasis by Don Carlos was an exclusive no-children hotel on the other side of the spa. It was only four storeys high and had its own entrance. Around the back of both hotels was the leisure deck with a full-length outdoor pool and luxury sun loungers. From there, the grounds sloped down the hill towards the sea, tree-shaded gardens on the left, and the Tennis Club Don Carlos on the right. At the bottom of the hill, the Nikki Beach Club was the Don Carlos stretch of seafront. It was all very nice. Only wealthy guests need apply. There were no working classrooms here.

Ben put a foot on the low wall and refastened his shoelace. He scanned the side of the main hotel all the way to the top. The penthouse suite. For some reason, the designer had put the balconies on the east and west sides of the building, ignoring the obvious that guests preferred a sea view. The sea was to the south but that side housed the lift shaft and stairways. The north face had the scenic elevator, another missed opportunity. Ben wouldn't be using the elevators.

The deepening blue sky reflected off the mirrored balcony panels and tinted windows. Climbing up the wall would leave him exposed to anyone looking up as they walked towards Elviria. Unlike the hotel in Leeds, there was nobody for him to bribe at Don Carlos. The five-star hotel prided itself on being private and exclusive so even the unofficial resort workers grapevine couldn't help get Ben a room adjacent to the target suite. No, he'd have to do this the hard way, and there was only one place to start. The tree-shaded gardens around the back.

He finished tying his shoelace and stood up. Time to go to work.

* * *

THERE WAS A POINT halfway up when Ben thought this was the best job in the world. He felt like Tom Cruise in one of those *Mission: Impossible* films, clinging to the side of the Burj Khalifa or any of the other buildings he'd climbed before becoming Jack Reacher. Then his foot slipped and he rethought that; maybe this was the most stupid thing in the world, climbing the outside without wires or a safety net. He did the thing they always told you not to do, but that he loved. He looked down. The view was spectacular. Not quite the Burj Khalifa but pretty good for the Costa del Sol.

The approach and beginning had been simple. As with all hotels, security was only a physical presence in the lobby and bar. Although the grounds were enclosed and had closed gates and wire fences, they were only there to keep uninvited guests from accidentally cutting corners, and weren't a serious attempt to secure the premises. The drive-in gates were automatic barriers that stopped cars without the code. They didn't stop pedestrians squeezing through the gap at either end.

From there it was easy to walk around the leisure deck to the rear gardens, hiding in plain sight as he wandered the grounds. Nobody challenged him. Nobody saw anything out of the ordinary. In fact, there was hardly anyone to see him anyway. After a few minutes to establish his presence and make sure nobody was watching, he approached the southeast corner where the trees came all the way to the hotel and hauled himself up onto the first balcony.

Speed was the essence now. The best way to get caught would be to take it slowly and give passersby time to notice him. No, it was better to build up momentum and keep it going. The balconies were head height with a bit more for comfort. Standing on the mirrored panel gave him the reach to grab the next balcony and pull himself up, then it was just a case of repetition.

Reach.

Pull.

Stabilize.

Reach.

Pull.

Stabilize.

It was all going well until his Tom Cruise moment halfway up. His foot slipped on the mirrored panel, and mortality came rushing in. It didn't matter if you were on the Don Carlos or the Burj Khalifa; any fall above five storeys and you were dead. Ben grabbed the bottom of the next balcony and regained his footing. His balance settled down and he took a deep breath. Momentum stalled. He was hanging off the side of the building for the whole world to see.

"You cannot avoid the inevitable, my friend." Eduardo's voice popped into his head, and Ben was forced to smile. Eduardo might have been referring to the naked flesh and upcoming hen party, but he could just as easily have been discussing gravity. *"I can avoid whatever I want."* Ben didn't feel so confident about that now. He looked down at Avenida Marbella Arbolada to make sure nobody was looking up, then turned his attention back to the job in hand. Building momentum. He started again, reaching, pulling and stabilizing, one balcony at a time. Fifteen minutes later, he hauled himself over the final balcony and flopped to the ground. His Tom Cruise moment was over. Now it was time to become Raffles.

* * *

BEN WASN'T SURE exactly when he decided to do something foolish but he was pretty certain the Robin Hood jibe had a lot to do with it. The Tom Cruise moment might have played into his decision as well, but he must have been contemplating the foolish thing before the climb otherwise, he wouldn't have brought the foolish thing with him.

The balcony door had been easy. Like he'd said to the runaway suitcase family, the *"Locks aren't very secure."* The sliding door opened with minimal effort but he stood on the threshold for a long moment before going in. He knew what Max Overend had told him to steal and exactly where to find it. He also knew there was enough money that only taking a third of it meant the theft wouldn't be noticed straight away. That was the thing about stealing from the rich, they often didn't realise just how wealthy they really were. The thing that stuck in Ben's throat wasn't who he was stealing from but who he was giving the money to.

He found the safe where all hotels kept their safes. The Don Carlos wardrobe was better appointed than most and the clothes hanging from the coat hangers were more expensive, but the safe was standard resort quality. The digital reader glowed in the depths of the wardrobe. Ben knelt down and flexed his fingers. He didn't need to. All hotel safes have a default code so that staff could reset the safe if a guest forgot the combination. Each resort changed the manufacturer's code but it was always simple so the staff could remember it. It only took Ben five attempts to find the staff code and open the safe.

Max Overend had been right.

There was a lot of money.

Robin Hood wavered. He thought about his brother dying in prison for a widescreen TV and a DVD recorder. He thought about Eduardo and the simple things that kept him smiling. Life was full of highs and lows. If you didn't aim too high, you could avoid hitting the lows, but where was the fun in that? Ben reckoned that the Laguna Park manager's highs were pretty high. He smiled at the low he was about to bestow upon him. He looked at the money one last time, then did what he came here to do.

Chapter Five

THE SHIT DIDN'T HIT the fan until lunchtime the following day and the only reason Ben lasted that long was because he didn't sleep at Laguna Park that night. He knew Max Overend would be on the warpath, so he took himself out of the firing line by staying with his waitress in Elviria.

"What is problem, my good-looking man?" Carlita Suarez was sleepy after working a late shift at the restaurant, but she was awake enough to recognise a sea change when she saw one. "You going dump me?"

That was her default setting whenever Ben went quiet or introspective. He wasn't a moody person, but sometimes his past caught up with him, and his mind closed in. Carlita was pretty in a plain sort of way, Ben supposed in another attempt to not stand out. He didn't want the most beautiful girl on the coast, he wanted to blend in. When you're on the run, you don't advertise yourself.

"No Carlita. I'm not going to dump you."

"You sure?"

"Go to sleep."

He left her in bed and went to the kitchen. Hacienda Elviria was up the hill from the Centro Commercial and across the N-340 from the restaurant she worked at. The long, straight Avenida cut through the trees of Aventura Amazonia, but the trees couldn't hide the tall, straight edifice of the Don Carlos hotel. Even from this distance, the five stars glinted in the morning sun. Ben turned away from the window and poured himself a fresh orange.

Carlita was a lovely girl, but he sometimes wondered if he only stayed with her to give himself an excuse to not fraternize with the women around the pool. Eduardo seemed to have his priorities right, practicing the Four Fs that were probably different in Spanish. Find em, Feel em, Fuck em, Forget em had never been Ben's preferred option. He wanted something deeper, but getting involved wasn't a good idea when you were living under the constant threat of exposure and the potential need for a quick getaway. His little stunt last night made the quick getaway more of a possibility.

"Good-looking man." Carlita's voice drifted from the bedroom. "My good-looking man. Come back to bed."

Ben finished his drink, then put the empty glass in the washbasin. He didn't consider himself to be a good-looking man, but there were some benefits to hiding in plain sight. He threw one last glance at the Don Carlos and decided to take advantage of one of the Fs.

* * *

"AND YOU DIDN'T THINK that would come straight back to me?"

"It was more of a spur-of-the-moment thing."

"Not that much of a spur-of-the-moment thing that you didn't go prepared."

"I had them with me anyway."

"When you were going to burgle the penthouse suite. You had a bag full of Laguna Park advertising leaflets."

It was shit fan hitting time in Max Overend's office. Eduardo had tried to head Ben off at the pool and almost managed to divert Ben's attention by pointing out that the hen party had checked in and was looking very promising. Fourteen women all the way from America, with the bonus for Eduardo that they all spoke Spanish. From around Los Angeles or the Mexican border, he reckoned. A long journey to the Costa del Sol, and with more money than your average hen party. He used that to distract Ben before casually mentioning that Max was looking for him. "We should keep him away from sharp things."

"He's that angry, huh?"

"Good job, the darts is finished for this week."

Ben glanced at the wall where they usually set up the dartboard, then smiled at Eduardo. "I dropped off some leaflets last night. Might have a few more signing up for the next competition."

A sharp double-hand clap sounded from the retaining wall overlooking the swimming pool. Eduardo's shoulders sagged as he turned away leaving Ben to look up towards the central walkway. The resort manager looked down at his entertainment staff. "You." He didn't need to point for Ben to know who he was talking to. "My office. Now."

Overend spun on his heels and marched up the slope to the Laguna Park reception. Five minutes later, he was slapping an advertising leaflet on his desk so hard that it stung his hand. "And you didn't think that would come straight back to me?" Leaving Ben to explain exactly what he'd done instead of stealing the money.

* * *

HOW IT WENT WAS like this. Ben stared at the money in the safe for a good long time before plucking up courage to give Max Overend a great big two-fingered "Fuck you." As fuck you's go, he thought it was pretty cool, playing into his Robin Hood sensibilities while letting the target know he'd been targeted.

The Laguna Park advertising leaflets outlined all the activities available on various days of the week. They included darts, table tennis, swimming, and a tennis lesson with the club pro. The club pro was Benjamin Green. The painted tarmac court was no competition for Don Carlos Tennis' six clay courts and two hard courts, and the tennis pro wasn't really a tennis pro, but it was enough of a connection for Ben to circle Tennis on the top leaflet before leaving a stack in the safe next to the envelope of money. He closed the safe and reset the combination then, just in case the target didn't use the safe when he got back from dinner, left a trail of leaflets from the door to the wardrobe.

Satisfied that the "Fuck you" wouldn't be missed, Ben locked the balcony door, put on a bright yellow Pizza Delivery jacket from his backpack, and adjusted the baseball cap down over his eyes. He gave one last look around to make sure the room was tidy then went out the door into the corridor.

"You didn't go over the balcony?"

"No need. Once you're inside the room, you can unlock the door."

Overend didn't look convinced. "Nobody spotted you in the lobby?"

Ben shook his head. "Hotel security's about stopping non-guests getting in. If you're coming the other way, they assume you've already been checked."

"In a Pizza Delivery jacket?"

"They get deliveries all the time. If anyone remembers, all they'll be able to describe is a white male in a yellow jacket."

"Your face will be on CCTV."

Ben looked at Overend as if he were talking to a child. "Next time you install security cameras, fit them at waist height." He pointed to the ceiling. "From up there, they're always looking down. Lower your head, and they can't see under the peak."

"So, they didn't recognise you?"

"They didn't see me."

"Except you circled your name on the leaflet."

"I circled Tennis."

Overend leaned forward and stabbed a finger at the desk. "One phone call to the guy you burgled in Leeds, and you'll be circling the drain." He gave Ben a stern look. "And any man who has three guards protecting one room, you know he can make it happen."

Ben leaned back in his chair opposite the desk and let out a sigh. Maybe giving Overend a giant "Fuck you" hadn't been such a good idea, but sometimes you have to go with your instincts. In this case, his instincts hadn't been best served. He was in a hole, and he'd just dug himself a bit deeper. Payment would become due. Pointing the finger at himself as the burglar hadn't been a smart move either. "How did you explain the leaflets in the safe?"

"Publicity stunt. Internal staff at Don Carlos."

"And he believed that?"

"No sign of forced entry. Nothing taken. What else is there to believe?"

Ben pushed back from the chair and stood up. "Well, I'm glad it all worked out."

Overend stood up as well. "You are going to repay me. Double. And soon." Ben waited for the hammer to drop. The manager gave a sly little smile. "You heard about the hen party from Mexico?"

Chapter Six

THE HEN PARTY HAD two rows of sun loungers reserved by the pool, but it took a while for everyone to get into their bathing suits and make their way down from their apartments. The organizer hadn't been able to book adjoining rooms, so the fourteen women were spread across Laguna Park with apartments on Terraces B, E, and F. Most were doubled up, with one apartment sharing three beds. The bride had a villa all to herself. That was the kind of hen party you could afford when you came from a wealthy family. Michelle Cordero Belen came from a wealthy and powerful family. That's why her father had insisted there be a bodyguard amongst the group. His daughter didn't know about that. It had been explained that thirteen, the original number, was unlucky, so they invited one more for luck. The one more was trained to kill. Michelle didn't know about that either.

* * *

"OKAY. NEXT QUESTION. What is the bride's favourite colour?"

Twelve pens scratched twelve answers, some resting the sheet of paper on their sun loungers and some lying face down and using the floor. Michelle Cordero Belen wasn't writing. She knew the answers. The bride-to-be scanned her friends and wondered how the organizer came up with the names on the T-shirts they were all wearing. One had WONDER HORSE written across her chest. Another read NUMBER TWO; that was the hen party organizer. Michelle looked down at her own T-shirt. SEXY

BITCH seemed a bit strong for a girl with a Catholic upbringing, but she supposed, considering her family, there was no point getting too religious. She mentally ticked off the answer everyone was scribbling. Red.

"Number Five. What is her favourite movie?"

Michelle reckoned most would say *The Godfather* since her father was the all-powerful ruler of the family business, but her favourite was actually *When Harry Met Sally*. She had even visited Katz's Deli in Manhattan once to relive the fake orgasm scene. Without the fake orgasm, she wasn't that much of an extrovert.

"Number Six. What poster did she have in her room at college?"

Michelle almost barked a laugh at that one. Most would be writing down her favourite actor at the time, which had been question number two. The real poster had led her roommates to think she was a lesbian, but in reality, it was her quirky sense of humour and her love of tennis. The poster was iconic by the time she went to college, even though it was from the 70s; the sun-dappled photo of a female tennis player scratching her naked ass while walking across the court. No panties. Pre-yellow balls.

"Number Seven. Where did she meet her first boyfriend?"

She didn't laugh at that one. Boyfriends had always been a touchy subject in the Cordero Belen household, not so much where she met them as how they ended up. How they mainly ended up was, badly. No wonder she was twenty-eight and still single. She'd met her first boyfriend at a swimming party when she was fifteen. The family bodyguard reported it to her father, and the boy quickly disappeared. At first, she thought he'd dumped her, but later, she learned Rodrigo's family relocated to another town. With a little pressure from her father. The same thing happened with every boyfriend until she was twenty-one, by which time she had developed a mind of her own and an aversion to any interference from El Jefe, as she referred to her father. After that, El Jefe was less hands-on, but she still suspected interference in matters of the heart.

"Number Eight. How did she meet her fiancé?"

Michelle sat up and swung her legs off the sun lounger. David Martinez was a different proposition. In fact, a proposition is exactly what this marriage was going to be. The answer that the rest of the group would be writing down was the official story given out by the family: Michelle Cordero Belen met David Enrico Martinez at a summer gathering on the Spanish island of Mallorca. The truth was that arranged marriages were still prevalent among powerful families. If two powerful families wanted to cement their ties, then marriage was the perfect glue. The days of having a mind of her own were coming to an end.

Sitting with her back to the sun she tuned the rest of the questions out. All she could hear was laughter and splashing and children playing. Music came over the poolside speakers. Then, angry voices brought the world back into her bubble.

* * *

BEN SHIFTED IN HIS SEAT atop the ladder and turned towards the argument. It was his turn as poolside lifeguard, and he'd been listening to the music while trying to ignore the hen party quiz. He didn't want to know where the bride met her first boyfriend or what poster she had in her room at college. He didn't want to know anything about the woman he was going to burgle. The sun was high, the sky was blue, and the pool was full of happy families enjoying their day.

All apart from one family. Raised voices cut through the hen party quiz and dampened the atmosphere. An eight-year-old boy didn't want to join the other kids who were gathering at the Crazy Golf for Eduardo's tournament. His father wanted the boy out of the way so he could enjoy the sun, and the mother was trying to keep them both happy. The father gave her a backhand across the mouth to shut her up and turned to his son. The boy's eyes were wide with shock but he still didn't want to play golf. Ben reckoned what he really didn't want to do was leave his mother. The voices got angry. The mother looked on in silent pain as the father/son relationship broke down even more.

A son that was being ordered to do what he didn't want to do, and a parent wielding overwhelming power. It was a family dynamic that Ben could relate to, although with him, there had been no father, and it was the mother who was the demon. He'd spent many an evening arguing against the Crazy Golf but he'd always ended up doing what his mother wanted. His brother went to prison, and Ben became a master thief. It wasn't the life he'd wanted any more than the boy wanted to play golf.

The boy made a stern face but couldn't hide the tears.

The mother gave a quiet whimper.

The father wagged a finger at the boy, then growled at the mother. Families on either side of them began to move away. Anyone within earshot went quiet, and people turned to see what was causing the trouble. In the comparative silence, a lone voice rang out.

"Number Nine. What is her favourite sport?"

Ben would have put money on it not being Crazy Golf. The boy began to cry and the mother tried to console him. The father spun around and raised his hand again, but he was too slow. Ben was down the ladder in a flash and shoulder-charged the man into the pool.

"Man overboard."

He took a lifebelt from the hanger and threw it at the man. The solid floatation aid hit him on the head, and he went under the water. Ben jumped in, grabbed him in a necklock, and swam him to the side of the pool. They weren't at the deep end, so the man tried to stand up, but Ben kept his arm locked tight around his throat and leaned close. "You touch her again, and I know some nasty Spaniards who will fuck you up. Nod, if you understand?"

The man was too busy coughing up water to answer, but when Ben released the pressure, he managed a weak nod. He flopped the man up over the side and climbed out after him. "Nothing to see here. Everything's alright."

Several people were looking at him. He waved for them to get on with their holiday. Sound returned to the poolside, and the mother dashed to her husband's side. The boy joined her, and they both hugged the man who had abused them. Ben shook his head. There was no pleasing some people. By the time he climbed back up the lifeguard's chair, the incident was forgotten, and everyone went back to what they were doing.

All except one. As he settled in his seat, he felt eyes burning into him, and he looked around. One of the hen party was sitting with her back to the sun, looking up at the lifeguard. The letters on her T-shirt read, SEXY BITCH. He didn't think that was very appropriate for somebody getting married.

Chapter Seven

THE HEN PARTY CROSSED the N-340 into Elviria later that evening. It was a pleasant walk along Avenida Marbella Arbolada, past the Don Carlos Leisure Club, and across the bridge over the motorway. Traffic was heavy going into Marbella, red brake lights indicating a holdup somewhere towards Los Pinos. The hen party took up most of the San Martino Restaurante Italiano around the back of the Centro Commercial. Number Two had considered Harmon's Irish Bar or La Fondue Steak House but felt that Italian was more suited to the evening.

"Aren't there any Spanish restaurants?"

The chief bridesmaid shrugged at the bride. "Seems like there's more Italians here than in Italy. The Elviria Restaurante across the highway was fully booked. So, no. No Spanish. It's either Italian, Irish, or Chinese."

"I don't like Chinese."

The bridesmaid held her arms out to the group. "Question Seventeen. What is her favourite food?"

Most of them answered in chorus. "Italian."

The bridesmaid nodded at the bride. "So here we are."

It was a lovely evening, the sun low in the clear blue sky as it dipped towards the horizon. The plaza was in shade but it was a long way from being dark, the warm evening air complementing the scent from the jasmine and flower borders. The maître d' ushered the group to outside tables that had been pushed together to form an L shape beneath the trees. Café bars and restaurants surrounded the terracotta-tiled square, the Irish Bar already livening up despite it still being quite early. The Ros Ka Sports Bar was showing a soccer match to the handful of patrons. The San Martino simply played piped music through discreet speakers hidden among the trees.

Menus were distributed. Drinks were served. The hen party settled into quiet contemplation as they chose their Antipasti, Primi, and Secondi dishes. Some ordered Contorni, but most agreed to share sides and vegetables. Dolci wouldn't be ordered until everyone had finished. Michelle didn't think she'd be able to eat dessert after a menu this size.

Somewhere across the plaza, a street performer played the accordion, the music mingling with the quiet, easy-listening tunes from the speakers. The musician moved from table to table at the other restaurants, keeping his distance from the more exclusive establishments. The accordionist kept his head down while his assistant, possibly his daughter, held an upturned hat out for donations. Despite the many rejections, they both kept smiling and nodding their heads. Michelle wondered what strength it must take to keep smiling through life's travails. Maybe she should ask how they did it because her biggest travail was just around the corner.

A gentle hand rested on her shoulder, and she looked at the friend who had organized this trip. Number Two had a sad little smile on her face. "You could always run away."

They both turned to look at Number Fourteen, the latecomer they were both growing suspicious of. The woman was sitting at the end of the table perusing the menu, but her focus didn't seem to be entirely in front of her. Michelle spoke softly so only the two friends could hear. "Where could I go that El Jefe wouldn't find me? Wedded bliss will go ahead. Even without the bliss."

Number Two held her menu up to block prying eyes and winked at her friend. "Let me see what I can do." She gave a little nod. "You deserve a little bliss before you get railroaded."

Michelle tilted her head and raised an eyebrow. "What did you do? They got special calzone?"

Number Two lowered the menu. "Eat. I'll tell you later."

* * *

CHAPTER SEVEN

"ABSOLUTELY NO FUCKING WAY."

"No fucking way is all the choice you have." Max Overend moved away from the view of the Don Carlos Hotel. "Unless you want the shit you pulled on the other tenth floor to revisit the shit you pulled on this tenth floor."

"The Don Carlos was the twelfth floor."

Overend waved the discrepancy aside. "If your Leeds target catches up with you." He made a high-diving motion with one hand and whistled all the way down. "See which floor he throws you out of."

Ben wasn't sitting in front of the desk this time; he was standing with his back to the office door. Dance music came from the reception bar, and he could hear children running and laughing along the corridor. This early in the evening, it was Children's Party Night. The shock he'd just got from Overend was enough to kill the party atmosphere.

"I thought you wanted me to repay you?"

"You will repay me."

"Double."

"Yes, double."

Ben shook his head. "Not like this. I'm a thief, not a..."

Overend moved behind his desk but didn't sit down. "This is punishment as well as payment. I'll allow a bit of discount in order to ramp up the punishment. You aren't going to repay me doing what you like doing. You're going to hate every minute of it."

Ben thought about the SEXY BITCH at the poolside and couldn't come up with a suitable retort. He wondered if Eduardo was free tonight.

* * *

IT TOOK ALMOST TWO HOURS for the hen party to get through Antipasti, Primi, and Secondi. Dolci was only ordered by three of them, the rest foregoing dessert for strong black coffee instead. There had been plenty of wine, and some of the women were getting frisky. Two women wolf-whistled at the waiter from next door, La Fondue Steak House's maître d' giving them a sideways look as he seated a family that included two young children.

"What's his problem?"

"He can be my problem anytime he wants."

Several of the hen party giggled. Three of them laughed out loud. Michelle turned in her seat and looked out across the plaza, sipping iced water to cleanse her palate after the coffee. The accordion played outside the sports bar, and the daughter collected donations. Michelle wondered how it was possible to feel so alone among so many people, many of whom were her friends.

An old man came through the passage from the Super Sol around the back of San Martino Restaurante Italiano. He looked very old, hunched over his walking stick as if it were the only thing keeping him upright. He wore thick glasses and a straw trilby but didn't have a shopping bag. His tweed jacket and creased trousers gave him the air of an elderly eccentric, a country gent who had seen better times. He crossed the road through the car park and stood opposite the plaza with its bars and restaurants. Music played, and people laughed. There was constant chatter and clinking of glasses, but the man stood alone. He looked to his left and then to his right as if he was waiting for somebody.

The accordionist struck up a jaunty tune.

Michelle looked at the sad-eyed old man.

Then the old man transformed into somebody different. Age fell away as he raised the walking stick and tucked the curved end under his chin as if playing the fiddle. He mimed to the accordion and danced a little jig, twirling around until he faced the plaza again. His face lit up, but his eyes were still sad. Nobody was watching apart from Michelle. He did one last twirl, then lowered the walking stick and became an old man again. He glanced to his left and to his right, but whoever he was waiting for never came. He walked through the car park and disappeared.

The sound of chatter and clinking glasses rushed back into the void, but Michelle's eyes followed the old man until he was gone. Now, *there* was somebody who was truly alone. She turned back to the hen party and refilled her glass of water. The ice had almost melted and she held the pitcher up for the waiter to refill. Evening had turned into night, and the bars and restaurants were getting into full swing. The gentle hand rested on her shoulder again. "There's no cheering you up tonight, is there?"

Michelle smiled at the friend who didn't know what it was like to be forced into marriage simply to merge the family business. It wasn't her fault. At least she would still be her friend. "You cheer me up." She waved a hand to include the hen party, Elviria, and Spain in general. "Thanks for doing this."

Number Two wagged a finger. "Oh no, you don't. You aren't getting out of this by pretending to be nice. We've paid for a big finish to put a full-body smile on your face." She leaned closer and told the bride what her present was.

Michelle's eyes widened in shock. "Absolutely no fucking way."

Chapter Eight

VILLA DEL SOL WAS ONE of three detached villas up the hillside at the western edge of Laguna Park. They were so exclusive that they had private entrances and weren't accessed via Terrace A, or B, or any of the other Terraces. This was the expensive side of the resort, each villa named after the sun the sea or the sand. Michelle Cordero Belen's villa was named after the sun.

The rest of the hen party left her on the central walkway as they drifted along Terraces B, E, and F to their apartments. Number Two was the last to go. She glanced up the slope to the resort manager's office, then gave Michelle a hug. She stepped back and held her friend at arm's length. Neither spoke for a long moment until Number Two broke the silence. "Think of him as Richard Gere in *American Gigolo*."

Michelle shivered. "More like *American Psycho*."

Number Two shook her head. "That was Christian Bale. No comparison."

"It's still sex for hire."

"It's sex. Settle for that."

"I don't want sex."

"Everybody wants sex."

Michelle let out a sigh. Her friend was right; everybody wanted sex, just not like this. She wanted to be wooed not, slam-bang, thank-you-mammed. She wanted a little romance, something that was sadly lacking in the run-up to the business merger wedding. She looked at the woman who had organized fourteen flights to the Costa del Sol and fourteen lots of accommodation. She had printed the T-shirts and written the quiz. It seemed she had also organized a collection and paid for *American Gigolo*; the least Michelle could do was show a little gratitude.

"How much did he cost?"

"A lot."

Michelle tried not to sound resentful. "So, he's a professional then."

"He'd better be." Number Two gave Michelle another hug, then let her go. "Look at it this way. When Harry met Sally, they didn't like each other."

Michelle laughed. It was her first smile of the night. "But was he right? Can a man and a woman be friends without sex coming into it?"

Number Two took a step back, then turned away. She spoke over her shoulder from the entrance of Terrace E. "You aren't going to be friends, so just enjoy Katz's Deli."

That seemed to be her final word, so Michelle waved goodnight, then skirted the poolside towards her villa. At least the moonlight glinting off the water felt romantic.

* * *

BEN FELT HIS STOMACH clenched as he stood in the shadows beyond the swimming pool. He'd considered getting Eduardo to take his place but knew that Max Overend would be monitoring. Eduardo might be Casanova to Ben's Robin Hood, but they weren't twins, and one of them was Spanish. The Sexy Bitch hadn't paid for Spanish. He watched her walk along the opposite side of the pool and felt his stomach clamp again.

How do I keep getting into this shit? He knew the answer to that. He kept getting into this shit because he came from a shit family with shit ideals and zero morals. Maybe if he'd had a father figure growing up, he might have grown up different, but having the mother from hell and a brother already on his way meant his only role models came from movies on TV. He couldn't remember any of them getting into a situation like this.

For the second time in two days, he considered upping sticks and making a run for it. Working at Laguna Park had its benefits, but it wasn't his life's ambition, showing kids how to play tennis while getting a tan by the pool.

Eduardo was a good companion and he liked Carlita, but neither of them was irreplaceable if push came to shove. Like Robert De Niro said, "Don't let yourself get attached to anything you are not willing to walk out on in thirty seconds flat if you feel the heat around the corner." Well, the heat was coming around the corner. If the guy in Leeds found out where Ben was, there'd be no lengths he wouldn't go to get back what was his.

He closed his eyes for a moment and thought about the long climb down from the tenth-floor balcony. Almost getting caught by the guard coming out of the toilet gave him no time to tidy up, so he snatched the package and went out through the sliding door. There wasn't time to clamber back up to his room; dangling legs would have been a dead giveaway, so he had climbed all the way down to the ground floor. Once he found out who he'd been stealing from he knew it was time to get out of Dodge. It took longer than thirty seconds, but he was out of the country in less than a week. The question was, was he willing to walk out on Carlita and Eduardo in thirty seconds flat? Knowing what the man from Leeds would do to him, the answer was yes. But would the man from Leeds find out where Ben was, if Ben did what Max Overend wanted him to do? The answer to that was less certain.

The Sexy Bitch followed the path from the pool towards the executive villas. Ben watched her with mixed feelings. She was very attractive, but the T-shirt put him off. Plus, anyone who was willing to hire a gigolo on her hen night wasn't somebody he felt an affinity with. He gave himself a metaphorical slap on the wrist. Men had been doing that sort of thing for years, why should a woman be any different? But the rules were different for women. They shouldn't be, but they were.

He stood by the pool for a while longer, giving the bride time to reach her villa and get changed. Would she get changed? Would she shower and freshen up? He didn't know how this sort of thing worked. Should he knock on the door and drop his trousers? Was he booked by the hour or for the night? Overend hadn't been specific. He guessed it was the customer's choice. He hoped she had a short attention span or a highly sensitive G-spot.

The moon looked cold and heartless as it glinted off the water. He circled the pool and followed the Sexy Bitch up the hill.

Chapter Nine

THE KNOCK ON THE DOOR caught her by surprise. Even though she was expecting him, Michelle wasn't prepared for the sharp intake of breath or the increased heart rate. It wasn't excitement it was apprehension. She couldn't believe her best friend had got her into this mess. For a moment she considered pretending she wasn't in but knew she wouldn't be able to explain that in the morning.

The knock was quiet and respectful, almost shy. She supposed that was to not disturb the neighbours. This was the exclusive side of the resort, after all. She looked around the living room and was thankful that this was a duplex apartment with the bedroom upstairs. At least she wasn't going to open the door with the bed glaring at them from the corner of the room.

The knock sounded again, a little more insistent this time. She took a deep breath and crossed the room.

* * *

BEN KNOCKED FOR A second time and stepped back. The sky was dark with just a hint of light on the horizon, the last vestiges of daylight clinging to the bottom of clouds that always drifted in at night. Palm trees stood out against the dying light. Occasional streetlamps picked out the Avenida around the back of Laguna Park, and pathway lights dotted the walkway and terraces. The other two villas were close enough to see but far enough for privacy. Standing on the doorstep he wanted more than privacy, he wanted the ground to open up and swallow him.

He heard movement inside Villa del Sol and held his breath, as if making no noise would negate his knocking on the door. His heart was racing, and he tried to calm it down, changing from holding his breath to taking long, deep breaths, in through the nose and out through the mouth. It was a good relaxation technique. He'd read that that Yorkshire cop in America used it all the time before going into action. This felt like he was going into action.

A shadow moved behind the door and there was more noise as a key turned in the lock. There was a pause. The door didn't open. The handle didn't turn. Ben took one last breath but didn't breathe out. The moment stretched until it felt awkward. Maybe she'd changed her mind. That was fine as long as she didn't ask for a refund. Max Overend wasn't in a refund giving mood.

The shadow moved away from the door, and Ben let out his breath. Crisis averted. There was a clattering noise inside the villa, then the shadow came back, and the door opened.

* * *

TWO PAIRS OF EYES blinked, then stayed open. Two sets of lungs held their breath. A man and a woman stood on either side of the doorway, and neither of them knew what to say. Michelle's nerves were still jangling from the noise of dropping her keys in the fruit bowl. Ben's nerves were just jangling. He tried not to look the Sexy Bitch up and down, but his eyes couldn't help taking in her sumptuous curves, slim waist and steady eyes. Michelle didn't look him up and down because the obvious thing to look at stood out in the gloom.

"I didn't order pizza."

Ben looked down at the bright yellow Pizza Delivery jacket that he'd forgotten he was wearing. "Ah, yes. Sorry. It was getting a bit chilly."

Michelle noticed sweat beading on his brow, the evening being as warm as every evening at the height of the season. Ben noticed it, too, and wiped the sweat away, feeling even more awkward than when he'd knocked on the door. "I could go get one if you're hungry."

"You think I want pizza?" She cringed as soon as she said it.

Ben nearly repeated what he'd once heard about sex being like pizza, there was no such thing as bad pizza, but caught himself just in time. He saw something flicker behind the Sexy Bitch's eyes that might have been embarrassment. She didn't blush but her eyes were a long way from feeling comfortable. They still stood opposite each other, him on the outside and her on the threshold.

Ben swallowed to moisten his dry mouth. "You've already eaten?" He looked down at his feet, avoiding her eyes. "Stupid question. Look at the time. Of course, you've eaten."

Michelle looked out past Ben and checked the sky, just for something to do. She looked down at her feet, then glanced at the keys in the fruit bowl. She didn't know what to do with her hands or where to look, so she forced herself to look him in the eyes. "How does this work?"

Ben let out a sigh. "I was hoping you'd tell me."

"You don't know?"

Ben shrugged. "I feel like that kid asking Bruce Willis about the limo service because he usually drove a cab."

"You like *Die Hard?*"

"Everybody likes *Die Hard.*"

Michelle relaxed slightly. "I prefer *When Harry Met Sally.*"

Ben tried for light and funny but cringed as soon as he said it. "It's a good job we're not friends then. Since a man and a woman can't be friends without sex coming into it."

Michelle tensed. "Yes. About that."

Chapter Ten

IF THIS WAS A romantic comedy this is the part where opposites attract before doing something that tears them apart. But this wasn't *When Harry Met Sally*, this was a woman whose best friend had hired a gigolo and a man who'd been forced into being that gigolo. She was from a wealthy family in Mexico and he was from a broken home in Yorkshire. They were the very epitome of opposite, but they definitely didn't attract.

No, this wasn't a romantic comedy. It wasn't boy meets girl, boy loses girl, boy gets girl back, it was boy avoids being thrown off a tenth-floor balcony and girl is forced into an arranged marriage. In that respect, they had more in common than they thought, they just didn't know it yet. So, it started with an awkward silence then a tactical discussion. Over orange juice.

* * *

"LOOK, I DON'T WANT to hurt your feelings but this wasn't my idea."

"It's your hen night."

"Doesn't mean I want to sleep with you."

"Doesn't mean I want to sleep with you either."

"You're being paid. You'll do as you're told."

Michelle was embarrassed at her forthrightness. She'd always been headstrong but it came to the fore when dealing with men. She reckoned that was due to having a father who tried to micromanage her life and tell her what she could and couldn't do. Bottom line was, if she were told one thing, she'd do the opposite. That wasn't a good combination with a reluctant gigolo.

The gigolo didn't look as if she'd hurt his feelings. He threw up a sarcastic salute, the American way not British. A casual flick of the wrist not full military. "Waiting to be told, ma'am."

Michelle felt anger flush her cheeks and struggled to think of something for him to do. "Pour me a fresh orange. Ice, no lemon."

Ben closed the door as he stepped into the room. "Shaken not stirred?"

She gave him a hard stare. "Straight not sarcastic."

Ben went to the kitchenette and opened the fridge. The layout was the same in all the apartments, just more luxurious in the villas. The drinking glasses were in a cupboard to his right. He took out a tall, heavy-bottomed glass, then turned to the bride-to-be. He held up a second glass and raised his eyebrows. The woman's expression softened and she gave an almost imperceptible nod. Ben dropped ice into both glasses and poured fresh orange juice from the carton.

The glasses clinked but the drinks didn't break the ice. The trouble was that Michelle didn't want to explain about the arranged marriage and Ben didn't want to tell her he was a thief living under a cloud. They both had reasons for being in the situation they were in but those reasons were separate and exclusive. This was the bride's party though, so Ben handed her the glass. "Well, Sally. You've met Harry. Now what?"

The soft expression disappeared. "We're not going to be friends."

Ben shrugged. "We're not going to have sex either." He raised his glass. "So, bottoms up."

Michelle didn't raise her glass, unsure if he was being facetious. She sat on the settee and took a cold refreshing drink, avoiding the gigolo's eyes. Ben took a drink as well and could feel the embarrassment coming off the bride in waves. He glanced at the woman who didn't seem like a Sexy Bitch and felt sorry for placing her in this awkward situation. He couldn't leave too soon, or Max Overend would have his head, but he felt he should offer. "I'll drink up and go if you like."

The woman's head jerked toward him. "You can't go yet."

Ben looked at her. "You paid me. You can do what you want."

"I didn't pay you."

"I am being paid though. So, you're the boss."

The woman looked uncertain what to do. She took another drink to cover her indecision. Ben did the same. The moment stretched until the silence felt uncomfortable. Michelle made up her mind. "I didn't pay you, but I don't want to embarrass the people that did. If you go too soon it could be awkward tomorrow."

Ben thought about the tenth-floor high-dive. "Awkward for me too."

Michelle looked at him. "For your reputation?"

Ben shook his head. "I don't have a reputation."

She indicated his yellow jacket. "You're not a regular pizza delivery."

Ben shrugged. "I'm not a regular gigolo either."

"So, what are you a regular?"

Ben still wasn't ready to explain. "I don't even tell my friends."

Michelle put her glass on the coffee table. "We're not going to be friends."

Chapter Eleven

"A THIEF?"

"Burglary mainly."

"Are you any good?"

That wasn't a question he was ready to answer. The police had never caught him, and his name didn't appear on any criminal databases, so he supposed that made him pretty good. He could get into practically any building, locked, alarmed, or otherwise protected, so he supposed that made him even better. But he was hiding in plain sight at a holiday resort where the manager held his life in the palm of his hand and could crush it with one phone call. That definitely brought him down a peg or two from good.

"I have my days."

"But now you're a gigolo."

"I'm not a gigolo."

Michelle tilted her head. "You're not a pizza delivery guy either, but you wear a pizza delivery jacket."

Ben shrugged. "They don't do Part Time Gigolo jackets."

* * *

IT WAS ALMOST ONE in the morning, but it didn't feel late. They'd been dancing around what to do for almost an hour, drinking two glasses of fresh orange and a Pepsi each. Neither of them felt like drinking anything stronger. Both wanted to keep their wits about them. The last of the late-night revelers had made their way home half an hour ago, the laughter and raised voices only interrupted by a crashing waste bin on the main walkway. Nobody made a noise coming towards the villas. People who could afford to stay at this end of Laguna Park were inherently quieter. Much more respectable types. Apart from those hiring gigolos for late-night sex. There was no late-night sex at Villa del Sol.

Ben had taken the yellow Pizza Delivery jacket off and was sitting at one end of the settee. Michelle was still wearing the Sexy Bitch T-shirt at the other end of the settee. There were no other chairs in the living room, so they couldn't sit any further apart. They were each backed into their corner with their knees together and feet drawn up to the base of the settee. They looked like Quakers at Sunday meeting, apart from the Sexy Bitch lettering.

"And you've got to do what this guy says?"

Ben stifled a burp from drinking Pepsi too fast. "He's my boss."

"He's resort manager. But that's not why, is it?"

Ben had kept it simple when explaining why he was moonlighting as a gigolo tonight. He'd told the bride he was a thief back in England but not why he was hiding out in the south of Spain. There was no point mentioning the angry man in Leeds or the potential for high diving. He did mention breaking into the penthouse suite at Don Carlos and leaving advertising leaflets for Laguna Park, but played it like a stunt gone wrong and the reason why Max Overend was pissed off at him. "He could make life awkward."

"There's that word again. Awkward. Why can't life be simple?"

Ben saw the opportunity to turn this around. "You're getting married. That should be fairly simple."

Michelle gave him a hard stare. "*Die Hard* is simple. Harry meeting Sally is anything but."

Ben wasn't going to give up that easy. "You mean your eyes didn't meet across a crowded room, and the heavenly choir began to sing."

Michelle's stare didn't soften. "Are you always this facetious?"

"I just thought getting married was a love-at-first-sight kind of thing."

"You've never been married, have you?"

"Have you?"

"That's not the point."

"What is the point?"

Michelle took a sip of Pepsi, but her drink was empty, so she toyed with the glass while she considered, what was the point? The answer she came up with was, *I have no idea.* She stopped playing with the empty glass and pushed it across the coffee table. She took a deep breath and sat up straight. "There are as many reasons for getting married as there are for hiding at a holiday resort."

Ben puffed out his cheeks. "Things are complicated, I'll give you that."

Michelle nodded absent-mindedly. "Complicated isn't the half of it. Give it six months, and the heat will be off for you. You'll be able to go back to your normal life. Getting married, that changes everything. There's no going back from that."

Ben looked at the woman in the Sexy Bitch T-shirt. "Is that why your friends hired a gigolo for one last night of freedom?"

Michelle snapped back to the hard stare. "That's why I don't want a smart-ass sticking his nose in where it doesn't belong."

Ben was startled by the ferocity of her tone. He held his hands up in surrender but didn't speak. Michelle looked at her watch, then tapped the face. "Half past one. That's long enough." She nodded at the front door. "Time to leave."

Ben put his glass on the table and stood up. Being dismissed like the hired help rankled even though he didn't want to be here. He was also beginning to feel a bit sorry for the bride, who obviously didn't want to be a bride.

The bride raised her voice. "Go."

Sympathy evaporated. Ben picked up the yellow Pizza Delivery jacket and opened the door. He turned back to look at the woman on the settee. She pointedly avoided meeting his eyes, and he couldn't think of any reason to stay. The door clicked quietly as he stepped onto the patio.

* * *

HE WAS HALFWAY TO the swimming pool when his spider senses began to tingle. The night was dark and still, stars twinkling between gaps in the clouds. There was no breeze to rustle the leaves but *something* rustled the leaves.

A stone rattled on the concrete path, and he turned towards the sound. It was the classic decoy manoeuvre. As soon as he turned to his left, a dark figure darted out of the bushes on his right. Strong hands grabbed one arm and twisted it up his back; then one hand clamped his mouth so he couldn't call out.

"You just made the biggest mistake of your life."

The voice was deep and husky but unmistakably female. The strength and violence were distinctly unfeminine. Ben wasn't sure which mistake she was referring to because he'd made so many, but his mind came to one conclusion: *he's found me.* His second thought was, *Max Overend, you bastard.* The resort manager had obviously grassed him up to the man in Leeds, and now the man in Leeds had sent this female ninja. The female ninja leaned close and spoke directly into his ear.

"If you make a sound, I will break your arm. Nod if you understand."

Ben nodded as best he could with the hand clamped over his mouth. The woman slowly removed the hand, ready to clamp his mouth again if Ben called out. He didn't, so the hand was moved to his shoulder to add leverage to the arm being twisted up his back. The pain hovered on the edge of broken bones.

"You will not visit the bride again."

Ben's mind went blank. What did the man in Leeds have to do with a bride from Mexico? Then, he quickly re-evaluated the situation. This wasn't about Max Overend ratting him out it was a female ninja bodyguard situation. His voice wouldn't come at first, his throat dry and sore from the shock. He moistened his lips and tried again. "I'm just the entertainment staff."

The ninja woman applied pressure to Ben's arm, and it twisted further up his back. Ben groaned at the pain. The woman stayed close to his ear. "You are not to entertain the bride again."

"Okay, okay."

The pressure eased, but the woman did not. "I will break your arm as a warning. If you do not heed that warning." She paused to let the first part sink in, then lowered her voice. "I will kill you."

Ben could only repeat himself. "Okay, okay."

The ninja woman twisted Ben's arm up his back again and stopped at the point of breaking it. "Do I need to break your arm?"

Ben shook his head. He couldn't speak through the pain.

The woman did. "Stick to teaching Ping-Pong."

Ben knew he shouldn't, but couldn't help himself. "I teach tennis. Eduardo does the Ping-Pong."

The arm twisted all the way up his back, and he screamed out in pain.

Chapter Twelve

BEN WOKE UP THE next morning to an aching shoulder and a raging argument. The shoulder he could live with because it meant the ninja woman hadn't broken his arm. The argument felt like something was irredeemably broken.

"And you expect me to believe that?"

"It's the truth. Honest."

Ben tried to ignore the fact that every time somebody said "honest" to him, it was followed by a lie. Or preceded by a lie. Either way, it was a word that usually strayed a long way from the truth. As it was, he knew which truth Carlita would least like to hear, so he'd skirted them both. He hadn't told her that the previous evening he had broken into a penthouse suite and opened the safe, and he didn't tell her that that burglary had forced him into becoming a gigolo for the night, leading to him coming home late and cradling his arm.

"I had to work late. Ask Max."

The excuse sounded lame even as he said it. He remembered his brother using a similar line whenever the police came around. The police hadn't believed it then and Carlita obviously didn't believe it now. Being born into a family of thieves and liars did nothing for his credibility and even less for his self-esteem. If low self-esteem was a glass-half-empty scenario, then Ben's glass was not only empty but broken. Like this relationship.

Carlita stomped around the kitchen, cleaning last night's supper things while looking out across Elviria. Ben considered putting his arms around her and trying to make things right, but one arm ached, and he thought she was beyond consoling anyway. It would take more than flowers and a bottle of wine to fix this, and he wasn't sure how much he wanted to fix it. That was the problem right there, his inability to commit to a lasting relationship, another side effect of living in the Green household. How could you commit when half your family died in prison, and the other half blamed you for it?

"I've got to go."

That was the nearest thing to the truth he'd said all morning. He wasn't due to start lifeguard duties until midday, having swapped the morning shift with Eduardo, but he had a bone to pick with the bride who didn't want to be a bride. Namely, which one of the hen party was the ninja bodyguard woman from last night?

He kissed Carlita on the back of the head and felt her body stiffen. She didn't respond. He stepped back and looked around the apartment he had never felt truly at home in. The sigh was partly one of resignation, but mostly a sigh of relief. He went out of the door and didn't look back.

* * *

"I TOLD YOU. It is not good restrict yourself to one in a sea of plenty."

Eduardo hadn't needed Ben to tell him that things weren't good back home, the Spaniard could see it from a mile away. Ben hadn't mentioned his night as a gigolo or the reason he was standing next to the lifeguard's chair, even though it was Eduardo's shift at the poolside. Of the acres of naked flesh on the sun loungers, there was only one group Ben was interested in.

"Just because there's plenty of fish doesn't mean I'm fishing."

Eduardo smiled down from his perch atop the chair. "Not fishing, barrel shooting. You said it yourself."

Ben kept his eyes on the hen party. "I'm not shooting barrels either."

Eduardo noticed where Ben was looking. "Then you should keep your eyes off the barrel, my friend. Those are my fish."

Ben looked up at the Spaniard and shook the ladder. Eduardo grabbed the sides of the chair and gave him a stern look. Ben nodded towards the poolside bar. "You fancy a cold one?"

"You are a cold one. What you need is warming up."

"Is that a yes or a no?"

"Yes. Coca, no ice."

Ben reached up and pinched the muffin top bulging over the side of Eduardo's shorts. "Diet Coke?"

Eduardo slapped Ben's hand away. "A woman needs something to hold on to when she rides the tiger."

Ben laughed. "Two Cokes it is then."

He went the long way around the pool to the makeshift bar in the shade of the restaurant. Ingrid was already popping the top off two Coca Colas, the part time Swede knowing exactly what these two drank when they worked the pool. Ben wasn't watching Ingrid; he was scanning the hen party as they stripped off their T-shirts and lotioned up. The Sexy Bitch was at the far end, a little apart from the rest. The other T-shirts read Love Bunny, Unemployed Lover, and All You Need Is.

Ben stopped in midstride as he rounded the corner. At the opposite end of the second tier, a hard-faced woman kept her T-shirt on. She looked pale and drawn and didn't seem to be enjoying the sun. It was the T-shirt that caught his eye. He couldn't believe she was being so obvious. He read the logo again, NINJA BITCH, and felt a shiver run down his spine.

* * *

"WE NEED TO TALK."

"No, we don't."

"About last night."

"Last night was farewell gigolo."

"Not the gigolo part. The ninja bitch who nearly broke my arm."

It had taken over an hour for Ben to get Michelle Cordero Belen on her own. He had to wait until she'd finished three bottles of water and a lemonade before she finally split from the hen party and headed for the poolside changing rooms. Ben cornered her between the vending machine and a pile of spare sun loungers. Out of the sun and away from prying eyes.

"I can't believe she's wearing Ninja Bitch on her T-shirt."

The bride snorted a laugh. "The Ninja Bitch is my third cousin, Maria. We gave her that T-shirt because she is timid as a mouse."

Ben considered the pale-skinned woman with the hard face and thought she looked anything but timid as a mouse. She was still more of a suspect than the girl in the Love Bunny T-shirt.

"Well, somebody jumped me on the way back from your villa. And she was very insistent."

The bride didn't laugh this time. "Insistent how?"

Ben checked that nobody was listening, then leaned closer. "Insistent like, twisting my arm up my back."

The bride's expression became blank while she weighed up all the options and came up with a credible counterargument. "You broke into the penthouse suite at Don Carlos and pissed off your manager. That's two people who want to break your arm right there."

Ben shook his head. "It's not the arm breaking. It's what she said."

The bride raised her eyebrows but kept quiet. The silent question hung in the air until Ben answered. "She said, 'I will break your arm as a warning. If you do not heed that warning. I will kill you.'"

"But she didn't break your arm."

"She came pretty close."

"Not much of a warning then."

"Enough to take it seriously."

A faint smile played across the bride's lips. "And you think my timid mouse cousin did that to you?"

"Timid on the outside doesn't mean timid on the inside."

Again, the faint smile. "Like gigolo on the outside hides burglar on the inside."

Ben was getting tired of going in circles. "This wasn't about being a burglar."

"And you know this, how?"

"Because she told me, that's how."

"She said it wasn't about Don Carlos?"

"She said, 'You are not to entertain the bride again.'"

Ben thought he saw something flicker behind her eyes, the faintest look of worry, but then it was gone. She put on a brave face and tried to make light of the situation.

"You did not entertain me."

"She doesn't know that."

The light went out of the bride's eyes as she lowered her head. When she looked up again, the determination returned.

"Meet me in Cabopino. This afternoon. Four o'clock."

Chapter Thirteen

MICHELLE SPENT THE REST of the morning, alternating between anger and denial. The bright colours around the poolside and the heat from the sun should have painted a picture of warmth and tranquility, but her mind was racing, and it wasn't racing anywhere good.

Her first thought was that her father would never stoop so low, but then she remembered what line of business he was in and knew he had stooped much lower and much harder. But not with his daughter, surely? Again, the denial, quickly followed by the anger. He had interfered with her boyfriends in the past, why would he stop now? Especially with so much at stake with this marriage of two families. No, this was exactly the kind of shit her father would pull. And that made her angry. So, Cabopino. Now all she had to do was shake off the ninja bitch bodyguard.

* * *

CABOPINO WAS A SUN-DRENCHED harbour two miles east of Laguna Park, accessed on foot through Dunas de Artola Cabopino, the sand dunes that backed onto the nudist beach and family play areas. It was small and intimate and the perfect place for a romantic meeting. This wasn't a romantic meeting; it was a misdirection. Michelle kept that to herself, not even telling Number Two. In fact, she enlisted the help of the party organizer without the bridesmaid knowing she was helping. The main thing about misdirection is to have everyone looking one way while you go the other. Cabopino was two miles east, so Michelle had the hen party go five miles west.

"Marbella? Are you sure?"

Michelle smiled at her friend, feeling a twinge of guilt as they lay at the poolside. "Old Town. Up near the castle. It will be a great day out."

Number Two nodded and swung her legs off the sun lounger. "Okay. I'll book a minibus at reception."

She stood up and addressed the others. "Excursion time. We are going to Marbella for the afternoon. Narrow streets. Old Town. A good place to cool off. If anyone doesn't want to come let me know. I am booking a cab now."

Everyone shifted position on their loungers, some sitting up while others simply propped themselves on their elbows. Nobody shook their heads. Michelle paid particular attention to the late addition to the hen party; the one her father had enlisted to avoid unlucky thirteen. He was a superstitious man, her father. The woman glanced at the bride, then straightened her towel. Michelle began to pack her things. The woman did the same. Nobody was staying at Laguna Park. Everyone was going west.

* * *

NINETY MINUTES LATER, fourteen women trooped into Plaza de los Naranjos looking for a cold drink and something to eat. The hen party hadn't been impressed with Muralla del Castillo, the ancient castle of Marbella, which was now just a section of castle wall and decrepit ramparts and was much happier with the tree-lined plaza with its bars and restaurants. The narrow streets and quaint shops of Old Town could wait. It was time to eat.

"Which one do you want?"

"The one with most space."

"No, the one with most shade."

The discussion went back and forth, but approaching mid-afternoon, there was only one choice. Restaurante Mena was on the south of the plaza opposite the Town Hall and had the most vacant tables under orange umbrellas. The group found four tables under a gnarled olive tree and proceeded to move the chairs around to fit all fourteen. A flustered waitress came over and distributed colourful menus. Number Two organized the seating arrangements but Michelle was concentrating on Number Fourteen. Not the NINJA BITCH T-shirt; CUDDLY BON BON. The bride stepped aside to let everyone sit down, then handed a menu to the woman with the hard face.

"Could you get everyone ordered? Drinks and appetizers."

She waved a hand towards the restaurant. "I need the restroom."

* * *

THE WOMAN WITH THE hard face took the menus but kept her eyes on the prize. The Cordero Belen cartel had entrusted her with its most cherished possession, and she wasn't about to let ordering at a restaurant distract her. She shifted in her seat and adjusted her T-shirt. She was certain the name across her chest was a joke, but she wasn't one for jokes. CUDDLY BON BON was the exact opposite to the personality that Cordero Belen had employed. She was the cartel's only female Sicario and had made her first kill when she was twelve. Being an assassin to a drug baron was more than a calling it was a blood oath. She nodded and put on a friendly face, then passed the menus around.

* * *

MICHELLE DIDN'T ASK for the restrooms when she entered the restaurant because she knew where the restrooms were. They were in the opposite direction to where she was going; out the back door and left along the alleyway. She glanced over her shoulder to make sure the bodyguard was still at her table, then went deeper into the restaurant. She couldn't risk being seen, so she dodged right, away from the front door. Once she was sure nobody could see from outside, she paused to get her bearings.

The interior was small and simple. There were half a dozen tables, but Restaurante Mena was mainly a street café. There was a bar and service counter on the right, with the restrooms just beyond that. An illuminated Fire Exit sign highlighted a narrow door in the back wall next to the kitchen. The kitchen door was open and trailed multi-coloured plastic strips to keep the flies out.

She knew where to go, but it wasn't her interior bearings she getting straight, it was the route to the taxi rank she'd seen up by Muralla del Castillo. There had been three cars parked in marked bays on Calle Portada, their drivers drinking coffee and smoking dirty brown cigarettes. The question was, did the back-alley lead to the road, or was it a cul-de-sac? She didn't think they would have a Fire Exit leading into a dead end, so she headed to the door.

A figure blocked her path, and she took a sharp breath. The flustered waitress looked even more flustered.

"Do you want drinks before you order?"

Michelle nodded towards the outside tables. "The big woman is taking the orders."

The waitress waved a hand, and Michelle followed her gaze. She could see the tables through the window. The seat with the menus was empty.

* * *

CUDDLY BON BON WAITED until the bride went inside, then put the menus down and stood up. She didn't ask for somebody else to place the orders; she wasn't interested in ordering. Bright sunshine in the plaza made the shadows inside the restaurant darker. The bride merged into the background three paces through the door, then disappeared. The bodyguard gave her time to clear the doorway, then stepped away from the tables.

Laughter and girl talk mixed with the clink of cutlery as the hen party rearranged the dinner settings. Birds chirruped in the trees. Somewhere on the access road, a motorbike backfired with a single throaty bang.

The bodyguard crossed the plaza to the restaurant. She didn't want the bride being on her own for too long. Bodyguards never left their charges alone for any length of time. It annoyed her that she'd missed the gigolo transaction until the bride was alone with him in her villa. She wasn't going to let anyone kidnap her in a public restaurant.

She reached the front door just as the rusty motorbike pulled up, loaded with crates of fruit and vegetables on the luggage rack. A skinny Spanish boy flicked out the kickstand and hefted the delivery in his arms. The bodyguard tried to beat him to the door, but he was already blocking the way. He shrugged an apology and smiled at the writing across her chest. She didn't know what Cuddly Bon Bon translated to in Spanish but was sure it wasn't, Pissed Off Sicario.

The boy went through the door, and the bodyguard followed. The bride was nowhere in sight. A quick glance around the interior pointed the way and the bodyguard didn't ask permission before charging through the Fire Exit door.

The alley was empty. It was straight and long and only went in one direction. There were no other alleys branching off from the main path. The bride couldn't have gone that far. The bodyguard cursed under her breath and went back inside. The fly curtains were still settling when she realised her mistake.

Chapter Fourteen

BEN FOLLOWED THE RAISED wooden footpath through the sand dunes, avoiding the nudist beach and the bouncy castle and coming out at Playa Cabopino just before four o'clock. He skirted the lower car park and cut through Andy's Beach Bar into the sheltered marina. The sea wall curled around the mouth of the harbour, protecting the private jetties and moored yachts.

Music pounded the air inside the beach bar but quickly fell into the background once he stepped onto the harbour front. Cabopino had a way of doing that, mixing oiled bodies and party time with the quiet privacy of the boating community. A red and white power cruiser reversed gently into a berth halfway along the jetty, its twin engines throbbing and bubbling in the newfound quiet.

Ben checked his watch. He was right on time, but he hadn't seen the bride along the walkway or the beach. He glanced behind him in case he'd missed her in Andy's Beach Bar but didn't think she was the beach bar type. A smaller motorboat pulled out of its berth and made the sharp right-hand turn around the boatyard towards the exit channel. A family chided their son for standing too close to the edge. Ben checked his watch again, considered why he was there, and thought maybe he was standing too close to the edge as well.

* * *

THE TAXI ALMOST RAN him down. Five minutes after he arrived at the marina. Three-quarters of an hour before he made the biggest decision of his life. Almost a week ahead of an ending that would suck the life right out of him. He'd always thought, after growing up in the Green family, that there wasn't much life left to suck. He was wrong.

Ben crossed the concrete access road that was for residents only, or for boat trailers using the dual slipways beside the boatyard. The narrow road ran all the way around the marina but couldn't come full circle because there was no bridge over the exit/entrance channel. Ben looked at the green and gold décor of Albert's Bar & Grill and decided on the friendlier colours of La Despensa next door. The Italian restaurant's outside seating was sheltered by a bright red canopy and several striped umbrellas, casting the diners in shades of red and yellow. It was the red and yellow he was looking at when the taxi came through the twin archway of the security gate. Too fast.

Panicked eyes stared at him through the windscreen as the driver slammed on the brakes and sounded the horn. Ben held up a hand of apology even though it wasn't his fault. He didn't point out the speed limit sign at the entrance that restricted traffic to five kilometres per hour. The driver's eyes went from panicked to angry to accepting, but it was the passenger's eyes Ben was focussing on. The woman paid the fare, then got out.

Ben nodded at her. "You trying to knock me off now? As well as having my arm broke?"

Michelle Cordero Belen closed the passenger door. "If I wanted you knocked off, believe me, you'd be knocked off."

* * *

DESPITE ALMOST RUNNING him over, Michelle was actually glad to see the gigolo who wasn't really a gigolo. She'd been thinking about what to say to him all the way over from Marbella, the taxi driver distracting her with his constantly burning cigarette. What she'd decided was to play her cards close to her chest and not reveal anything about the family business or what a nest of vipers the burglar had got himself mixed up with. She felt responsible and yet it was not her fault. You can't choose your family. She felt sure that was something he would understand.

That feeling was even stronger now things had settled down, and they were sitting under the red canopy drinking wine and Coca-Cola. Wine for her, Coke for him. They toyed with a plate of mixed starters while they decided what to eat. She was hungry, having missed out on lunch with the hen party at Plaza de los Naranjos.

He surprised her by beating her to the punch. "I've got a confession to make."

She wasn't going to be outdone. "Me too."

He waved a hand. "Ladies first."

Michelle shook her head. "I'm no lady."

* * *

BEN THOUGHT HE SAW a hint of sadness behind her eyes and felt his anger melt a touch. He had agreed to meet the bride fully intending to give her a piece of his mind. She was arrogant, wealthy and full of her own importance. She used people when it suited her, and discarded them when it didn't. That wealthy indifference almost led to him having his arm broken and his dignity stripped. He didn't have much dignity to start with, and couldn't afford to lose any more of it.

Add to that she almost ran him over arriving at Cabopino, and had shown no sign of remorse. This was a woman he had absolutely nothing in common with, and even less attraction to. So why did he feel sorry for her? He hadn't learned that in the Green family playbook, that Robin Hood instinct to take from the rich and give to the poor.

But Michelle Cordero Belen *was* the rich.

So why did her eyes say she was the poor?

He felt a sudden urge to unburden himself but didn't know why. He had kept the family history to himself for so long, it felt like a stone weighing him down. The secret of who he was and why he was here was a crushing pressure that tightened his chest and made it hard to breathe. Not always.

Most of the time, he could disguise the pressure he was under, but other times, he wanted to tell somebody and get it off his chest. He hadn't even mentioned it to Eduardo, the only person he considered to be a friend on the Costa del Sol.

And now he was considering telling this woman from Mexico, a woman who had a bodyguard that had threatened to kill him and a hen party that hired gigolos. It made no sense, and yet it did. It was like women telling secrets to the hairdresser or men unburdening themselves at the barbers. Telling a stranger your darkest secrets made complete sense, because there was no way for it to come back on you. You were never going to see the stranger again.

"I've got a confession to make."

It felt good just saying it. Then, the bride caught him by surprise.

"Me too."

Chapter Fifteen

"AND SHE NEVER forgave you?"

"For him dying in prison? Not my fault."

"For him going to prison in the first place."

Ben shook his head. "What she couldn't forgive was me putting stuff back instead of stealing it."

Michelle looked at him across the table. "She wanted the entire family to be thieves. Not just your brother."

They had finished their appetizers and were waiting for the main course. Ben didn't think time had ever flown so quickly. He had kept the story brief and to the point. Childhood, elder brother, and apprenticeship in crime. Robin Hood, brother in prison, and the Green family fallout. Finally, continuing in the family business and becoming a master thief. All in less than fifteen minutes.

Ben shrugged. "She *was* the entire family. I'm just something she had to put up with."

Michelle took a sip of red wine. "But you don't like being a master thief."

Ben looked at the woman he was growing increasingly comfortable confessing to. "Didn't. Thing about repetition is it develops muscle memory. You get enough muscle memory, and you get really good at what you're memorizing. When you get good enough…"

He shrugged again. "It's hard not to like what you're good at."

"So, you're not Robin Hood anymore."

"I'm a thief and a burglar." He let out a sigh. "I just chose the wrong person to steal from."

"The guy with the bodyguards in Leeds."

Ben rattled the ice around his glass. "Two bodyguards in the corridor should have warned me. I didn't know about the third inside the room. But the corridor?"

He pushed the glass away. "If you're big and powerful, you hire a bodyguard to guard your body. It's only people bigger than that, hire them to guard their prized possession."

The bride lowered her eyes for a moment. When she looked up, he saw that look again, the one that said she was a poor girl, not a rich bitch. "You met the bodyguard protecting my father's prized possession."

Her eyes seemed to be pleading. "How big and powerful do you think that makes *him*?"

* * *

MICHELLE FINISHED HER WINE and waved for another glass. The waitress brought a fresh Cola as well, even though the gigolo hadn't ordered one. Michelle waited for the waitress to pour the drinks and leave. Ordering a refill was a delaying tactic. She used the time to evaluate Ben's confession and weigh it up against her own. His story was different to hers but surprisingly similar. Once the bubbles had settled in his Coke, she leaned back in her chair and looked him in the eyes.

"Families. They don't always want what's best for you." She swirled the wine in her glass. "Mine is more interested in the business asset than the daughter."

Another fifteen minutes. Another story told in brief. Michelle was the only child of a man who wanted sons to carry on the family business. Her father was a businessman in a shady business that she didn't need to explain. He was Mexican. Aside from the Columbians he was the biggest threat to American drug trafficking. But he wasn't satisfied with America; he wanted to conquer the world. He doted on his daughter, vetting her boyfriends and keeping her away from predators. She had all the privilege a rich twenty-eight-year-old could hope for, but none of the freedom. She rebelled. Her boyfriends paid the price.

Ben looked shocked. “He killed them?”

Michelle’s eyes were sad. “He disappeared them. Their families moved away. The boys never contacted me again. I doubt he dumped them in a vat of acid, but they certainly got the message.” She looked at Ben. “Hands off.”

Ben nodded. “Or your ninja bodyguard will break my arm.”

“Worse.”

“I thought you said he didn’t dump them in a vat of acid.”

Michelle took a drink. “My therapist says I’m living in denial.”

“You have a therapist?”

“Had. He disappeared her as well.”

She looked at the lifeguard turned gigolo, who was really a master thief. She could see he had questions and knew which one to answer.

“So, no boyfriends, you ask. How come I’m getting married?”

Ben shifted in his chair. “Business asset.”

Michelle nodded. “A marriage of convenience. A merger of two families. A daughter finally proving useful. Who needs a son, when your daughter can expand the empire?”

She smiled but the smile didn’t go anywhere near her eyes. “Families. They always want what’s best for the family.”

* * *

BEN DIDN’T KNOW WHY he did it, but he did it anyway. He reached across the table and took Michelle’s hand. She resisted at first, then let him hold it. He could feel the tension vibrating through her bones. After a few moments, the tension eased, and the hands rested together in a mutual need. He patted it with his other hand, gave it a gentle squeeze, then let go. By the time he sat back in his chair, he was already formulating a plan.

Three-quarters of an hour after he arrived at Cabopino.

Five minutes before the biggest decision of his life.

“When is the wedding?”

“Two weeks.”

"But he's not your boyfriend."

She gave him a look that said, as if that matters. "He's my fiancé."

"Have you met him?"

That didn't matter either, but she nodded anyway. "His family have a place near Palma in Majorca."

Ben turned his hands, palms upwards. "And?"

"And what?"

"Do you like him?"

Michelle looked exasperated. "What difference does that make?"

Ben turned his hands from questioning to placating. "Point I'm making is. If you like him, does it matter he wasn't your boyfriend before you met. Arranged marriages happen all the time. Law of averages says some of them turn out fine."

Michelle let out a sigh. "I don't like the law of averages."

Ben lowered his voice. "But do you like him?"

Michelle leaned forward, resting her arms on the table. "He has the same dead eyes as my father. No. I do not like him."

The plan was taking shape in his head. Forty-nine minutes after he arrived at Cabopino. One minute to decision time. When he spoke, it was as if he were talking to himself.

"Families. They fuck you every time."

Michelle nodded. "They certainly do."

Ben firmed up his gaze. "So why don't we fuck 'em back?"

Chapter Sixteen

AS BAD IDEAS GO, fucking 'em back was right at the top of the list, but just like all the bad decisions Ben had made in his life, this one seemed like a good idea at the time. Running off with the bride-to-be felt like that scene at the end of *The Graduate*. Pissing off her father was more like *No Country For Old Men*, a cartel boss sending an implacable hitman to chase down the money. In this case, it was the daughter, not the money, although in the grand scheme of things, they amounted to the same thing. Only it wasn't Javier Bardem in a fright wig; it was the ninja bitch in a Cuddly Bon Bon T-shirt.

Avoiding the ninja bitch was the first part of the plan.

Having enough money to go on the run with was the second.

Ben took care of the second part first.

* * *

SPORTS COORDINATOR AND ENTERTAINMENT were separate functions of the same person. Benjamin J Green. Sports were strictly daytime activities, but entertainment included children's parties and evening functions. He shared the evening functions with Eduardo Perez. Ben felt guilty at dropping Eduardo in the shit, so he gave him the heads up as they were clearing away the rubbish after the *Star Wars*-themed party. The reason he had time to give Eduardo the heads up was because the safe he was going to rob wasn't available until after lights out.

"Eduardo. Something I've got to tell you."

Eduardo stopped pealing silly string off the wall. "That you sorry for taking the gigolo job over me?"

Ben dropped a Darth Vader mask in the bin liner he was carrying. "You know about that?"

"I know about everything when it comes to servicing our clients."

"I didn't service anyone."

"And yet you met her in Cabopino this afternoon."

"You know about that as well?"

Eduardo gave Ben a steady look. "Everything."

He softened his expression. "What I don't know is what you intend to do next. Because I get the feeling you intend to do something. And I think, as a friend, I should warn you against it."

Ben looked at his only friend on the sunshine coast. He sighed and gave him a gentle nod. "You're right on both counts. But let me tell you, as a friend, the less you know, the better."

Eduardo dropped the bag of silly string and leaned against the wall. His eyes showed surprise and sadness. Mainly sadness. "You're saying goodbye?"

Ben felt a weight he didn't expect to feel. "I'm saying the less you know, the better. And if anyone asks, you don't know anything. But yes, I didn't want to go without..."

He didn't finish. The two ignored the cleaning and stared at each other like only friends can without it getting weird. After a couple of minutes, it did begin to feel weird, so Eduardo pushed off from the wall.

"When?"

"Least is better."

"Who with?"

"Even less."

Eduardo had one last question. "You got travelling money?"

Ben shrugged. Eduardo's mouth dropped open, and he glanced towards the office behind Laguna Park reception. Ben was beginning to think his friend was right when he said he knew everything. He wondered how much he knew about the jobs Max Overend sent Ben on during the night and how much he knew about Ben's skills as a burglar and a thief. Eduardo proved just how much he did know.

"Can you steal cars as well?"

Ben tilted his head. "I'm not going to hire one."

Eduardo turned serious. "No. And don't book anywhere needs your name and passport. Cash only. How far?"

It seemed the less you know the better wasn't proving a hindrance to Eduardo asking questions. Ben felt his resistance crumble.

"Up the coast. Road trip. Nothing specific."

Eduardo looked around for a notepad and pen. He couldn't find one but found a *Star Wars* colouring book and crayons. He tore a page out, scribbled an address, and handed it to Ben.

"If you get that far. Look this up. There will be help."

Ben looked at the address. "That's a long way."

Eduardo gave Ben a hard stare. "If you do this thing, I do not know what you are going to do. A long way is where you need to go. Because Max, he is not a very nice man, I think."

Ben nodded and put the folded paper in his pocket.

"You don't know the half of it."

* * *

THE NOT VERY NICE man locked the office safe, and the keypad made an electronic beep as it flashed twice. Max Overend moved away from the wall safe and knelt beneath the leg space of his desk. He listened to make sure there was nobody outside, then unlocked his private safe in the floor, dropped the money he'd taken out of the official safe, then locked this one as well. Smoothing the throw rug, he pushed himself up using the desk, then slipped the key into his pocket. He didn't believe in keypads and codes for his personal security. You don't employ a burglar, then trust your fortune to a keypad that the burglar could crack in thirty seconds.

The evening entertainment had finished almost an hour ago and the staff had cleaned up and gone to their chalets. The takings had been counted and separated, half in the office safe and half in his. That was enough for one night. He turned the light off and locked the office.

* * *

BEN SAW THE OFFICE light go out, but wasn't going to be rushed. The key to being a successful burglar wasn't being able to get into any room or building, it was making sure nobody came back and caught you because they'd left something behind. Ben reckoned on half an hour then doubled it, watching from a bench up the hill from the Supermercado. A warm sea breeze rustled the palm fronds that lined the road, the trees throwing patches of light and dark between the streetlamps. The bench was in the dark.

He glanced across the road at Laguna Park and tried to place the villa where the bride was packing. He wondered again if this was a good idea, then brushed his doubts aside. Of course it wasn't a good idea, but since when did that make any difference?

Ben watched Max Overend drive his company car out of the entrance and head across town to his off-site apartment. He waited twenty minutes to make sure he didn't come back, then started to make his preparations. The bag of tools was heavy. He wanted to be ready when the hour was up, so both parts of the plan could work almost in unison.

Chapter Seventeen

MICHELLE WAS READY TO play her part in the evade and escape operation. The first thing had been explaining her sudden disappearance from Plaza de los Naranjos and avoiding the accusing stare of Cuddly Bon Bon. The explanation had been easier than the accusing stare. When she met the rest of the hen party back at Laguna Park, she said she'd got carried away with a local shopkeeper and lost track of time. When she returned to the restaurant, the others had gone, so she made her own way back to the resort.

The undercover bodyguard had to accept that in public because she couldn't exactly kick off with the other women watching. To that end, Michelle made sure she was never alone with the ninja bitch, and invited a few of her friends to the villa for a nightcap. When they all left, it was late and dark and time for lights out. Cuddles would have to wait until morning.

Michelle locked the front door and turned the lights out, apart from a night-light in the bathroom. She packed her flight bag with a few essentials, including toiletries and a change of clothes. She left the rest of her luggage behind as a decoy to buy a little time before the flare went up. She looked out of the balcony window towards the nearest row of holiday apartments. The one she wanted was as dark as hers. There was no twitch of curtains. There was no glow from the bathroom night-light. She wondered if ninjas slept with their eyes open.

The kitchen clock ticked downstairs. Michelle lowered the toilet seat and sat on the lid. Bars on the bathroom window made it feel like she was in prison. Looking back on her life it felt like she always had been.

* * *

AFTER THE PENTHOUSE SUITE at Don Carlos and the tenth-floor hotel room in Leeds, breaking into the manager's office at Laguna Park was a piece of cake. Holiday resorts spend money on the swimming pool and the bar, a bit less on the restaurant, and hardly anything on the chalets. They spent nothing at all on security. After all, what was there to steal in the resort manager's office?

Ben used his key card on the main entrance, then went behind the unmanned reception desk; Laguna Park reception wasn't a twenty-four-hour job. He popped open the key cabinet in five seconds and was unlocking Max Overend's office in ten. That's how easy it was to break into the resort manager's office.

Ben closed the door but didn't turn the lights on. There might not be anyone around, but burglars don't like the light. He reckoned it was hardwired into his DNA, or maybe his mother had beaten it into him. Whatever it was, he waited until his eyes adjusted, then used the light spilling in from the street and reception. He looked out of the window at the gilded tower of Don Carlos, its five stars gleaming in the night. He checked the turnaround and footpath, then turned his attention to the wall safe.

Office safes are bigger than the ones fitted in the rooms, but they're basically the same. Digital keypad. Electronic beep when unlocked. Double beep when locked. Supplied by the same company that provided half the security on the Costa del Sol. Same selection of combinations or simple variations thereon. Ben knew the security guy, and could guess the staff code in less than five minutes. He put the heavy bag down on the floor and looked at the glowing keypad.

The security guy had told him something else as well. Ben looked at the office safe for a few more seconds, then turned his back on it. He dropped to one knee and ducked under Max Overend's desk.

* * *

CUDDLY BON BON WATCHED the bride's villa from her kitchen window. She was a professional, so she didn't hold a grudge, but her pride had been dented, and the last thing you want on your tail is a dented assassin. If the package hadn't been so highly valued by the Cordero Belen cartel, the bodyguard would have exacted her own price for slipping the leash, but the bride was El Jefe's daughter. The price would have to be exacted in a different way. Right now, the Sicario was undecided which way that would be.

The other drinkers had left the villa half an hour ago, and the lights were turned off not long after. The curtains were drawn, but there was some light from deep inside the villa. Upstairs, probably the bathroom. Kitchens and bathrooms. Strange places to be spending the night, watching from darkness into darkness. A cat hissed somewhere along Terrace B. A dog barked, and the cat hissed again. Stalkers and their prey. It was a busy night. The trouble with dogs is they never know what to do if they catch the cat. The bodyguard could sympathise. She settled in for a long wait while she made up her mind.

* * *

BEN OPENED THE HEAVY-DUTY canvas bag and laid his tools out on the throw rug beneath the desk. Digital keypads are easy, and traditional twist-and-turn combination locks are a bit more long-winded, but he could open either of them in less than fifteen minutes, given enough peace and quiet to work in. Opening a safe that used a key could take a bit longer. If you didn't have the key. Ben didn't have the key.

The next part was tricky and needed a whole selection of lock picks and torsion wrenches. It needed deft touch, a keen ear and more time than Ben had allotted for this part of the operation. The location precluded drilling and hammering, and he didn't work with acid or other corrosive substances. Thankfully, Max Overend was as arrogant as he was overbearing. He thought having a safe fitted into the floor would make it a floor safe.

Ben settled into a crouch in the footwell. He remembered a burglary at a sub-Post Office back in Leeds where the thieves spent all night cutting through the joists in the floor in order to take the safe away with them. The safe had been encased in concrete and hung into the basement like a giant wasps' nest. The wooden joists had been easy enough but the concrete was laced with iron rebar that was sunk into the foundations. They almost demolished the building and still didn't get the safe.

The security guy who fitted Max Overend's safe had taken the resort manager's money and sold him a curate's egg. The lock itself was solid and hard to pick, but the safe was fastened to the floor with four screws. Ben selected the biggest screwdriver and put all his weight behind it. Twenty minutes later, he had the safe in his bag and the office key back in the key cabinet.

He smiled as he crossed the turnaround to where he'd parked the stolen car. He almost wished he could be there when the manager saw the Laguna Park leaflet in the cavity where the safe had been.

Chapter Eighteen

MICHELLE NEARLY JUMPED OUT of her skin when Ben appeared in the bathroom door. She didn't scream or yelp or clamp a hand over her mouth; she just slapped him across the face.

"What the fuck?"

Then they both laughed when they spoke at the same time with the same WTF. The tension broke. The waiting was over. The nightlight provided a cocoon of safety Michelle was beginning to feel comfortable in. She let out a sigh, then looked towards the darkened stairs from the front door.

"You didn't?"

Ben glanced down the stairs. "Front door? You kidding? I think that woman sleeps with one eye open."

Michelle was only half joking. "Both eyes."

Ben gave her an encouraging smile. "Doesn't matter how many eyes. If there's nothing to see."

Michelle looked for the bag, but he was empty-handed. "Did it go alright?"

Ben nodded. "Muscle memory."

He dropped to a crouch so he was on the same level as the bride. "You still okay with this?"

She leaned forward and rested her elbows on her knees. *Was* she still okay with this? She had done plenty of things to piss her father off, but this was the biggest fuck-you stunt she'd ever pulled. She considered that for a moment, then thought about the enormity of the thing he was making her do. Life changing.

She looked Ben in the eye. "Yes."

"There's no going back for me now, but you. You've still got time."

She'd made up her mind. "I don't need time. Let's get on with it."

They stood up in unison and almost banged heads. That made them laugh again. Ben stepped aside to let her out of the bathroom, and Michelle smiled. Maybe this road trip was going to work out fine. Then there was a knock on the door, and the ninja bitch shouted through the letterbox.

* * *

"WHAT TIME DO YOU call this?"

"I call it time to get a few things straight."

They were standing in the entrance hall that led into the open-plan living room. There was a low partition wall with a plant pot and ashtray. There was no smoking in the villas so the ashtray was for spare keys. Michelle had the keys in her hand.

"Thing I want to get straight is straight off to bed."

"After."

Michelle didn't throw a nervous glance or look away. She stared Number Fourteen in the face and didn't give any indication there was someone else in the villa. She'd been brought up by a drug lord, she knew how to face off against the domestic staff.

"Who do you think you're talking to? This is my…"

The eyes that stared at her were cold and merciless. This wasn't facing off against the domestic staff; it was being fronted by a trained bodyguard. The Sicario pointed at the settee, and they both sat down. One at each end of the couch. The same as before only different. This time, it wasn't an unwanted gigolo but a dangerous woman. The dangerous woman was relaxed but alert. Her eyes scanned the lounge and kitchenette.

"Let's get one thing straight."

"We talking that straight thing again?"

The woman held up a finger, and Michelle shut up.

"You know who I am now, so let's cut the bullshit. I'm not here for you. I work for your father. To make sure this marriage goes ahead."

"You think I'm going to get kidnapped?"

"I think you need to be careful."

Michelle gave a mischievous twinkle. "I was careful."

The woman's tone didn't change. "Today was not being careful. And hiring a gigolo was poor judgment."

"I didn't hire the gigolo."

"But you did spend the night with him."

The twinkle left her eyes. "You know exactly how long I spent with him. You almost broke his arm on his way back." She knew she'd made a mistake as soon as she said it.

"So, you have seen him again."

Michelle backpedalled. "You saw us. At the pool."

"Not at the pool."

Michelle didn't answer, so the woman continued.

"Here's how it's going to go from now on. You will not go anywhere without me being included. You will not be out of my sight for longer than it takes to have a pee or powder your nose. And you will not see the pool guy again."

She leaned forward to close the gap on the settee. "I can do worse than break his arm."

Michelle stared back at the face of death. "Yes. My father's been doing that my whole life."

The woman's face almost became human. "It's for your own good."

Michelle shook her head. "It's for the good of the business."

A faint smile played across the woman's lips. "Same thing."

She stood up and waved towards the back of the villa.

"And don't go thinking of sneaking out the back door. There isn't one. I checked. Bars on the windows. Your only way in or out is past me."

She went to the door and looked back at the bride. "Now we've got that straight." She nodded towards the stairs. "You can go straight off to bed."

* * *

THE FRONT DOOR CLOSED, and Ben came out of the bedroom. He felt a shiver run down his spine that had nothing to do with the air conditioning. He waited until the bride locked the door, then came down the stairs, quietly, one at a time. He stayed away from the lights to avoid throwing shadows on the curtains and leaned against the wall. The bride came towards him and was about to speak when he held a finger to his lips.

The bride stopped in mid-step.

Ben listened at the door.

When he nodded, the bride spoke in a whisper.

"How *did* you get in?"

Ben smiled. "Same way we're going to get out."

He didn't explain, just showed her. Then they were off into the night in a stolen car with a safe full of money.

II

COSTA DEL DIABLO

"I know where to find something you're missing."
— Max Overend

Chapter Nineteen

"THIS IS RECOMMENDED practice, is it? Changing cars so soon?"

"Number plates, not the car. We'll change the car later."

They had followed the coast road east and north through Cala de Mijas and Fuengirola before hitting the tourist hub of Benalmadena. Twenty-five miles. Not far enough to be safe, but enough distance that they could stop for breakfast and change number plates. Ben had parked in a side street opposite Parque de la Paloma and quickly switched plates with another hire car from the same company. Three-quarters of the cars on the Costa del Sol were hire cars. They all looked different but the same. When the police finally started looking for this one, they'd be stopping an unsuspecting tourist first.

"Ready for something to eat?"

"I'm ready for some sleep."

Ben crossed the road and entered through the ornate park gates. Chickens walked the garden paths, and overweight rabbits rested in the shade. It was another beautiful morning with blue skies and warm sun, even though it was only quarter to nine. Holidaymakers were still in bed, but the Café de Auditorio was already busy. Breakfast before it got too hot was a local tradition.

"You can sleep in the car."

"We're not in the car."

Ben stopped and turned to face the bride. "Having second thoughts?"

Michelle shook her head but didn't look convincing.

Ben glanced around the beautiful gardens and wasn't that sure himself.

He let out a sigh and looked at Michelle. "Sticking it to your father is a big deal. I can always drop you off, and you can go back."

The shake of the head was more positive this time. "My father isn't someone you stick it to then go back. His guard dog isn't either."

"She might not know you've gone yet."

Michelle gave Ben a hard stare. "She knows. And it won't be your arm this time. Does she strike you as someone who makes idle threats?"

Ben rubbed his arm. "I'm not going back."

Michelle hugged herself as if protecting her arms. "Her theory will be I can still get married with a broken arm."

"Your father would have your arm broken?"

"My father would do whatever it takes to make the deal go through."

"But the ninja bitch wouldn't do that off her own bat."

"Bat?"

"Her own decision."

Michelle lowered her arms. "As of now, the ninja bitch is the last person you need to worry about. My father doesn't live in the land of second chances. She is burned."

She nodded towards the Café de Auditorio. "So, you're right. We'd better eat. Because the people he sends next will pull your teeth out one by one, then hang you upside down until you bleed to death."

Chapter Twenty

PABLO CORDERO BELEN put the phone down and looked out across the expansive grounds of Villa Real. The Martinez cartel had loaned him their family retreat so he would be close to hand for the wedding. Majorca was a beautiful island but the telephone call had dimmed that beauty. He picked up the baseball bat he took with him everywhere and gave it a few loose swings in one hand. Gentle swishes of the bat that had smashed more skulls than Pol Pot.

Then he swung it hard and fast, bringing it down on the coffee table hard enough to shatter the lacquered top and bounce the telephone onto the tiled floor.

"Hijo de puta."

Even under these circumstances, he couldn't bring himself to swear at his daughter, but calling the man who had run off with her a son of a bitch was only the start of the degradation he was going to visit upon him.

"Alejandro."

His right-hand man came into the room and didn't even look at the destroyed table. Cordero Belen stood on the balcony and watched the sea lap against the private beach. He stopped swishing the bat and leaned it against the wall.

"Get me three men."

That was all he needed to say.

* * *

NINJA BITCH LISTENED TO dead air down the line for a long moment before hanging up. She knew how it went from here. She had failed. Cordero Belen would call in his crack team and the female Sicario would be sidelined. Consuela Mendoza didn't want to be sidelined.

She looked at the cell phone in her hand, then put it away. She hadn't thought of herself as Consuela for a long time and definitely didn't consider herself to be Cuddly Bon Bon. Ninja Bitch was a name she would have agreed with if she'd known it was being used, but what she really thought of herself as was, Terminator. Not that muscle-bound lughead Schwarzenegger, but someone who executed her orders and terminated anyone who got in her way. Right now, the person who had got in her way was Michelle Cordero Belen, but killing her would terminate the wedding, and the wedding was the future. No, she couldn't terminate the bride, but she could make the gigolo pay while returning the bride to the fold.

Mendoza looked around the bedroom in Villa del Sol. Clothes were hanging in the wardrobe, and the drawers were still full. The bride's suitcase stood in the corner of the room, no doubt a half-hearted attempt at throwing her off the scent, but the flight bag was missing, and the bathroom was empty. There were no toiletries, and the hairbrushes were gone. Mendoza's reading of the bride was that she never went anywhere without her hairbrushes.

She searched the cupboards and dressing table, then checked under the mattress. Passport and travel money were missing as well, and there was no sign of her cell phone. The phone didn't mean anything, everybody took their phone when they went out, but nobody took their passport unless they didn't plan on coming back. Mendoza went back upstairs and looked at the tiny safe in the bottom of the wardrobe. The door was unlocked with instructions how to change the password flashing on the keypad.

No, the bride had flown the coop, and there was only one suspect for who she had flown it with. She had told all that to Cordero Belen, and he was no doubt mobilising his team right now. Soon, a hit squad would be scouring the Costa del Sol for the missing pool attendant and the bride-to-be, and what they brought back wouldn't resemble the gigolo she had spent the night with.

Mendoza wasn't bothered about the condition of the gigolo, but she wanted to be the one to mete out justice. The hit squad would be called in from Mexico, or maybe had been travelling with him to Majorca. They would have to fly to the mainland, then pick up the scent. That gave Mendoza a head start and knowledge the hit squad didn't have. She knew who the gigolo's friend was at Laguna Park.

Chapter Twenty-One

BEN DIDN'T FEEL COMFORTABLE until they'd skirted Malaga and continued east on the coast road. He stuck with the coast road to avoid the tollbooths and cameras on the A-7, and he kept out of Malaga because the airport was the first place the cartel would be looking for a quick escape with the runaway bride. This wasn't a quick escape it was a road trip.

The runaway bride was a sleeping beauty for most of the drive, Michelle being exhausted from the overnight tension and the confrontation with Cuddly Bon Bon. Ben let her sleep. He had enough to think about without having her tell him about being hung up to dry with his teeth pulled out.

* * *

"YOU CAN OPEN IT, can't you?"

"I didn't dig it out the floor for a souvenir."

"So, what's taking so long?"

Ben held a finger to his lips but didn't make a shushing noise. They had pulled off the N-340a after several unavoidable stretches of the A-7, and were sitting in a coastal park at Roquetas de Mar just before Almeria. A hundred miles, and a three-hour drive. The coast road wasn't conducive to fast driving. Castillo de Santa Ana overlooked the Real Club Nautica marina, but nothing overlooked the open boot of the hire car.

"Safecrackers don't usually work in a public car park."

"So maybe you should have cracked the safe in the office."

Ben didn't explain the priorities of speed versus stealth, and the fact that safecracking in the dark was like everything else in the dark, harder than in the light.

"Why don't you take a spin around the castle or something?"

Michelle stepped away from the back of the car and scanned the seafront. The promenade was lined with palm trees and there was a concession stand over near the castle. She wiped sweat from her forehead with one finger and flicked it onto the concrete. It hissed like fat in a frying pan.

"You want an ice cream?"

Ben glanced at the concession stand. "Smoothie. Banana and strawberry."

Michelle put her hands on her hips. "They don't teach manners in Yorkshire, do they?"

Ben let out a sigh. "Please, and thank you."

"It's please when you're asking. Thanks, when you receive."

"I'm saving time. I'll have it open when you get back."

Michelle nodded as if she believed him, then set off along the walkway. Ben turned his attention to the floor safe in the leather holdall. He flexed his fingers and leaned into the car boot. It had been a while since he'd done this, but he still had the tools. He hoped he still had the skills as well. Once Michelle had left, he set to work on liberating Max Overend's ill-gotten gains.

* * *

THE BANANA AND STRAWBERRY smoothie helped calm Ben's nerves as the odd couple sat on a shaded bench. Palm trees marched off in both directions along the walkway, mercifully free from walkers in the heat of the midday sun. He had dropped the safe into deep water over the promenade wall when no one was looking and was sitting with his back to the car. That's as far as he was going to get from the leather holdall that wasn't just a tool bag anymore.

Michelle sat up straight. "How much?"

Ben didn't repeat the amount. "More than I've been stealing for him."

"How much more?"

"A shitload more."

He took too deep a suck on the straw and felt the cold freeze his brain. Fingers of pain dug into his temples and he closed his eyes. Shutting out the world around him had been a defence growing up, but closing his eyes now just meant he wouldn't be able to see what was coming. He kept that thought to himself, because what was coming was Trouble with a capital T.

While he waited for the pain to subside, he did some rough calculations, working backwards from the Don Carlos through all the times Max had given him targets to hit. Maybe a dozen. Not more than fifteen. Some scores bigger than others but all of them moderate to sizeable. There had been a small rake off for Ben but everything else went in Max Overend's floor safe. Ben knew that Max was skimming off the Laguna Park takings as well but didn't know how much that amounted to, but gave it a conservative figure then added it all together. Even if he rounded it up, the total was nowhere near what was packed in the leather holdall.

"Shit."

"You suck too hard?"

Ben nodded and opened his eyes. The brain freeze wasn't the shit he was talking about. He took a deep breath and let it out slowly. The only explanation for a small-time crook like Max Overend having this much cash was that Laguna Park wasn't a holiday resort it was a business expense. A tax write-off. Taking in enough money to show legitimate profit and appease anyone looking at the books. Money came in, and money went out. Where it came from was probably the same place as Michelle's father's. Drugs. Smuggling. Organised crime. Ben knew that three cartels ran the drugs trade in Southern Spain, but he didn't know who they were. Max Overend was laundering money for one of them. When it went out, it was clean. Unless somebody dug up the floor safe and ran off with the money.

Chapter Twenty-Two

MAX OVEREND PUT OFF making the call as long as he dared. He'd never been a daring kind of person, that's why he was happy to let others do the dangerous stuff and simply bank the spoils. A bit of a sideline to his main job, which was cleaning money for a group of people he never wanted to meet. Compared to that, running a holiday resort was a piece of cake.

He sat in the office with his feet either side of the hole where the safe used to be and put the phone down again. No, he wasn't a daring person, but there was no avoiding telling them about the burglary and the fact that the burglar had ignored the official safe and only taken their money. The Laguna Park leaflet stared up at him from the bottom of the hole. The bottom of a hole was exactly where he was unless he could spin the story to cover himself.

There's been a burglary.

That happens. Doesn't mean he had anything to do with it. Okay, so maybe he could have alarmed the office, but holiday resorts are busy places, and alarms don't like movement. That could be his argument there. The mocking leaflet he could leave out of the report.

The burglar was a member of staff.

That would be harder to explain, if he mentioned it at all. He considered that. Why tell them that Benjamin Green was a thief in hiding that Max had put to work feathering his own nest with a few local break-ins? It's not like the people he worked for were here looking over his shoulder. How would they find out? Nobody here was going to tell them because nobody here knew, apart from the offending person himself, and he'd run off with the safe.

Max shook his head. No, that wouldn't work. The people he worked for would catch the thief as sure as day followed night, and when they did, the thief would talk. He might play the strong silent type for a while, but eventually, he would talk, one broken finger at a time. Max shook his head again and corrected himself, one amputated finger at a time. Ben would talk, and the next thing they'd ask would be, why Max hadn't told them.

It wasn't my fault.

Businesses get burgled all the time. You don't blame the Supermercado manager when the supermarket gets broken into. Imagine what would happen if every time a TV shop or car showroom got burgled, the owners blamed the man who ran the day-to-day business. It wasn't his fault, so why should this be Max's?

The sigh exploded from his lips, and he sat back in his chair. The desk was supposed to make him feel like a movie mogul, but now it felt like a prison, hemming him in. There was no escaping the fact that this was his fault. What had he been thinking, blackmailing a thief to steal for him and not expecting the thief to keep on stealing? That's what thieves do. You dumb piece of shit. As soon as they started chopping off Ben Green's fingers, the next amputation would be further up the tree. Decapitation, not amputation. The head, not a finger. Max rubbed his neck and gave a little cough to clear his throat.

Then, a thought struck him. An idea so simple in its purity.

The dogs would be unleashed once Max had made the call, and those dogs would track Ben down and make him talk. If they got to him first. But they weren't the only dogs interested in finding the thief from Leeds.

Max nodded at his own ingenuity. He'd have to make the call, yes, but it didn't have to be the first call. He took a leather notebook out of his desk and found the name he was looking for. He picked up the phone and dialled the UK number. A gruff Yorkshire accent answered after four rings, and Max calmed his voice.

"I know where to find something you're missing."

Chapter Twenty-Three

BEN PULLED OUT OF the car park, took the second exit at the roundabout to bypass Castillo de Santa Ana and the yacht club marina, and headed into Roquetas de Mar. From there, it was a straight road back to the N-340a and a right turn towards Almeria. The leather holdall was safely hidden in the boot, but its presence oozed menace. It wasn't so much an elephant in the room as something far deadlier, with teeth, which could get them both killed.

Neither of them spoke about the elephant.

Neither of them spoke at all.

Not until Michelle saw the road sign at the N-340a and patted the dashboard.

"So now it's changing car time?"

Ben pulled onto the N-340a and headed east. Just five miles to Almeria.

"Changing, crushing, and disappearing car time."

Just the sound of that made Michelle nervous.

"With that guy, you mentioned earlier."

Ben didn't answer. Earlier felt like a lifetime ago.

* * *

BEN FINISHED THE banana and strawberry smoothie and dropped the plastic cup in the waste bin next to the park bench. Fifteen minutes after he'd told Michelle how much money was in the bag, and ten minutes before driving through Roquetas de Mar towards Almeria. The bride spoke in a calming voice because Ben seemed anything but calm.

"You need to slow down, or you'll get brain freeze."

Talking about the smoothie, but not really. She looked at the pool attendant turned gigolo who was really a thief, but he wouldn't meet her eyes. Ben stood up and took the car keys out of his pocket.

"Slow down, and we'll get more than brain freeze."

This time, he did meet her eyes. "This changes everything. It's not just your father coming after us now."

Michelle dumped her half-finished ice cream in the bin and stood up, too. "My father's coming after me. The money guys only want you."

Ben waved a hand to indicate each of them. "Either way. Whoever finds one of us, the other gets caught in the crossfire." He gave a sad little sigh. "I should drop you off."

"And miss the road trip?"

"This isn't *When Harry Met Sally*."

"It's not *Die Hard* either."

"It's closer."

Michelle didn't fold her arms and stamp her foot, but she did stand firm. There was a set to her jaw and a look in her eyes that said she wasn't for budging. Ben held her gaze as long as he could, then glanced at the car. When he looked back at her, she had folded her arms and was tapping one foot. He took a deep breath and nodded.

"Okay. We're going to have to lose the car."

"What? We're walking now?"

"Changing. There's a fella I know in El Puche."

"Pooch?"

Ben waved towards the main road. "The man from Almeria. Pedro."

Michelle smiled. "Are you Don Quixote or Sancho Panza?"

"We're not tilting at windmills."

She put on a serious face. "The donkey, then."

Ben gave up. He pointed at the car. "El Puche."

* * *

CHAPTER TWENTY-THREE

PABLO CORDERO BELEN swished ice around his glass of lemonade and waved for Alejandro to come out onto the tiled balcony. The polite knock belied a strength and cruelty that had served Cordero Belen well over the years. He trusted Alejandro with his life and, more importantly, with the life of his daughter.

The ice clinked against the glass. Cordero Belen stopped swishing. The look on Alejandro's face gave nothing away, but he wouldn't have interrupted El Jefe's meditation if it weren't important.

"They are going to see a man called Pedro at El Puche in Almeria."

Cordero Belen nodded. "Are you still tracking her phone?"

Alejandro didn't nod. He didn't do anything. "And listening."

El Jefe looked out across the bay and watched a ferry coming across from Valencia. The sea was turquoise near the coast and deep, unrelenting blue further out. The sun glinted off the waves as it headed west. He wagged a mock admonishing finger.

"They say if you eavesdrop, you will only hear bad things."

Alejandro kept his face straight. "I am your filter from bad things."

Cordero Belen's shoulders sagged. The pressure of running the family business was only outweighed by the stress of running the family. He loved his daughter, but she was also an important asset. He didn't want to see her get hurt, but sometimes there were bigger considerations. He took a drink of lemonade.

"Do it."

Chapter Twenty-Four

SILENCE AND THE LACK of movement. Those were the two things that were sending warning signals through Ben's system as he sat across the Andarax, watching the back of the Auto Repair yard. On the map, the Andarax was a wide blue river flowing into the sea at Punta del Rio. In reality, it was a dry riverbed with a ribbon of water that was barely a stream. It reminded him of the giant storm drains they called rivers in Los Angeles, only dirtier and more uneven. Bushes clung to life at the water's edge. Lizards scampered for shade.

The rest was silence and lack of movement.

Ben shifted his position behind the retaining wall across the bridge. The car was parked in the shade beside Floristeria Montseflor, the bride standing against the boot as if guarding the money. Ben turned his attention back to the breakers yard where he was going to kill the car and get a clean one.

From this angle across the dry riverbed the neighbourhood looked to be split into two contrasting halves. To the right of Colegio Publico El Puche, the walled-in community resembled a shantytown, all makeshift dwellings that were somewhere between canvas tents and corrugated roofing. To the left, off Calle Mar de Alboran, the sprawl of adobe tenements looked like Bedrock from *The Flintstones*, interconnected concrete blocks with stairwells and walkways and dark foreboding passages.

Malaguenas Autos was at the far left of Bedrock, just off the roundabout across the bridge. The first row of apartments looked derelict, with windows boarded up and twirls of barbed wire across the rooftops. The breakers yard had a broad wooden gate that was so parched that all the paint had flaked off years ago. There was an office or workshop just visible over the cracked concrete wall. There was no sign of movement, which brought him right back where he started. Silence and lack of movement.

There were no children playing in the street. There was no foot traffic or cars driving past. If this were the land of tumbleweeds, there would be tumbleweed rolling across the open ground between the yard and the bridge. The first sign of life was three streets to the right; a woman hanging washing over the balcony and wafting flies off her face. A child barely old enough to walk was pulling a three-legged wooden horse up the stairs at the end of the block.

Nobody moved at Malaguenas Autos. There was no activity inside the breakers yard. It was hard to tell from this angle, but it looked like the gate was slightly ajar. A mangy dog trotted along the footpath, stopped to cock its leg against a lamppost, then wandered over to sniff at the open gate. It stuck its head through the gap, then yelped and ran off down the street.

Noise and movement. Things were looking up, but not in a good way.

Ben scanned the main gate one last time, then glanced at the woman hanging her washing out. The child had almost reached the top of the stairs. The three-legged horse banged in the silence. More noise. Ben noted several loads of washing hanging from half a dozen balconies. Washday in the tenements. He turned to look at Michelle waiting patiently at the car. Floristeria Montseflor provided a little shade, but the florist was just a narrow shop that fronted acres of covered land, like greenhouses with nylon sheeting instead of glass.

Flowers and washing. It might be sexist, but Ben had an idea. He pushed off from the retaining wall and crossed the road. Michelle was about to speak, but Ben held a finger to his lips and went into the florist.

* * *

BEN HAD BEEN LOOKING out for trouble all his life. Casing a target was second nature, and assessing threat levels, exit strategies, and points of entry was par for the course. He supposed cops had a similar instinct for danger, except for Ben, cops usually *were* the danger. Not always, like the bodyguards in the hotel corridor. Or the cartel hit squad that had been sent to retrieve the runaway bride.

Yes, he'd been casing joints his whole life.

But this was the first time he'd done it with a flower barrow and a smile.

The wheels creaked as he pushed the wooden barrow across the open ground between the roundabout and Calle Mar de Alboran. It felt like he was crossing no man's land towards enemy lines. The ground was too uneven to use as a car park and it didn't look like anyone in the tenements owned a car anyway.

A cat hissed and darted from its place in the shade. The splintered waggon wheels wobbled but didn't give way. Ben found himself turning around and pulling the barrow over some of the rocks, leaving his back exposed but displaying less of a threat if anyone was watching. By the time he reached the road, sweat was running down his neck and soaking into his shirt.

He paused on the blindside of Malaguenas Autos to catch his breath, but mainly to scan the side wall. There was still no movement in the yard. He wiped the sweat off his brow and proceeded to do a circuit of the perimeter, anti-clockwise away from the front gate, keeping his distance from the wall.

The first two sides were straightforward, just follow your nose and avoid the potholes, but the third was up against the nearest row of Flintstones tenements. The apartments were boarded up, but the stairwells were clear. The chipped adobe homes were like spilled concrete building blocks, jutting out at irregular intervals and accessed by stairwells and walkways. Ben wasn't interested in the ground-level passageways; he wanted the view from upstairs. He turned backwards again and pulled the barrow up one step at a time. He wondered if the child with the three-legged wooden horse had reached his mother yet.

The first row of apartments might have been derelict, but the walkways accessed all areas. As in all close communities, word spread like wildfire. The first woman came out of nowhere just as Ben reached the top of the stairs. She smiled and jabbered and bought three bunches of flowers that he didn't recognise. He wasn't a florist. By the time he was halfway along the walkway, he'd made forty-five euros and cemented his cover. Nobody was looking at the flower seller unless they wanted to buy flowers.

Ben threw occasional glances over the wall. The yard was empty.

Two women helped him down the stairs at the far end, and he gave them the last three bunches free of charge. They grinned like it was the best day of their lives and waved him off. With the empty barrow providing less cover than when he'd set off, he walked slowly along the front of the breakers yard and made a big show of stopping to catch his breath again. He pantomimed wiping sweat from his brow, and glanced at the dried wooden gate.

It was open maybe two feet.

There was no movement on the other side.

He scanned the street, then looked at the far end of the bridge. He couldn't see the car or the woman he'd run off with. That was a good sign. If he couldn't see it then the hit squad hadn't seen it either. If the hit squad were here. His instincts might have been wrong. This was an unusual situation; he'd never gone on a road trip with a drug cartel's runaway bride before. Maybe he was overreacting.

He didn't wave at the bride to say it was okay. He wasn't sure it was okay yet. There was still the small matter of why Pedro wasn't busy repairing cars in the middle of a workday afternoon. It was past siesta. This wasn't mad dogs and Englishman time. The midday sun had long since moved across the clear blue sky.

He lowered the handles of the flower barrow and took a step towards the gate. A lizard scampered across the splintered wood and hid in a crevice. Heat bounced off the bleached concrete. He wondered what the mangy dog had seen to send it whimpering, then leaned closer to look through the gap. Strong hands grabbed him by the collar and dragged him in, and the gate slammed shut behind him.

Chapter Twenty-Five

"THE GOOD NEWS IS you can keep the forty-five euros."

There was a pause for effect.

"The bad news."

The man didn't have to say what the bad news was; he simply indicated the inert figure dripping blood from the chair it was tied to. Ben looked at Pedro Malaguenas and shuddered. The bad news was very bad indeed.

* * *

THE SNATCH SQUAD WAS a two-man team with a third man providing Overwatch from the roof of the tenements. Barbed wire had been a problem for the third man but at least it provided cover since Ben hadn't thought to look at the rooftops. The other two had been waiting in the blind spot between the gate and the wall nearest the adobe buildings. There was no angle from the upstairs walkway and the only way to see them was if you stuck your head through the gap in the gate. The dog hadn't liked the reaction from the snatch squad. Ben had liked it even less.

Now they were sitting in the makeshift office that was really just a corner of the workshop, exchanging pleasantries about keeping the flower money. The snatch squad were standing. Ben was tied to a second chair with one of the squad behind him. The Overwatch guy had come down from the roof and was standing guard just inside the front gate.

The Team Leader moved away from Ben's chair and stood behind Pedro. He slapped the dripping head from side to side with a wet smack. The face was a bloodied pulp. Ben tried not to look at the weeping stumps where the fingers had been cut off with pruning shears. The fingers were scattered on the floor around the chair.

"So, the question you have to answer is this." He let go of the head and it flopped on Pedro's chest. "Where is the girl?"

He scuffed the toe of his shoe through the scattered fingers. "And you need to answer soon."

In the past, Ben had always been able to talk his way out of trouble. Looking at Pedro, this wasn't one of those times. The Team Leader slapped Pedro's lifeless form again. "I bet he wished he'd told us when you were coming."

Ben shook his head. "He wasn't expecting us."

"A surprise?"

"A change of plan."

The Team Leader waved a hand around the workbenches and power tools. "Dump the car. Have it cut up. Get a clean one."

"That was the idea. Yes."

"But that requires that you bring the car."

Ben had no energy to shrug. "Something didn't feel right."

"So, you came to check it out."

Ben nodded. The chair creaked. It seemed like every piece of wood in El Puche was dry, splintered, and weak. He was running a few things through his mind, the main one being, if Pedro didn't know they were coming how come the snatch squad got here before them?

The Team Leader took his silence for resistance. "You parked the car."

He stood in front of Ben. "And came on foot."

He brought a pair of pruning shears from behind his back. "Which brings me back to my question. Where is the girl?"

Ben tried to buy some time. "With the car."

"And where is the car?"

Ben kept his hands balled into fists to hide his fingers. "Parked."

The Team Leader unlatched the shears and the blades sprang open. He moved closer but wasn't ready for finger-cutting just yet. He massaged his brow with the fingers of his free hand as if deep in thought.

"You came across the bridge with a flower barrow."

He nodded at the man behind Ben's chair. "Check local florists."

There was some tapping and swiping before he answered.

"Floristeria Montseflor. Other side of the Andarax."

"And where is her phone?"

Some more tapping and swiping.

"It's not that accurate."

"But she's here."

"Close."

Now Ben understood how the men had tracked them, but not how they knew they were coming to Malaguenas Autos. There were some muffled sounds coming from the phone-man's earphone. He pressed the earbud deeper into his ear so he could hear.

"She's talking."

"Who to?"

"To herself, it sounds like."

The Team Leader looked nonplussed. "What's she saying?"

The phone-man sounded embarrassed. "Yippee-ki-yay, motherfucker."

Ben knew exactly what she was saying. He heard the roar of the engine as the car changed into low gear. He shoved back with his chair and the main gate smashed open.

Chapter Twenty-Six

MICHELLE SAW BEN GET yanked through the gap and the gate close behind him. For a moment, she thought he'd stumbled and fallen through the opening, but that moment was brief and quickly dispelled. She dropped to a crouch behind the retaining wall and peered over the top. A man lowered himself off the adjoining rooftop, then came down the stairs at the end of the block. He didn't go fetch the car, going through the gate instead, but she knew their car would be nearby.

"Mierda."

Even from being a little girl, and despite being taught English practically from birth, whenever she was in trouble she always swore in Mexican. This didn't feel like the time to say "shit," so she said it again. "Mierda."

Malaguenas Autos was too far and the dry riverbed too wide to hear if there was any shouting coming from the enclosed yard, but she was sure Ben wouldn't go down without a fight. Unfortunately for him this wasn't like being a thief in Yorkshire, the gigolo was in deeper shit than that. "Mierda."

Third time lucky. She walked around the side of Floristeria Montseflor and jumped in the stolen hire car. The heat was sweltering so she wound the windows down, but it didn't make any difference. This could be one of those, out of the frying pan into the fire situations, another expression she'd picked up during her English lessons. She shook her head and started the car. It was time to use the other lessons she'd been given from an early age.

* * *

A TACTICAL DEPLOYMENT THAT her father used regularly was a three-man team moving fast and loose. That meant a single car for easy access, and one man providing Overwatch for the other two. The extractions rarely needed more than two men. The third was there for backup and as a replacement if one of the pair got injured. Once Overwatch wasn't required the third man became security, providing a lookout while the other two tortured, beat, or kidnapped the target. In this situation the lookout wasn't looking out, he would be protecting their backs. That meant covering the gate.

She came out of the back street onto Calle Mar de Alboran and drove on the opposite side of the road to get a straight run at the gate. The wood looked dry and frail but she didn't have time to check. She started muttering under her breath to build herself up. Part of her mind was replaying lines from *When Harry Met Sally* but thinking about Ben being tortured behind the wooden gate, she slipped into *Die Hard*.

"Yippee-ki-yay, motherfucker."

The words coincided with her mounting the kerb and hitting the gate at an angle. Wood exploded inwards as the car burst through the gate, taking the lookout down at the knees and peppering him with splinters like shrapnel.

One down and two to go.

The car skidded sideways until she regained control. A few dabs of the controls and she aimed at the workshop. She hoped the wooden structure was as parched as the front gate. This time, there was no kerb to mount. She went straight through the office window into darkness.

* * *

BEN SHOVED HIS CHAIR backwards into the man behind him as the car smashed through the side wall and the window. The workshop was no more than a wooden shack with scale; big and wide with sagging roof beams. Lack of rainfall and baking heat had sucked all the moisture out of the wood. The car drained everything else. The wall splintered into a thousand fragments. The window just splintered.

The strain on the chair broke the legs, releasing the rope that bound him. Ben rolled sideways and swiped the phone-man's legs from under him. He grabbed what remained of the back of the chair and pressed it down on the man's throat. There was a gurgling cry, then he dropped the phone and blacked out.

The car shoved the workbench across the floor, knocking Pedro's body over and dropping the Team Leader to his knees. He was about to get up when Michelle opened the driver's door and slammed him to the ground. She used the door three more times to make sure he didn't get up again, then held a hand out to Ben.

"Get in if you want to live."

Ben struggled to his feet. "That wasn't *Die Hard*."

"I wasn't trying for *Die Hard*." She waved a hand for him to hurry up. "I'm trying to get you out of here alive."

Ben agreed, but there was just one thing. He kicked the bits of broken chair aside and searched the floor but debris from the wall made it difficult to see. He swept some of the wood away from where he thought the phone had landed but couldn't see it.

Michelle's hand waving grew more frantic. "Now."

She put the car in reverse and did a half circle to face the hole in the wall. The man she'd hit with the car door was starting to come around and the lookout in the yard got to his knees. Hire cars aren't as deadly as those big black Suburbans in the movies. It was the difference between being hit with a baseball bat or a baguette. A baguette doesn't keep you down.

Ben found the phone and picked it up. He turned towards the car but a hand grabbed his ankle. The phone-man was groggy but strong. His eyes weren't focussed, but he knew what he was holding, the man they'd come here to question. Only they didn't need to question him anymore because the girl they were looking for had just driven through the wall. So, he didn't need to keep the pool guy alive.

The gun came up slowly, the man aiming with his senses, not his eyes. All he had to do was shoot just above his hand and he'd hit something. The barrel wavered. The car door slammed open. Ben tried to kick himself free but the hand held his ankle in a death grip.

Everyone was waking up. The guy in the yard was swaying but on his feet. The phone-man was trying to line up a shot. The Team Leader was on his knees brushing debris off his back.

The barrel stopped wavering and pointed just above Ben's knee. The eyes came into focus with the hint of a smile. Ben froze. Then Michelle stamped on the gun hand and twisted the gun out of his grip. She slammed the butt into his face and the other hand released Ben's ankle. They were back down to two again but those two looked pissed off and ready to rumble.

Michelle jumped in the car and Ben climbed in the passenger seat. She drove out through the hole in the workshop and crunched gravel and wood across the yard. The lookout dived to one side but got clipped by the front nearside wing. The car skidded slightly then steadied. She went out through the gate and turned left away from the bridge.

The flower barrow stood forlornly on the pavement. The women had gone back to hanging out their washing. Michelle cut left at the Colegio Publico El Puche and disappeared into the back streets. Ben tried to be helpful.

"They'll be coming after us."

"Not unless they've got four spare tyres." She indicated the florist knife in the footwell. "And not once did you tell me how they found us in the first place."

Chapter Twenty-Seven

"PITY. I REALLY LIKED that phone."

"I really liked Pedro."

"Sorry. Yes, all because of my phone."

They had cut back on themselves, then abandoned the coast road, heading up into the hills and turning west through Desierto de Tabernas on the A-92, not the highway but the old road that threaded its way alongside the main transport route. Going back towards Malaga before dumping the phone in a skip behind an old western saloon. The area was steeped in the history of the Spaghetti Western, with a theme park and several fake cowboy towns replicating the American West. In many ways, they looked more authentic than the real thing. Or at least more like the Old West of the movies.

Once they'd got rid of the phone, setting a false trail heading west, they could turn east again on the N-342, but not until they'd talked about the other elephant in the room, Michelle's evasion technique and the reason the snatch squad had known where to find them. They had that discussion at a gas station in Abla, just off the highway and a million miles from anywhere.

* * *

STEAM HISSED FROM THE ruptured front grill, and the left-hand light cluster was broken. If that wasn't bad enough, the rear bumper was hanging off, and the front nearside tyre had a slow puncture. Hire companies in Spain were notorious for renting damaged cars but this car was crying out to be stopped by the police. Ben and Michelle couldn't afford to be stopped by the police. They hadn't committed any crimes they could be arrested for, but the Cordero Belen cartel no doubt had fingers in many pies, one of them being local law enforcement.

Ben looked at the damage. "Round the back down the arroyo he said."

Michelle gave Ben a wary look. "And you trust him?"

Ben shrugged. "He runs a petrol station in the middle of nowhere. Who else is there to trust?"

Estacion de Servico Cepsa was a three-pump gas station at the side of the road into Abla. The mountain village climbed a hump in the land half a mile further on, all adobe buildings and cracked concrete, but the Cepsa signage looked clean and fresh. They weren't parked next to clean and fresh; Michelle had pulled around the side between the Aire & Agua stand and the Aspirador. The vacuum cleaner looked as banged up as the car and twice as rusty.

"We're not looking to keep it, but..." Ben indicated the desert terrain and lack of infrastructure. "Who's going to find it out here?"

Michelle still didn't look convinced. "Assuming he's got something to replace it with."

Ben held up his hands. "I'm not the one battering rammed The Alamo."

"Nobody survived at The Alamo."

"Pedro didn't survive at Malaguenas Autos."

They fell silent. Both of them knew how serious the situation was and who was responsible. Ben felt like telling her it wasn't her fault, but was struggling with his own guilt. It might have been Michelle's phone they were tracking, but they were tracking her because of him. He deflected his thoughts by surveying their surroundings. They were sitting on the dusty porch of an adobe building that might have been the original gas station. The roof had sagged, and one wall was leaning precariously from the gable end. The porch was only missing a rocking chair and a hitching post. He almost expected Clint Eastwood to come around the corner with a poncho and a cigarillo.

He puffed out his cheeks. "So, this battering ram technique. You learn that at finishing school?"

It was supposed to take her mind off having her phone bugged, but he regretted saying it when he saw her shoulders sag.

"Sorry. Bad joke on a bad day."

Michelle looked up from staring at her feet. "You want to know about bad days?" Her stare was hard enough to cut glass. "Let me tell you."

* * *

THE FIRST TIME MICHELLE knew she was different from the other kids was when she was picked up at school by a group of armed men wearing body armour. She was eight years old. The Cordero Belen family name was a big thing with the teachers, but it wasn't the only big name at her school. Her best friend was from a family whose name was only ever whispered, but she didn't know why. The day Michelle was taken home by an armed escort was the day she found out.

Her friend had been kidnapped, and her family was all over the news.

Michelle was a quick learner. It didn't take long to realise that the chaperone who went everywhere with her was really a bodyguard, and the news made it clear how Pablo Cordero Belen made his fortune. Her father's face was on the news almost as much as the whispered family cartel. Michelle's friend looked happy and smiling in the news photos. When she was returned home after an armed siege and a street battle that left five dead and fifteen injured, the smile was long gone. Not long after that, her friend left school in favour of being home tutored.

Michelle refused to leave school; it was where her friends were. Even at the age of eight, she was headstrong and stubborn. That's when she started taking private lessons, things they didn't teach at Instituto Simon Bolivar. Things that made her faster, stronger, and even more headstrong.

Just over a year later, the whispered family cartel was massacred in a widely publicised coup. By then, her friend was no longer her friend, but the news that she had been caught in the crossfire still shook her world. Speculation was rife that the Cordero Belen cartel had folded the business into its own and became so powerful that *her* family name was only whispered.

She was now ten years old.

Her kidnap evasion training went into overdrive, and she had two chaperones instead of one. By the time she was twelve she was proficient in self-defence and could disable an attacker with a pen or just about anything out of her geometry kit. When she was fourteen, she could drive as fast in reverse as she could going forward. By sixteen she was back to having one chaperone. She didn't need two.

She could field strip an M-16 with her eyes closed and knew each component of a Beretta, a Sig Sauer or a Smith & Wesson. She could hit a stationary target at a hundred yards and a running man at ten. So far, she hadn't needed to do either, until she ran one man over and hit the other man with the car door. Now hitting a running man at ten yards seemed a distinct possibility.

* * *

BEN WAS STUNNED TO silence. He looked out across the scorched hills and leaned back against the wall. Powdered whitewash dusted his shoulders but he didn't notice, his mind was playing a dozen scenarios and none of them came out good.

"Couldn't you have told me before I stole the car and broke into the safe?"

"You were always going to steal the car and break into the safe."

Ben couldn't argue with that. He knew that sooner or later, he was always going to flee Laguna Park, and when he did, he was going to take Max Overend's money with him. What he was really doing was delaying having to express the sympathy he felt building inside him. He might have had a tough childhood, but his life had been nothing compared to Michelle Cordero Belen, daughter of a drug lord, and a trained assassin. Or at least how to avoid assassins.

"And you had to do all that at ten years old?"

"Eight through sixteen. Right up until now."

Ben gave her a sideways look. "Should I watch my back?"

She kept a straight face. "You're not trying to hurt me."

He held his hands up. "I'm not trying to do anything with you."

She nodded and let out a sigh. "I know."

Her expression softened. "That's why I like you."

They both went quiet. The air was thick with unspoken sentiments, the most pressing of which was that they both liked each other, but what were they going to do about it? Ben felt the hairs bristle at the back of his neck, and he wanted to look her in the eye, but he lowered his head and stared at his feet. He made little stamping motions and watched the dust puff around his shoes. He did a little tap dance. More dust. He swallowed to moisten his throat, then glanced at the wrecked hire car.

"Round the back down the arroyo."

"You've already said that."

He stood up and brushed the whitewash off his shoulders. "Let's go buy a car."

Chapter Twenty-Eight

PABLO CORDERO BELEN SLAMMED the phone down. He didn't call anyone a hijo de puta this time, the slamming was enough to vent his frustration. He glanced at the baseball bat but thought better of destroying any more of his host's property. He took a deep breath and looked out across the Badia de Palma instead. The bay was calm and clear and a dozen shades of blue. A Balearia Abel ferry cut through the water on its final leg from Valencia on the mainland and took a left turn towards the ferry terminal at Portopi. Catedral de Mallorca looked down from its perch across the bay in Palma. The cathedral looked a hell of a lot calmer than the man staring out from Villa Real.

"Alejandro."

The balcony door opened, and Alejandro crossed the tiled floor and waited. It wasn't his place to ask, just wait to be told. He didn't have to wait long.

"Two more men."

Cordero Belen tapped a paradiddle on the phone with three fingers. "They're to take the ferry to Valencia and wait."

Alejandro had been with the family long enough to brave the question. "Is she coming to Valencia?"

"She isn't going the direction she dumped her phone."

He stopped his finger-tapping. His daughter was well trained; he knew because he'd paid a lot of money for that training. Kidnap protection, evasion tactics, and self-defence. She had been taught by the best. Now, it was time for the best to get back in the game.

"Where is Esteban?"

"Retired."

"Retired where?"

"Mexico."

Cordero Belen gave Alejandro a hard look.

Alejandro expanded. "Sabinas I think. North. Up near Boquillas Crossing."

Cordero Belen nodded. "At the border. Good. Get him to Houston and have my private jet bring him here."

He gave Alejandro the hard look again. "Yesterday."

Alejandro left to make the arrangements and Cordero Belen felt a tug at his heart. His daughter had been troubled her whole life, but she was still his daughter. He was proud of her independence, and it would break his heart if he had to punish her, but you don't become the head of the most powerful family in Mexico by being lenient on wayward daughters. This merger was even bigger than absorbing the whisper family's territory. This was international.

"Mierda."

This time he did swear, echoing his daughter's curse while thinking of the son of a bitch who had distracted her. He had dealt with hijo de putas before, the many boyfriends who had tried to win her heart, but that had always been back home in Mexico. It was different dealing with an Englishman in Spain. Everyone was abroad. Nobody was on home turf.

"Shit bitch motherfucker."

Swearing in English cleansed his palate. He hoped that was the only cleansing he would have to do before this was over.

* * *

CONSUELA MENDOZA WIPED THE blood from her hands and considered her next move. She knew that Cordero Belen's snatch squad had failed to snatch the bride because she made a point of knowing everything. She could even speculate as to how the bride had avoided being snatched;

the training she had been given by Esteban Salazar, a retired legend in the close-quarter protection community. Decades of service had earned him the nickname El Zorro Plateado, The Silver Fox. She also knew what Cordero Belen's next move would be; send two more men to augment the original snatch squad and bring Salazar out of retirement.

If Salazar was The Silver Fox, then Mendoza was beginning to think of herself as La Perra Ninja, The Ninja Bitch, because the person she was questioning told her the runaways already called her that. Sometimes parallels are part of life; she dressed in black at night and could stalk a snake in the long grass. The snake she was stalking at the moment was Benjamin Green, former lifeguard and tennis pro.

It was time to light a fire under the snake.

She looked at the person she'd been questioning. Eduardo Perez had told her everything she needed to know after breaking his toes, one at a time. Some people broke fingers or cut them off but that was too obvious and left the authorities in no doubt that something bad had happened. Broken toes don't look much different to unbroken toes but elicit the same response. They hurt like hell.

The address Eduardo had given her was a long way from where the runaways were last seen but they were heading in the right direction. Almost being caught in El Puche would certainly drive them forward, after the obligatory detour to throw their pursuers of the scent. The bride should have known better; El Zorro Plateado had taught her whatever tactics she employed. Whatever she knew, he knew first. The secret now was to promote an urgency that forced them to use Green's get-out-of-jail card.

She looked at the man slumped on the kitchen chair, his head on back to front where she'd broken his neck. She'd have to straighten that before sending the message to light the fire, and she'd have to wait until dark before she could set that in motion. Until then, it was time to eat. Torture always made her hungry.

Chapter Twenty-Nine

ROUND THE BACK DOWN the arroyo was a bit further than just around the back of Estacion de Servico Cepsa. The dirt track was a deep cutting leading to another dry riverbed, this one not as wide as the one in El Puche but just as parched. If the main road through Abla was two-lane blacktop this was dirt and stone with a covering of dust. The dust plumed around the back of the car as Ben negotiated the narrow-gauge road, having taken over the driving again. Kidnap resolution tactics weren't required this time. Michelle shouted a warning.

"Watch out."

The car hit a boulder and the rear bumper fell off. Ben stopped and picked it up. There was no room in the boot so he put it on the back seat. He returned Michelle's condescending look with a raised eyebrow and a tilt of the head.

"I wouldn't have to watch out if you hadn't wrecked the car."

"You wouldn't be here if I hadn't wrecked the car."

They were back to arguing again, their default setting it seemed, rather than admit there was any kind of emotional connection. Ben concentrated on avoiding any more boulders. Michelle focussed on anything but Ben.

The garage was at the end of the cutting alongside the dry riverbed. There was no name and no signage. The land had been cleared and levelled to allow parking for several cars, half of which were in need of repair while the other half had En Venta signs on the windscreens. They looked like they'd been For Sale a long time. The garage itself didn't look much better, a ramshackle mixture of adobe walls, corrugated sheeting and wooden fencing. The house by the river was more traditional, if a little small. The front porch would have had a river view if there'd been a river to look at. Sitting on the bench seats now would just get you dusty.

"Good choice." Michelle being sarcastic again.

Ben was more realistic. "We don't have a choice."

On that, they both agreed. Ben pulled into a space at the far end of the En Venta cars and turned the engine off. There was no steam now, the radiator having burned dry. The car shuddered and settled on its axels. The exhaust coughed once then everything went quiet.

An old man came out onto the porch and stood in the dying rays of the setting sun. He took a drink from a tall glass, then put it on the porch rail. The steps creaked under his weight, then he crossed the turnaround and stood in front of the car.

"Your little mule is past repair."

Ben got out and waved at the other cars. "It's a new mule we need."

Michelle got out and stood beside Ben. The old man looked at the couple who were pretending not to be a couple. They looked tired and careworn but stood together. The old man let out a sigh.

"You need more than a new car, I think."

* * *

ENRICO AGUILAR PUT THE food on the table and looked out across the river. He had brought the table onto the porch because there wasn't enough room for three people in the kitchen. The sun had set but the desert landscape was still shades of grey and blue. Stars were beginning to puncture the darkening sky but it was still clear blue with a few ribbons of cloud along the horizon.

"Ice cream does not count as food."

He was responding to Michelle saying when they'd last eaten. The steaming bowl of chilli and rice made her stomach rumble. Aguilar set a plate of nachos next to the bowl and distributed plates and cutlery.

"I have learned, over time, to always have a bowl of chilli on the boil. You never know when you are going to eat."

They hadn't told him why they were here or what trouble they were in, he simply intuited it. Helping weary travellers seemed to be his mission in life as much as repairing broken cars. Broken people were more challenging, and the first step towards repairing them was chilli and rice.

He held up a finger. "One moment."

He went inside and came out with a tub of soured cream. "Now we can fix you."

He said a little prayer in Spanish and crossed himself. His grey hair shone in the evening light and there was a twinkle in his eyes. It looked like repairing people was better than selling cars. Ben looked at Michelle, and this time, there was no sarcastic response. She nodded and gave a little smile. Ben smiled back. Then they ate in silence.

After the meal, Michelle offered to wash up, but Aguilar shook his head.

"There is only one woman washes my dishes."

"I am only one woman."

Aguilar smiled. "But you are not *that* one woman."

Michelle looked at the old man and nodded. There was no need to ask where that one woman was, any more than Aguilar had to ask what kind of trouble Michelle and Ben were in. It didn't matter. The old man lived alone, that was all. How he came to live alone was irrelevant. Aguilar stacked the plates and took them inside.

He raised his voice through the open door. "You can have the spare room."

Michelle stood in the doorway and looked at the cramped interior. "There's a spare room?"

Aguilar stopped washing the plates and turned towards her. "Any room that isn't used is spare." He indicated the sky above the front porch. "I like to sleep under the stars."

"What if it rains?"

"Did you not see the river?"

"Oh. Yes."

He finished washing and stacking, then came back out onto the porch. The sky had darkened and stars punched pinpricks in the night. Moths danced around the porch light and a gecko scurried across the wall into the shadows. The gentle hum of traffic on the A-92 sounded in the distance. Soon, the hum would stop for the night, leaving only cicadas and bats. He indicated the table and the runaway couple sat. Closer than the first time. Aguilar smiled. He did a lot of smiling.

"Now, cheese and wine."

The smile turned sad. "Then we will talk."

* * *

THE LANDSCAPE WAS ALIVE with the chirruping of night creatures. Ben wondered how hard you'd have to rub your legs together to make that much noise. Wondering about the crickets or whatever they called them in Spain was just his way of avoiding the main question.

"The bad people that are looking for you. Are they very bad?"

Michelle nodded. Ben listened to the crickets.

"And they want to hurt you?"

Michelle twirled her empty wineglass. "They want me back. It's him they want to hurt."

Aguilar considered that, then proved again how intuitive he was. "Su padre?"

Michelle nodded again. "My father."

The old man pushed a piece of cheese around his plate. It was a small piece of cheese. He patted it back and forth between the fingers of both hands, like a cat toying with a mouse.

He stopped patting. "And those people are the ones who damaged your car?"

"Actually, I damaged the car running over those people."

"But they still won't hurt you?"

Michelle held a hand out and made it quiver. "If they have to."

"If you ran them over, I think have to is what they will do."

"Maybe."

"Either they will or they won't. There is no maybe."

"Yes, then."

"You ran them over in Almeria?"

"El Puche."

"But you're heading east, so you turned west. Diversion."

Ben stopped contemplating the cricket and joined the conversation. "That's why we need a new car."

Aguilar turned his attention to Ben. "I don't have new cars."

Ben shrugged. "A car they aren't looking for."

Aguilar toyed with the small piece of cheese again then stopped and flicked it hard into the night.

"And your little mule. It stays here? Where the bad men will never look."

Ben and Michelle nodded in unison.

Aguilar was looking at them both now. "Do you know how many bad men have come to Abla looking for cars?"

They didn't shake their heads.

Aguilar leaned forward and rested his elbows on the table. "The same as have come looking for fugitivos."

He held one hand up and formed a zero with the forefinger and thumb. Ben frowned.

Michelle looked at the old man. "Your point being?"

Aguilar pushed back from the table. "My point is. They are looking north, south, east, and west. For you. In any car. Anything moving. Anything with two people. Your car is already history to them. It is the roads they are searching. But they won't come looking in Abla."

Ben thought he knew where the old man was going, but Michelle gave Aguilar a questioning look. The grey hair looked even greyer in the porch light and the twinkle in his eyes grew brighter.

"So, rest in Abla. Let the dust settle. Wait them out."

Chapter Thirty

"THIS IS GETTING TO be a habit. You coming to my room at night."

"I'll sleep in the other room."

"There is no other room."

Michelle had a point, but Ben wasn't ready to give up yet. "I'll sleep on the floor."

The old man had refused to let them help with the washing up again, and had moved the table back into the kitchen. The living room was cluttered with furniture and mementos from a past life, a life with the only women he allowed to wash his dishes. There was no room for a makeshift bed, so they would have to share the bedroom. Ben was beginning to think the old man had the best idea, sleeping under the stars. In Leeds you couldn't see the stars. It must be a romantic way to spend the night.

He brought himself up short at the thought of, romantic. Under the present circumstances it shouldn't even be on the radar, and was the last thing he needed when people were trying to kill him and kidnap her. He wondered if her kidnap resolution training had taught her how to deal with that, the growing attraction between two people on the run together. Shared experience, mutual danger, and close proximity could all conspire to push those people together. Like Stockholm syndrome, only different, the victim falling in love with the kidnapper.

Ben broke it down into something closer to his experience: that bomb on the bus movie with Keanu Reeves and Sandra Bullock. Him saying that relationships based on tense experiences never work, and her saying they'd have to base it on sex then. The sexy bitch and the good-looking man were in a small room with one bed, how hard could it be?

"The floor." He even pointed to a corner of the bedroom for emphasis.

Michelle gave him a steady look. "You repeat yourself a lot, don't you?"

"I'll repeat this. You're not Sally, and I'm not Harry."

"You never said that before."

"But I'm repeating it anyway."

Michelle twirled a hand at the size of the room. "And this isn't Katz's Deli."

Ben didn't even want to think about Michelle faking orgasm. He didn't want to think about orgasms at all. Except he did. He really did. That's why he clenched his jaw and spoke through gritted teeth.

"Your father wants to pull my teeth and hang me up to bleed out. So, forgive me if I don't order pastrami on rye."

"That's what Katz's Deli is famous for."

There was mischief in her eyes. "That and the orgasm."

"Fake orgasm."

She raised an eyebrow. "You've seen it then."

"Not as much as *Die Hard*." He pointed to the floor again. "And right now, I'm going to make fists with my toes."

Michelle moved closer to him. "You're not suffering from jetlag."

"I'm suffering from Cartel and Money Laundering syndrome. The symptoms being an acute awareness of my mortality."

There was just enough room for him to step around her and walk to his corner of the floor. He stepped to one side and made his move, but his trailing hand brushed her hip as he went past, and they both stood still.

* * *

MICHELLE FELT THE HEAT from his hand as it brushed her body, and the flirty humour evaporated in an instant. She stood facing one way, and Ben faced the other, but they both stopped just out of reach of the body heat that the hand had caused. She had already admitted to herself that she found his honourable behaviour attractive. He was good-looking in a strange, unsexy way, and he *was* English. That accent worked on Americans and Mexicans alike, but the whole gigolo and hen party thing had soured any possibilities of involvement. It simply wouldn't work.

So why had she been teasing him just now? What was the point of making him feel uncomfortable if it wasn't to make him notice her in a romantic way? Or was this just another of her mini rebellions? A statement to her father that she would choose her own boyfriends and damn the consequences.

Except this time, the consequences would be pulled teeth and bleeding.

She looked at the wall above the bed to avoid looking at Ben. The paint was clean but cracked, and there was a carved wooden crucifix halfway above the pillows. A crude figure hung from the cross, and she thought of that English cop who kept turning up on the news back home. The one that was always causing trouble across the border and getting caught on camera with his arms out like Jesus on the cross. It would take a lot to get resurrected from this, the teeth pulling not the body heat.

She tried to think what she wanted from this. Was she looking for a long-term boyfriend, or was this really just a fuck you to her father? She knew how it had started, but it felt a long way from that now. Some of that was the adrenaline rush of putting her training into practice, but most of it was the quiet unassuming Englishman who had just brushed her hip. Maybe this could resurrect the little girl who believed in love at first sight and that there was someone for everyone.

She took a deep breath and let it out slowly. Once her pulse had stopped racing, she turned around.

* * *

BEN WAS ALREADY FACING her. He had turned around almost as soon as he'd touched her hip. He knew this was a bad idea, but his life was littered with bad ideas. As bad ideas went, this one felt a lot safer than putting Laguna Park leaflets in a Don Carlos hotel room safe. Still, this felt like a bad idea.

"This isn't what I wanted."

"Who said it's what you're going to get?"

Arguing again. It seemed like she couldn't help herself.

Ben looked her in the eye, a slow steady look that took in every part of her face. He noticed she had a scar on her chin, and her nose was slightly crooked. Broken, maybe during her childhood training? There was a little pulse in the corner of one eye and a flaw in the iris. It was a slightly different colour than the other one.

"I'm not a good investment."

Her tone softened. "I've never been a safe bet either. Ask any of my..."

She didn't continue. They both let out a sigh and nodded. Ben took a step closer and was raising his hand when there was a knock on the door. The old man's voice was loud and insistent.

"Hey, amigo. You worked at Laguna Park, didn't you?"

Chapter Thirty-One

THE TELEVISION WAS OLD and faded but there was no mistaking the image on the screen. Ben felt cold despite the heat inside the house by the river. There was no rushing water to soothe his nerves. The river was as dry as his heart. A newsreader explained about the tragic accident in Spanish without subtitles while a handheld camera captured the scene. Ben didn't need subtitles to know what had happened, and he didn't need a close-up to know who the paramedics were loading onto the gurney, but he got a close-up anyway.

Eduardo Perez stared up at the camera until a hand pulled the cover over.

"Fucking shitty death."

The old man didn't need a translation. Once again, he had intuited that the bad news on the TV was linked to the runaway couple. He didn't need any intuition now because there was no doubt the dead man was Ben's friend. Ben stared at the screen.

"Bastard fucking bitch."

No doubt at all.

* * *

CONSUELA MENDOZA WATCHED THE wall-mounted TV in her apartment on Terrace B with a blank expression and no emotion. Walking distance from Villa del Sol. Not much further from the poolside lifeguard chair. A long drop onto hard tile. It hadn't been easy carrying the overweight Spaniard, but nobody had seen the Ninja Bitch planting the evidence. Soft pool shoes hid the broken toes. Anybody looking could see the broken neck.

Mendoza checked her watch and wondered if Benjamin Green was watching the news live or if he'd see it in the morning. It didn't matter which. She had lit the fire. Now, all she had to do was watch him run for cover. Right to the address that Eduardo Perez had given her after the fourth toe.

* * *

"YOU CANNOT AVOID THE inevitable, my friend."

Eduardo certainly hadn't been able to avoid it, but the question was, would it have been inevitable if Ben hadn't run off with the bride? Ben slumped into a kitchen chair and felt guilty about mentioning Eduardo's weight that day by the pool. He felt guilty about a lot of things but mainly, what he felt right now was angry.

The way the news played, it was like this.

With the help of a translator.

Tragic accident with a touch of irony; a lifeguard breaking his neck falling off the lifeguard chair. The timeline was vague, but the implications were clear. According to witnesses the victim was well known for partying and drinking to excess. It was believed that once the resort had shut down for the night, Perez had continued at a private party in one of the villas. When the party shut down, he set off back to his apartment but detoured past the pool. There was no evidence but the report suggested he was singing and swaying and generally acting like Eduardo. He climbed the ladder to the lifeguard's chair and did a bit more singing and swaying. Until he swayed too much and fell out of the chair. It was a long way down. And hard as stone. His neck didn't stand a chance.

There was some screaming and shouting from the guests, and the entire bottom row of apartments was awakened. Somebody from Terrace B found the body, although they couldn't say where the screaming had come from. Policia Local and an ambulance arrived about the same time as the television news, so the blue flashing lights made a dramatic opening to the news coverage, and the reporter even managed to get them in the background when she signed off with the tragic irony angle.

"I feel sick."

The old man turned the TV off, and Michelle pulled a chair next to Ben's. She placed an arm across his back, and he turned to rest his head on her shoulder. There was no sexual frisson. The body heat didn't spark any Harry Met Sally vibes. This was just one person comforting another person who had suffered a tragic loss. There was nothing ironic about that.

After a few moments, Ben blew out his cheeks, nodded, then sat up straight. Michelle's arm fell away from his back, and it was as if they'd never touched. Ben flexed his shoulders and twisted his neck one way then the other. Bones cracked in the silence. He shifted in his seat so he could look at Aguilar and Michelle.

"This changes everything."

Aguilar shook his head. "It changes nothing, amigo. If they have done this thing, it is because they do not know where you are. I argue that things are just the same. Bad men never come looking in Abla."

It was Ben's turn to shake his head. He glanced at the old man, then focussed on Michelle. "If she got to Eduardo, then she knows where we're going."

"El Puche?"

"The other where."

"Your friend gave you an address?"

"And Ninja Bitch has got it."

"You don't know that."

"We've got to assume."

Michelle stared him straight in the face. "If you assume, you make an ass out of you and me."

"That's not funny."

"It's not supposed to be. Don't assume. Hope for the best and plan for the worst. The best is, he didn't tell her. The worst is, she knows the address. If we plan for that then we're in the driving seat. We'll be looking for her, not her finding us."

"I don't feel in the driving seat."

Michelle leaned forward and kissed him on the forehead. "You're not. I am. Let's put all that training my father paid for into action."

The old man slopped out a bowl of still-warm chilli and sat at the table. It seemed he was right when he'd said, always have a pot of chilli on the boil. He took three mouthfuls while he watched his guests, then swilled it down with a glass of lemonade. The room was quiet. The TV clicked as it cooled, but the enclosed space didn't cool much.

"So, you won't be staying in Abla?"

Michelle's expression was hard as nails. "No."

Aguilar pushed the bowl away. "I'd better get your new mule ready then."

He didn't wash the bowl. "But not until tomorrow. Get some sleep. You're going to need it."

Chapter Thirty-Two

DAWN BROKE TO THE sound of a cock crowing and a drill drilling. Ben hadn't noticed any livestock but knew where the drilling was coming from. He swung his legs off the bed and sat up, surprised that he had slept so soundly. He glanced over his shoulder. Michelle was still asleep. That surprised him as well. They had both slept on the bed, and there hadn't been any funny business. Maybe Billy Crystal was wrong, and you could be friends without sex getting in the way.

Ben shook his head to clear it. This was nothing to do with friendship. It was about survival. He stood up, went to the window, and peeked through the curtains. The cock-a-doodle-do stopped, but the drill didn't. The old man must be an early riser because it looked like he'd been working through the night. Michelle awoke with a jerk, then sat up in bed. For a blissful moment she looked like any beautiful woman waking up in the morning, then she remembered where she was.

The drilling changed into hammering with periods of angle-grinding.

"Don't they have cockerels to wake you up around here?"

* * *

BEN CROSSED THE COMPOUND, kicking up puffs of dust in the dirt even this early in the morning. There was a water tank above the workshop and a weathervane above the tank. Wind coming off the hills made the blades creak as they spun. The heat would have been perfect for Laguna Park. At a backwater garage, it was just hot.

"You don't waste any time."

Enrico Aguilar brought his head up out of the engine compartment and wiped an oil-stained hand across his chin. The grey hair was lank and flattened with sweat. The twinkle had left his eyes.

"Time is in short supply."

Ben stood in the doorway and nodded back towards the house. "Chilli for breakfast, is it?"

A smile played across the old man's lips. "No. There is bacon and eggs. You're in the tourist mecca. Full English available everywhere."

Ben indicated the car Aguilar was working on. "Little mule?"

Aguilar wiped his hands on a dirty cloth. "With an extra kick."

The car was one from the En Venta line, second from the left. It looked like an ex-rental with the usual quota of dents and scratches. The paintwork was bright red with a sheen of dust, and was faded by the sun. That was good; it would stand out among the crowd and, therefore, be completely invisible. Cordero Belen's men would be looking for something that blended in.

"Kick how?"

"Let me show you."

The kick wasn't so much a kick as a head-butt. Like a raging bull getting its head down to charge the toreador or whatever they had in the bullring. Aguilar had reinforced the front and rear bumpers and given added strength to the driver and passenger doors. He had tuned the engine to get the most out of the horsepower, but the added weight was going to drain fuel like a greedy drunk. Ben wasn't worried about the cost of refuelling; he doubted he'd be worried about the cost of anything ever again. If he survived long enough to reach ever again.

The old man patted the rear of the boot. "I saw what happened to the back of your other car." He kicked the bumper. "This will go through walls." He pressed down on the springs. The car was sitting low on the suspension. "But if you want to outrun them. Forget about it."

Ben opened the driver's door and looked inside. "I don't plan on seeing them, never mind outrunning them." He scanned the interior, half expecting an instrument panel. "No ejector seat?"

The old man didn't know his James Bond. "It doesn't even have airbags. So, if you ram anyone, make sure you're wearing your seatbelt." He tapped the side of his head with one finger. "And don't drive angry. What happened to your friend. That was to make you run. Think first. Payback later."

Ben closed the car door and looked over the roof. "That's a lot of advice for a place where bad men don't come looking."

Aguilar's face looked a hundred years old. The lines around his eyes crinkled into something resembling a wise old smile. The twinkle was tempered by sadness. "There are always bad men. It is outsiders we avoid."

"We're outsiders."

"That you are."

"So why are you helping us?"

The old man pushed off from the car and dropped the cloth on the workbench. "Because for every man and woman trying to make their way in this world, there is another man and woman that went before. When you find the one who will wash your plates, you deserve all the help you can get."

Ben didn't enquire about the one that went before. "The other car?"

"It never existed."

"For spare parts?"

"For earth and rust and landfill."

Ben nodded. "Then for that, I'll pay double."

The old man's smile returned. "You will pay triple. Don't forget the chilli."

Chapter Thirty-Three

MAX OVEREND WATCHED THE clean-up operation and felt the bottom drop out of his world. He'd finally plucked up courage to tell his investors about the burglary and fully expected there to be repercussions, but this wasn't it. This was something else. He stood at the balcony behind reception and looked down at the resort that was rapidly turning into a war zone.

The rows of terraces fanned out from the central walkway as it sloped all the way down to the restaurant and the pool beyond. In the clean light of day, Laguna Park looked the same as any other day in the Spanish summer. The horizon was clear, and the red tiled roofs contrasted with the perfect blue sky and the luscious green of the trees. Holidaymakers went about their business oblivious to the death that walked among them.

"Green, you bastard."

It was easier to blame his pet thief than accept responsibility himself. So far, Overend's sideline had cost him his head of entertainment, the assistant lifeguard, and a safe full of money he couldn't afford to lose. The first and the third parts of that could be laid at his door, employing a thief and using him to feather his own nest, but Eduardo Perez falling out of the lifeguard chair was as likely as slipping on a bar of soap.

Surely, it was too soon for his principals to have retaliated. He'd only told them last night, after giving the man from Leeds a head start. He'd explained about Ben Green going missing but not that he knew he was a thief. That might come out in the wash, or it might not, but he was banking on having plausible deniability. *"I didn't know he was a thief."* Having two parties looking for the missing gigolo was bad enough, but now he had to factor in this third person. It was like one of those *Agatha Christie* mysteries. Who killed the lifeguard at the swimming pool? And was it linked to the runaway bride? That was the fourth factor. The hen party had been asking at reception if anyone had seen her leave. Max Overend didn't believe in coincidence. The gigolo breaking into the safe on the same night as the woman he'd been hired to service disappearing was too obvious for words, not to mention all that happening the same day the body of the gigolo's friend was found beside the lifeguard chair.

The other thing to consider was what the third person might have learned from Perez, because he had certainly been questioned before he took the high dive. Taking the worst-case scenario, it was likely the attacker had been given the address that Perez had no doubt shared with Green. It was the obvious place to start and it was undoubtedly where the gigolo was heading now.

The only thing in Overend's favour was the fact that Green probably didn't know who had given Perez the address in the first place. The assistant lifeguard had a shady past of his own, but wasn't in the same league as Benjamin Green. Whether he knew or not, the address was Green's only means of escape. Passports and transport with no questions asked. Overend almost felt guilty giving that information to the man from Leeds but not to the money launderers. A head start was one thing, but he wanted to slant the odds in his favour. The fly in the ointment was this third party, because now there were too many people heading to Barcelona.

Chapter Thirty-Four

"DO YOU THINK WE should have stayed a while?"

"We don't have a while."

"Want to know what my training says?"

"I know what your training says. It says the news was to spook us into breaking cover. That we will either run straight into a trap or turn tail and run the opposite direction. Either way, blind panic leaves you blind. We're not running blind."

They were on a long, straight run through dry grassland. The high plains were parched and colourless apart from patches of scrub brush on either side of the road and the tall white blades of the wind farm that stretched to the horizon on the right. To the left the snow-capped mountains of the Sierra Nevada stood out in the distance. Abla had disappeared in the rear-view mirror twenty minutes ago.

"Blind rage is the same as blind panic."

"We know what we're looking for. That's not blind."

Ben was driving because this was the driving stretch of the journey, not the tactical evade and destroy section. That would be Michelle's field of expertise. Ben was beginning to wonder what his field of expertise was, but then he remembered the holdall in the boot. The bag was filled with his field of expertise and was the reason they could afford to pay three times the price for a second-hand car with extras.

"He really called me the woman who'd wash your plates?"

"It wasn't so much about the plates."

"What was it about then?"

Ben glanced at the woman beside him. "You know what it's about."

Michelle turned in her seat so her back was against the passenger door and looked at the man she'd spent the night with twice but hadn't really slept with. He was right; she did know what it was about. It was about two people who hadn't wanted to be together being forced together due to circumstances beyond their control; actually, circumstances entirely of their own making. It was about those two people realizing they had more in common than they thought, and a growing affection neither could deny. It was about Harry meeting Sally.

"That was nice of him."

Ben nodded. "Don't get your hopes up. I don't think it worked out too well for the last dish washer."

"But it was good until it wasn't."

Ben glanced at Michelle again. "It was good."

"And he doesn't see us as Bonnie and Clyde."

"He sees us as two people who need his help. So, he helped."

"That was nice of him too."

Ben kept his eyes on the road. The A-92 continued its gentle climb into the hills and curled right towards Guadix and the place where they could turn east again. They hadn't discussed the plan in detail but it pretty much relied on driving to Barcelona and getting new travel documents and transport. Until then it was the open road and a lot of driving. And something else.

"Are you sure about this next part?"

Michelle swivelled to face forward again. "I want to see what he's got lined up against us."

"I thought we'd seen your father's men."

"That was his snatch squad. I want to see his base team."

"Isn't that with him in Majorca?"

Her expression hardened. "It's on the mainland. Close to hand but ready to move. Good transport links. Air, sea, and road."

"And going straight to them?"

"Head on. Last thing they'll expect."

Ben let out a sigh and put his foot on the accelerator. The weight of

Aguilar's improvements strained at the engine, but the car surged ahead.

"Once more unto the breach, dear friends."

Michelle shook her head. "Once more unto Valencia."

Chapter Thirty-Five

"SHE IS COMING TO Valencia?"

"It is what I would do. And she will do what I would do."

Esteban Salazar was tired from the long flight, but travelling in Cordero Belen's private jet was a lot better than travelling long haul with American Airlines. The tall grey Mexican hadn't needed to book extra legroom because he was the only passenger, it was all legroom. El Zorro Plateado was as rested as he could expect to be after such a long flight. Being dragged out of retirement wasn't up for discussion; when you worked for Pablo Cordero Belen you were never retired.

"How many men do you have there?"

Cordero Belen glanced over his shoulder. "Alejandro?"

"Including the two you sent to enhance the first team?"

"Without them."

Alejandro stood in the shade at the back of the veranda and did some quick calculations. Valencia was less than two hundred miles to the west but the men they had with them in Majorca would be no help on the mainland.

"Four. In the safe house. Two more at the hotel. The first team have been hospitalised."

Salazar nodded his approval. "She took out your snatch squad?"

Cordero Belen sat still. "Don't get too smug. It's what I paid you for."

"Except she is using it against you."

"Not against me. She was protecting this new man."

The Silver Fox was an old and trusted member of the family. He could say things that no one else could say, not even Alejandro. He looked at the man he had known since before he was a man and chose his words carefully.

"She always wanted to make her own choices."

Cordero Belen sensed judgment in the words. "Meaning?"

Salazar had started, so he had to finish. "Maybe it is time for her to..."

Cordero Belen slammed his fist on the coffee table. The silence that followed was as brittle as frozen glass. A ferry sounded its horn across the bay. There was no sound at all on the balcony overlooking Palma. The man in charge of ninety per cent of the drugs in Mexico left the fist on the table, then slowly opened it and laid his hand palm down, fingers outstretched. The appearance of calm was diluted by a twitch in the forefinger. To cover the twitch, he drummed his fingers.

"Do you know how much money we made last year?"

It was a rhetorical question, so nobody answered.

"And do you know how much we could declare as legitimate income?"

Again, no reply.

"I could buy a small country three times over. Except you need legitimate income to become an international financier. Legitimate income is what David Enrico Martinez's family possesses."

He stopped drumming. "Do you know which white powder Spain and Italy are built upon?"

Nobody was going to speak, so he stopped asking questions.

"Concrete. Spain. The Balearic Islands. Tenerife. Three-quarters of Italy. The power in Europe is construction and European construction is concrete. The industry has its fingers in every walk of life. In every level of government. In everything. Without concrete, there is no building. With no building, there is no expansion, and expansion is what all governments want. It is where they get their money. You cannot tax a man who has no income. Concrete is legitimate income. We buy into concrete and suddenly all our money is legitimate. Then I can buy that small country, three times over. Or anything I want. Legitimately."

He took his hand off the table and rested it in his lap. "This marriage is not between Cordero Belen and Martinez. It is between cocaine and concrete. It will go ahead, if my daughter wants it to or not."

He looked at the man who taught his daughter everything she knew. "I want this lifeguard dripping blood from the diving board, and my daughter back in the fold. You taught Michelle her moves. Deploy your counter move."

His face showed no emotion. "Or discover the other thing Italians use concrete for."

Chapter Thirty-Six

THE SUN WAS SETTING by the time the battered red car skirted Alicante and followed the coast road north. Valencia was almost three hundred miles from Guadix, and a lifetime away from the calm of Abla. Enrico Aguilar had been right about one thing: the little red car wasn't going to outrun anyone, but it was as solid as a rock. They refuelled three times on the drive across the hills, but the journey was all downhill, heading back towards the coast road.

They were sharing the driving, and Michelle was at the wheel when she stopped at the tollbooth on the AP-7. There was no need to hide the registration number anymore because the car wasn't stolen or on anyone's radar. She collected the ticket, and the barrier went up. Delivery trucks rumbled past through the far gates. Michelle followed the car lanes until they merged with the Autopista. There wasn't much traffic, so she kept in the slow lane.

She said, "At least we should blend in for tonight."

"If I wear a Kiss Me Quick hat and ask for English breakfast."

Michelle gave Ben a sideways glance.

Ben expanded. "Benidorm isn't my idea of the Spanish experience."

"We aren't looking for the Spanish experience; we're looking to blend. You're English, aren't you?"

"You aren't."

"If I put a Kiss Me Quick hat on, nobody will notice."

She ignored the first exit, which led to Cala and Las Lomas, and followed the sweeping curve of the AP-7 as it bypassed the neighbouring urbanizations in favour of the main resort.

"We need to be fresh for Valencia tomorrow. Plain sight only works if we're the same as everyone else in plain sight. Tourists. So, cotton candy and a hotdog. And a cheap hotel."

Ben said, "Benidorm is mainly resort hotels and rental apartments."

"Everywhere has a cheap hotel. If I had my phone, I could use Booking.com."

They both knew why she didn't have her phone.

Ben didn't belabour the point. "We'll do it the old-fashioned way."

Michelle flicked the indicator and eased onto the off-ramp. Salida 65 was a long, slow turn onto the slip road that fed the exit tollbooths. She pulled in behind two family cars and allowed herself to get boxed in by a rental. Just like the other tourists. Blending in. She inserted the ticket and paid the toll, following Avenida Comunidad Europea through Parque de Bomberos towards Benidorm. The tall, thin spires of the high rises stood out along Playa de Levante like a miniature New York. It was the very opposite of the calm, pleasant coastline of Laguna Park.

"How much does your local knowledge stretch to Benidorm?"

Ben was scanning the area to get his bearings. "It stretches."

Michelle slowed on the approach to the roundabout where the central pond had been drained for cleaning. A man wearing waders he didn't need was busy scraping the sprinkler nozzles for the ornamental fountain. There were a lot of nozzles.

"Near the beach but not too close. Good access in either direction in case we need a fast getaway."

"I thought we were blending."

"Plan for all contingencies. Then you only have to use one."

* * *

BEN RAN WHAT LITTLE knowledge he had and considered the options. There weren't many if they wanted to avoid the tangle of narrow streets in Old Town or the maze of tourist apartments along Avenida del Mediterraneo. The obvious choice was fully booked. That's how they came to be staying at the only low-rise hotel squeezed between Hotel Agua Azul and a beach resort that was nowhere near the beach.

"You're right; this is getting to be a habit."

They got a double room for one night and paid cash. Hotel Primavera was a small family-run hotel that looked like it needed a coat of paint and a lot of love. The lack of a refresh was mainly down to competition with the chain hotels and the lack of a swimming pool. The cramped footprint didn't leave room for a swimming pool. There wasn't room for car parking either, but there was an underground car park across the road at Plaza de los Reyes de Espana. Michelle didn't want to get trapped underground, so she parked a hundred yards away along the street.

Being a rundown hotel had two benefits: they could get away with just the holdall and Michelle's cabin luggage, and paying cash negated the requirement for a passport. Strictly speaking, photo ID was needed at all hotels, but when you're desperate for customers, legality goes out the window.

Room 107 was on the first floor rear with a view of the back of another building that was twice as tall and half as scenic, being mainly a rusting fire escape and boarded-up windows. It was either a hotel or commercial property, and in keeping with all service industries, the only part that needed to look nice was the part the customers saw. Nobody would see the back of the building unless there was a fire, and if that happened, the only thing they'd be interested in was the fire escape. Hotel Primavera only had a ladder and a soft landing.

Michelle looked at the double bed. "Déjà vu."

Ben looked out of the window. "So long as it's not El Puche all over again."

There was no diplomatic response to that, so they both ignored it and stowed their bags. The room had a built-in wardrobe, an old wooden chair under the window, and an adjoining bathroom. They didn't need anything else.

Except...

"Eat in or eat out?"

Ben was deferring to Michelle's tactical training, but he knew what his vote would be. Michelle scanned the room and came to the same conclusion.

"I don't think room service is high on their priorities."

Ben nodded. "Out it is then."

* * *

THE SUN WAS DOWN by the time they found a suitable tapas bar in the historic part of town. Historic because the tourist guide said it was, when what it really meant was the older part of Benidorm before the tourist industry exploded and turned it into Blackpool in the sun. It was still pretty much Blackpool in the sun, but with ornate buildings instead of concrete and steel.

"That looks nice."

Not Ben describing the tapas bar, but the dress Michelle was trying on in Zara before they went to eat. Walking down from the hotel, they both agreed they needed more than the single change of clothes that Michelle had packed. Ben didn't have a change of clothes at all, so they found Calle Gambo, the main pedestrian precinct leading from the modern tourist centre towards the ancient castle ruins at Balcon del Mediterraneo. Zara was a bit upmarket for Ben, but they did stock men's and women's clothes, and they were advertising Rebajas with up to seventy per cent off.

Ben bought two pairs of summer-weight trousers, a Weird Fish jumper, and three short-sleeved shirts. Michelle bought slacks, blouses, t-shirts, and assorted underwear. That prompted Ben to add socks and underpants before Michelle saw a dress with double discount. It was totally impractical for evade and destroy, but when she tried it on, practicality was pushed aside.

"Really nice."

Michelle did a little twirl in front of the changing rooms, and Ben felt his heart miss a beat. She looked more than nice; she was beautiful. Their eyes locked, and she stopped twirling. Neither of them spoke until Michelle broke the spell. She held up the shopping basket, then waved towards the checkout.

"Do you think they have a Kiss Me Quick hat?"

"If they did, I think you'd rock it."

For a moment, Ben felt like a regular guy with a regular girlfriend, and he suddenly knew how Billy Crystal must have felt when he realised Meg Ryan was more than Sally to his Harry. In the end they didn't need a Kiss Me Quick hat, carrying a handful of Zara bags marked them as tourists as much as everyone else crowding the narrow streets of Old Town.

Ben paid and slipped his arm around her waist as they went in search of a tapas bar overlooking the Mediterranean. The fact that she didn't struggle, and accepted the arm, was probably why he didn't notice the two men following them. The two men definitely didn't look like tourists.

Chapter Thirty-Seven

"AND HE SAID 'What, like they too big to carry off?'"

"You actually said that? Fat people don't get kidnapped?"

"It was in reference to him being out of breath going up the hill."

"How did he feel about that?"

"About them always taking the thin one? He said the downside was if a plane crash goes cannibal, fat kid goes first."

"So, you did call him fat?"

"I said he was carrying a few extra pounds."

Ben had been reminiscing about Eduardo Perez while they ate tapas at a restaurant overlooking the ocean. Placa de Castellar was a terrace bar on the stubby point of land jutting into the Mediterranean and had a view of the crescent beach and the Club Nautica de Benidorm. The horizon was aglow with the recent sunset.

"But now you feel guilty."

Ben toyed with his finger food. "I feel guilty about a lot of things."

"About your brother?"

"Not that."

"About me then."

Ben looked at Michelle across the table. "Yes."

Michelle rested a hand on his. "Like they said in that Ryan O'Neal movie. Love means never having to say you're sorry."

"*What's Up, Doc?*"

"The other Ryan O'Neal movie." She squeezed his hand. "You don't have to feel guilty about me."

They sat looking at each other across the table, hands entwined like any other couple basking in the sunset. Ben felt an urge to lean over and kiss her, but despite her bringing love into the conversation—a play on words he was sure—he didn't feel he'd earned the right.

Ben said, "I didn't want to meet you."

Michelle said, "*I* didn't want you to meet me."

Ben gave a sad little half smile. "I never used to get what I wanted."

Michelle looked deep into his eyes. "Back to your childhood again."

"Back to everything."

It was Michelle's turn to give a little half smile. "But two negatives make a positive."

Ben nodded. "I'm glad I met you."

Michelle let go of his hand. There was something she needed to clear up before committing fully. It was always like this when she got close to somebody.

"Let's go back to this guilt thing. You didn't bring anything on that hasn't been a long time coming."

Ben sat back, not sure how to take that. He kept quiet.

"I told you about my friend disappearing, right? About her coming back but everything being different. Well, the difference wasn't her it was me. I suddenly realised what kind of world I lived in, the power that some people have, and I started pushing against it even then. At eight years old."

Her face looked hard in the dying light. "Everything since then, boyfriends, training, temper tantrums. It has all been me fighting back. Against my father. Against that world."

She twirled a hand to encircle the pair of them. "This. Us. The runaway bride. It isn't your fault."

She held his hand again, more gently this time. "But *this*."

Her expression softened. "Us."

There was a tear in her eye. "This is *all* your fault. Because I'm glad I met you, too."

The sky grew dark outside, and the lights came on in the tapas bar.

Coloured lights that were strung along the Placa de la Senyoria danced in the offshore breeze, giving the seafront a carnival atmosphere and complementing the music coming from several bars overlooking the beach. There was laughter and chatter and the clinking of glasses. Benidorm had always been a sea of party noise, but for the couple sitting at the table, the world grew quiet, and the lights faded into the background.

"That's the first time I've been glad to be guilty of anything."

"What are we going to do about it?"

Ben stood up, and Michelle came with him. "I'll tell you back at the hotel."

* * *

THE WALK THROUGH OLD Town was much better than the walk from the hotel. Ben carried all the Zara bags, and Michelle held him close. The body heat had reached melting point, and he could feel the muscles in her body move under his hand as they walked. Every few hundred yards, they stopped and embraced. The kisses were slow and gentle and promised passion beyond belief.

They passed their original choice, the Hotel Agua Azul, and crossed Plaza de los Reyes de Espana. Despite the romance blossoming right next to him, he couldn't resist glancing up the street. The little red car was still parked at the side of the road, facing a quick getaway. He stopped and kissed her again, more passionately this time, and she held him tight. Hotel Primavera looked like the Adams Family mansion between the high rises on either side. In Ben's eyes, that made it more romantic. He broke off the kiss and looked her in the eyes.

"You sure about this?"

Michelle almost looked angry. "Are you kidding me?"

They kissed again, and Ben practically dragged her across the street. A bell rang above the door as they entered the lobby, and the receptionist handed them the room key. They were so preoccupied they didn't see the look of fear in the woman's eyes. Ben transferred the bags to his other hand and waved Michelle forward to the stairs. He watched her lithe figure sway as she climbed each step.

The first-floor corridor was dimly lit, but Ben found their room and slipped the key in the door. It rattled and scraped and needed a gentle touch. He smiled, the master thief having trouble unlocking his own room. He opened the door and let Michelle go in first. Ben followed and turned the light on.

The pain in his head was sharp and debilitating. He just had enough time to see the knife against Michelle's throat before he hit the floor.

Chapter Thirty-Eight

"WHERE IS THE MONEY?"

The room swam in front of Ben's eyes as he adjusted his vision, but he didn't pass out. This was too serious to pass out. He felt himself being dragged backwards and sat up against the wall. The other man stood in front of the door with Michelle in a necklock and a knife against her throat. The room looked even more threadbare than when they'd left for dinner, made all the worse by the ransacked wardrobe and upturned bedding.

"Where is the fucking money?"

More insistent this time. The knife drew a bead of blood against Michelle's pale skin, her natural tan washed out by fear and panic. Ben knew the panic wouldn't last long; he'd seen her in action before, but this time, she wouldn't be able to hit one of them with a car door.

The man standing over Ben kicked him in the ribs, then knelt down and grabbed his hair. He bent his head to Ben's ear and lowered his voice.

"I will not ask again."

He clicked his fingers, and Michelle gasped. The trickle of blood was thin and weak and utterly terrifying. Ben glanced at the holdall sitting overturned on the bed. Michelle's flight bag was inside out with the lining ripped. Her cosmetics and single change of clothes were scattered across the floor. The holdall was empty.

"Last chance."

Ben held his hands out and made a placating motion. "Okay, calm down. I'll tell you. But let her go."

Bad breath and garlic chuckled in Ben's face. "She is insurance."

Ben was playing for time while he calculated angles and distance. He didn't need to work out who the two men worked for but he did wonder how they'd found him so fast. He considered playing the Cordero Belen card but decided to save that unless his first play failed. Starting point was slowing things down.

"Max lost his nerve, didn't he?"

Divide and conquer.

"He told you I broke into the floor safe and stole your money."

He shifted against the wall and turned to the man kneeling beside him. "Who do you think told me about the floor safe in the first place?"

He could see the story was getting some traction. "If I was going to rob Laguna Park, I'd hit the wall safe. Maybe clear a few thousand for travelling money. What you lost, what Max was laundering, that was a hell of a lot more. My half of that was better than travelling money."

"Your half?"

"I wanted it to be sixty/forty since I was taking all the risks, but Max insisted on half each. I guess he panicked and dimed me in."

"Dimed you in?"

"Sorry. Too many American movies. Sold me out."

Now, the man sounded more than interested. "He reported the burglary and the missing lifeguard. He didn't need to sell you out. Two and two makes four."

"And fifty/fifty makes a hundred. What? Did he hope you'd kill me before I talked?"

The talker stood up and moved towards the door. He exchanged a glance with the man holding the knife to Michelle's throat, and the knife wavered. It was a bit less tight against the skin. Ben checked the bathroom door and the window. Neither offered much hope. The talker turned to Ben again.

"He said not to take any chances. You were a dangerous fugitive."

Ben snorted a laugh and drew his legs up beneath him. He rubbed the circulation back into his thighs so the men would get used to the movement. "He never was playing with a full deck. I told him he'd be the first person they'd suspect. Since when did money launderers trust the man holding the money?"

Ben shifted into a kneeling position, checking the door, the bathroom, and the window. Two men blocked the door, and the bathroom led nowhere. That left the window with the fire escape ladder and the soft landing. Ben was counting on the soft landing, because he didn't think they'd have time to use the ladder.

"And since when did the recovery team not ask where the money was?" He tapped the side of his head. "He didn't think it through."

Mention of the money got the man's attention. "Which brings me back to my original question. Where is the money?"

Ben had been thinking about that, and came up with the only answer they might believe. He waved a hand around the room. "You didn't think I'd leave it in here, did you?"

He flexed his knees, and nodded towards the door. "It's downstairs. In the hotel safe."

Both men did what Ben expected them to do. They glanced towards the door and took their eyes off the man kneeling beside the bed. Ben gave Michelle a hard stare, and Michelle blinked her understanding. Timing was everything, the split second when the men were distracted, and the knife was lowered. Right now. Ben pushed up with his knees and...

The door burst open, hitting the talker in the face and knocking the knifeman to one side. Ben barely had time to register that he recognised the intruders before the two men who had been following them came into the room.

Chapter Thirty-Nine

SOMETIMES LIFE COMES FULL circle, and sometimes it doesn't. The bodyguards from the hotel corridor in Leeds looked bigger in the cramped space of the first-floor room. That was the coming full circle part. The not coming full circle part was this hotel room not being on the tenth floor.

Timing was everything.

Now.

But different.

Michelle kicked backwards and scraped her shoe down the knifeman's shin. He was already off balance having being slammed by the door, so losing one leg tipped him over the edge. He reached for anything to regain his balance, and Michelle grabbed the outstretched arm, bent the arm upwards and the wrist down under itself, forming a gooseneck, then twisted it sideways. The knife dropped to the floor.

The talker recovered first. He'd been hit in the face before, and used the pain to spark his retaliatory strike. He elbowed the first man to come through the door in the face, and brought his knee up into the stomach of the other. The first man had been hit in the face before as well, so he blocked and parried, forearm knocking the elbow to one side and strong fingers grabbing the talker's throat.

Despite being doubled over, the second man made a grab for Michelle but she was already halfway around the bed towards the window. The knifeman regained his balance and came up off the floor, shoulder-charging the second man in the ribs and sending them both across the room in a tangle of arms and legs.

Ben jumped up and rolled across the bed, landing on his feet on the other side. There were two men wrestling on the floor, and another two punching and gouging each other against the bedroom door. The door had slammed shut blocking the way into the corridor. The bathroom was a dead end.

So, it was the window or nothing.

Michelle had obviously come to the same conclusion, because she reached for the handle and twisted. The handle didn't turn. The two men near the door realised what was happening and tried to disengage or lose the prize. The prize for one was the money, and for the other, it was what Ben had stolen in Leeds. Either way, they both wanted to stop Ben escaping through the window.

Michelle twisted harder. The handle was painted shut. The talker elbowed the first man in the throat and brought his knee up into his balls. Squashed testicles worked every time, and the man dropped to his knees, freeing the talker to go after the thief. Ben shoved the bed across the room, then flicked it up and over.

Michelle tried one last time.

The paint wouldn't budge.

Ben picked up the chair and smashed window, using the legs to knock most of the glass out of the frame. He set it down, and Michelle used it as a step onto the windowsill. There was no time to turn and climb down the ladder, so she jumped. The bed was knocked aside, and the talker dashed to the window. Ben spun the chair behind him, the legs tangling below the talker's knees. The man tried to step over the fallen chair, but straightening up just tangled his legs even more. Ben checked the frame for broken glass, then dived out the window after Michelle.

Chapter Forty

"JUST HOW MANY PEOPLE are after you?"

"Not counting your father? Too many."

"And how did they find us?"

"That part's easy. They drew a line north from Laguna Park and came to the same conclusion we did. Benidorm's the best place to blend in."

Michelle mulled that over, then told Ben what was really troubling her. "If they anticipated our next move, how come my father didn't?"

She said what they were both thinking. "Because that would have been more than a sharp knife and fisticuffs."

* * *

THAT WAS AFTER THEY'D made their getaway, but before they found a place to lay low. As Ben expected, the soft ground beneath the window wasn't very soft, the freshly turned flower border breaking their fall but not doing much else. Michelle was up first and helped Ben to his feet. Together, they limped as fast as they could along the side of Hotel Primavera and up the road to the car. Michelle had the keys and got in the driver's side. This was more her level of driving than Ben's. The little mule kicked and jerked forward, building up surprising speed despite the added weight.

"Straight across the roundabout. Shortest route."

Michelle kept her foot to the floor. "They know the shortest route as well."

Ben looked over his shoulder at the Adams Family mansion. "They're busy seeing who'll come after us first."

The little red car screeched around the roundabout and took Avenida de la Comunidad Valenciana north, taking the long straight road out of town. A space-themed discotheque flashed by on the left, and several rundown karting tracks competed for customers on the right, all closed for the night or simply closed for good.

"And who exactly are *they*?"

"Not while you're driving."

Ben groaned as he slid his seat back and straightened his bruised legs. "They're going to be thinking where to stop us up ahead."

He flexed his knees. "So, we're not going to go up ahead."

"We are going up ahead."

Ben shook his head. "We're building a lead then we're going to disappear. Before those four back there, figure it out and come after us."

"After you. They're not my father's men."

"After me then."

Michelle saw the sign for the N-332 and glanced at Ben. "Just how many people *are* after you?"

* * *

AS SOON AS THEY got on the N-332 they got off it again. The first exit on the left towards Alfaz del Pi. Ben ran what little local knowledge he had and ruled out Albir and Altea on the right because he didn't want to get caught with his back to the sea. The coastal strip was narrow to the east of the main road, leaving few escape routes except back onto the N-332. Alfaz del Pi was up the hill giving options of going inland over the mountains, taking surface roads, or making a getaway on the AP-7.

Michelle did a quick circuit of the urbanization, which consisted of Avenida Pais Valencia running through the center, and apartment blocks scattered among the traditional buildings on the back streets. There was only one hotel, but they were off hotels. Ben was looking for something less obvious. He found it back where they started, just off the N-332 in an overgrown vineyard.

The abandoned villa looked like The Alamo, with the windows shuttered and part of the roof collapsed amid adobe walls covered in graffiti. A huge cartoon face peered over an imaginary wall like a colour version of the famous Kilroy Was Here artwork. The rest of the frontage was a mass of letters and words that Ben couldn't make out in the dark. The driveway was potholed and fringed by trees that needed trimming, with a chain across the entrance. The chain was padlocked, but the wooden gatepost was rotting. Ben yanked the chain out, then hung it back over the post once Michelle had driven through. She parked the car on the blind side, away from the road, and checked for alternative exits. It was hard to see in the absence of streetlights, but there was a dirt track to the right and a narrow-gauge railway bordering the north.

Michelle looked at the heavy wooden side door. "Can you pick the lock?"

She couldn't see the withering look Ben gave her in the dark.

"You pick the lock when you need to be quiet and don't want to leave evidence of a break-in. Tonight? When it's old wood?" He raised his foot and kicked. The frame splintered, and the door flew open. "Picked."

Michelle glanced at the overstuffed seats in the car. "Should we bring the money in?"

Ben opened the boot and took out the emergency blanket and a canvas tool bag. He looked at the back of the driver's seat to make sure the money and the passports weren't sticking out of the seam he'd opened. The passenger seat as well. They looked secure, so he slammed the boot shut.

"It's safe where it is."

He indicated the splintered door. "But we need some rest."

Michelle checked to make sure none of the floorboards were missing, then struck a match from the box she always carried with her, a holdover from the kidnap protection training. She also had a Swiss Army knife and a ball of string. The Silver Fox had never told her what the string was for. The flame showed her that the floor was tiled concrete, so she wasn't going to fall into the basement. The Alamo didn't have a basement.

She led the way, checking the empty rooms. Ben followed with the blanket and bag. The interior was surprisingly clean for an abandoned building, with a functioning kitchen and an old bed in the back room. The bedside cabinet had a melted candle in an ashtray and an alarm clock without a battery.

"Somebody lives here."

Ben checked the mattress. There was no bedding but the mattress was clean. "Somebody visits."

"Tonight?"

Ben shook his head. "Tending the vines, maybe? I don't know. But not in the middle of the night."

Michelle lit the candle before the match burned her fingers. The room was filled with stuttering light. Now that they'd stopped moving, her shoulders sagged, and she let out a sigh. "I wish I'd brought the Zara bags."

Ben thought she was being a typical woman, thinking about creature comforts over necessity, then he remembered her training. The Zara bags had clean clothes. Keeping fresh and alert was important if you wanted to stay ahead of the game. But he thought he caught a bit of the woman in her expression. He nodded. The dress had looked particularly nice.

"Let's go less upmarket next time."

Michelle gave a stern look. "I'm the daughter of a cartel boss. I am upmarket."

Ben brought a hand from behind his back and held up the last thing he'd grabbed before jumping out of the window. He had no idea why he snatched it but he'd stuffed it in his jacket after the fall. The dress was creased but still nice when he held it up.

Michelle gasped and felt a tremble of femininity. "Ben."

It was all she said before putting her arms around him and giving him a warm, slow kiss. After a moment, she broke the embrace and laid the dress on the bed. When she turned back to him, her face was all business.

"Now. Let's talk about what just happened."

Chapter Forty-One

WHEN HARRY FINALLY ADMITTED his attraction for Sally, he wasn't being hunted by Sally's drug cartel father, a money launderer he'd stolen money from, or a gangster from Leeds who wanted something else. Pillow talk was more of the romantic variety and with cleaner sheets. The Alamo didn't have clean sheets. It didn't have pillows either, so this was going to be a long way from pillow talk.

The candle flickered. The room was warm. Ben dropped the emergency blanket and the tool bag on the bed.

"Okay. The way I figure it is like this."

Then he spent the next half an hour laying out how he figured it.

* * *

HOW BEN FIGURED IT basically consisted of running through the list of suspects and explaining each party's motivation. He started with the one they both knew and understood, Michelle's father. The Cordero Belen cartel was acquiring or merging with an undisclosed Spanish concern, and the glue in the merger was the marriage of Michelle Cordero Belen and David Enrico Martinez. Running off with the bride put Ben at the top of the cartel's shit list and made him a prime candidate for having his teeth pulled and being hung to bleed out. That didn't happen at Hotel Primavera, so her father's men weren't part of the intervention in room 107.

Next came the money-laundering organisation that was behind Laguna Park and was paying Max Overend to run their operation. It was their money Ben had stolen when he dug the safe out of the floor under Max's desk. That, and whatever money Max had skimmed from the laundering and the holiday resort. Max had obviously reported the theft and fingered Ben, which was only to be expected. The fact that the first man through the door had asked where the money was pretty much identified the money launderers as the first party.

The second party needed more explanation. They wanted Ben for something completely different.

"You broke into their safe in Leeds, didn't you?"

"Yes."

"Then it's not all that different, is it?"

"It's not what I broke into. It's what I took."

Ben had been keeping that little secret for so long, he'd almost convinced himself he hadn't stolen it in the first place. When he'd opened the safe in the tenth-floor hotel room in Leeds, there was no money and no jewellery, but the thing he did steal was worth more than any of that. To the owner, it was priceless, and it was currently stuffed in the back of the passenger seat, along with two and a half million euros and a pair of passports.

"The notebook has more incriminating evidence than Capone's accountant. Names. Dates. Transactions. All of it."

"He wrote it all down?"

"He doesn't trust computers."

"What about his memory?"

"The only thing he remembers is me."

"And he knows where you are, how?"

Ben shifted on the edge of the bed they were both sitting on. The movement sent the candle spluttering. Light danced off the walls and made shadows dance at the edges of darkness.

"My guess is, Max told him, hoping he'd get me before his boss. That way, he wouldn't have to explain why he was using me for his own burglaries."

Michelle drew her knees up and hugged them. The change of balance tipped her towards Ben, and he put a hand out to stop her falling over. The heat from her body tingled the hairs on the back of his neck. He had to force himself not to shiver. She looked at her knees.

"That's why you had to take the gigolo job. Because he knew about Leeds."

Ben looked at her knees as well. "He knew why I was hiding out. And he knew who wanted to find me."

He raised his head to look in her eyes. "But not wanting to be a gigolo? That was ethics."

Michelle met his gaze. "Same reason I didn't want a gigolo. It didn't feel right."

"Didn't?"

"Not then."

"How about now?"

"Now you're not a gigolo."

"What *am* I?"

She lowered her knees and turned to him. Their eyes danced with candlelight in the confined space. The heat wasn't just the remains of the day or the flickering candle. Ben didn't know whether to lean in or back off. He'd never wanted to kiss anybody so much and yet be so unsure. They were being hunted by three different factions, with no real idea of how to get out of the predicament they were in. This was a relationship based entirely on a tense situation. If Sandra Bullock was right, there was only one thing to do.

Michelle must have read his mind because she leaned against him and eased him back onto the bed. With gentle fingers, she touched the side of his face, then bent over and kissed him. He didn't take much persuading to kiss her back.

Chapter Forty-Two

"WE LOST THEM in Benidorm."

Alejandro said, "You'd better not tell *him* that."

"No. He is exactly who I've got to tell."

Esteban Salazar had taken the call himself, having assumed control of the retrieval operation, and was standing in the long basement kitchen around the back of the villa. Alejandro put the breakfast tray down on the heavy wooden table and looked at the man everyone called El Zorro Plateado. Plain white archways made the kitchen look like something out of a Spaghetti Western, and he supposed that was appropriate, since the wedding was going to take place in Italy. Neutral ground. In just over a week. The Silver Fox looked calmer than Alejandro felt.

Alejandro said, "Well, make sure there's nothing breakable when you tell him."

* * *

PABLO CORDERO BELEN took the news calmly and quietly. He stood on the balcony beside the baseball bat and looked out to sea. It seemed like he received all his bad news overlooking Badia de Palma. Maybe that was a good thing, the myriad shades of blue having a calming influence on the rage that was building inside him.

"Tell me."

Esteban Salazar stood out of reach of the baseball bat, just in case. "Hotel Agua Azul had no vacancies."

"The hotel you predicted they would use."

"So, they checked in at Hotel Primavera next door."

"Which you also predicted."

Cordero Belen wasn't massaging Salazar's ego, just stating a fact. The story so far had gone according to plan, the hotel with the best transport routes, and the backup hotel if that was unavailable. All predicted by Salazar's expertise, and Michelle's adherence to her training. The next part was what Cordero Belen wanted to hear.

"And?"

"There were complications."

Salazar explained about his men losing Michelle among the tourists when they went out shopping, and returning to cover the hotel for when they got back. It was the getting back part that was the problem, because the new snatch squad weren't the only people waiting for them. Two swarthy Europeans were already in room 107, and two pale-skinned Englishmen were watching from outside. It was the two watching from outside they couldn't identify.

"Who were the first two?"

Salazar paused to gather his thoughts, then spoke quietly. Everything he did, he did quietly. The slow, calm voice demanded attention. "The gigolo stole money from Laguna Park. The resort is a front for a money laundering operation for a family in Southern Spain."

Cordero Belen knew that in Southern Spain, the drugs trade was run by three separate cartels. Jose Maria Peiro covered the tourist destinations along the Costa Del Sol. The Golandrinas Cartel supplied the mountain villages and inland towns. Rueda Mata was in charge of import and supply at the major commercial ports along the east coast. The three families enjoyed an uneasy alliance.

Cordero Belen said, "Which one was Max Overend laundering money for?"

Salazar said, "One of the smaller gangs. The three families know that in order to maintain peace, they have to throw some scraps from their table."

Cordero Belen waved to indicate the Martinez villa. "Not our Spanish family?"

"No. But they have sent men to recover the money."

"Do they think my daughter is involved?"

"Your daughter is with the man who stole it. It doesn't matter if they think she is involved or not, she will be collateral damage."

Still in that calm, slow voice. Still demanding attention. Cordero Belen was becoming anything but calm. His tone demanded attention as well.

"She will not."

Salazar ignored the interruption and continued with his report. "The other two we cannot identify. Almost certainly from England, so no doubt linked to the gigolo's past. They followed Michelle into the hotel, and that's where the complications set in."

* * *

THE BREAKFAST TRAY went sailing over the veranda and clattered in the courtyard. Broken plates dug into the lawn. A silver teapot embedded itself in the flowerbed. There was no roar of anger, just the flying tray. The man who was polishing the car in the turnaround, glanced up then went back to buffing the shine.

Alejandro was waiting in the kitchen. "So?"

Salazar pulled out a chair and sat at the table. "He took it well."

"But?"

"But things are different now. Michelle knows to be flexible once you've made contact with the enemy. Plans change. She knows people are looking for her."

"I thought she always knew we were looking for her."

"Other people. And because of them she knows they predicted her first move. She will know we predicted it, too. So, she will be unpredictable. There will be no more hotels. No more straight route from A to B."

Alejandro leaned against an archway over the oven. "She won't be coming?"

Salazar looked at Cordero Belen's right-hand man. "She will need more incentive."

Alejandro held his hands out in a question. Salazar answered.

"El Jefe is going to Valencia."

Chapter Forty-Three

DAYLIGHT SEEPED IN THROUGH gaps in the shutters and slowly brought Ben awake, one beautiful memory at a time. He remembered Michelle's lips on his and the feel of her soft, naked skin. It felt like silk and velvet rolled into one, with the bonus of a gentle pulse running through it as they made love. If the bomb on a bus scenario initiated their passion, it was ignited by Sandra Bullock's assertion that if relationships based on tense situations are doomed to fail, they should be based on sex. The sex was fantastic.

Then, the bomb on the bus woke him up fully.

* * *

BEN OPENED HIS EYES but didn't move as he assessed his situation. The first thing he noticed was he was lying on his side, curled up under the emergency blanket, and Michelle was curled up behind him like two spoons in a drawer. The bomb on the bus for them was the time bomb situation with her father and just about every other group that was hunting them. The fallout was Eduardo Perez being dead at Laguna Park, and Pedro Malaguenas being dead at El Puche. Ben felt guilty about both of them. The rest was car wrecks and jumping out of hotel windows. One of each.

A warm, dry hand snaked around his stomach and held him tight. "Were you dreaming about car wrecks and hotel windows last night?"

Ben snuggled backwards and felt her breasts crush against his back. "I was too busy to dream last night."

"After the busy. You were twitching in your sleep."

"Windows probably, then." He turned over to face her, and their legs intertwined. "I've spent most of my life climbing in and out of windows. Some low and some high. Jumping out of the hotel window was just the latest. Wouldn't surprise me if they crop up in my dreams."

"You don't remember your dreams?"

"I try not to remember anything."

Michelle hugged him so tight it squeezed the breath out of him. "That's not very promising."

Ben got his breath back and kissed her on the forehead. "What's not very promising is our situation." He kissed her again. "Because I don't think going to Valencia is a good idea."

Michelle loosened her arms and rolled onto her back. She stared at the ceiling while she considered what to say next. Ben waited. The morning after the night before was always a delicate balance. He didn't want to overbalance this. After a few moments, Michelle let out a sigh and spoke to the ceiling. "You remember what I said about my training?"

"That you started young. Not much more."

"Well, the man who trained me is a legend in Close Order Protection. At least in the cartels. He knows every move and countermove and can plan three steps ahead. He knows how to protect against a frontal attack, a pincer movement, or a surprise ambush. Nothing surprises him. Nobody second guesses him."

Ben leaned up on one elbow and waited. This didn't sound like it was going to end well.

Michelle turned her head and looked into his eyes. "I do what he taught me. Which means he knows what I know."

"I thought he was retired."

"There is no retiring from Pablo Cordero Belen." Her expression grew serious. "I think they brought him to Spain. They were waiting at the hotel we would have used."

"Hotel Agua Azul?"

"And they were watching our second choice. But complications set in."

She even used the same phrases as El Zorro Plateado.

Ben used his own. "The shitbags in the hotel room."

"The bags of shit. Yes. Plans changed. We had to improvise." She leaned up on one elbow to be on the same level as Ben. "Now my training dictates we change direction."

"So, not go to Valencia."

"Which he will expect."

Ben had a sinking feeling about this, so he didn't speak. Neither of them did, because they both knew they were still going to Valencia.

Chapter Forty-Four

VALENCIA IS THE THIRD largest city in Spain after Madrid and Barcelona, with about 800,000 people in the city limits, and over one and a half million if you include the surrounding urbanizations. Cordero Belen wouldn't be staying in the surrounding urbanizations, but still, finding one man among 800,000 was the epitome of looking for a needle in a haystack. Unless you knew where that needle liked to stay.

Tactics would dictate somewhere with easy access and available transport routes, close to the Autopista with open ground to the rear. A hotel near a park, or a rental villa. Short notice precluded the villa, so it was hotels or apartments. Probably hotels. So, Michelle should be looking near the zoo or the university. Except Pablo Cordero Belen liked a sea view, and Michelle was certain her father would bring himself front and centre to act as bait. So, the port it was.

* * *

"THIS ISN'T EASY ACCESS and good transport routes."

Michelle said, "No, it's the opposite. A bottleneck."

Ben shook his head. "It's not a bottleneck it's a dead end."

Michelle didn't seem bothered that Hotel Blasco Ibanez was a dead end, she was too busy scouting the location to see if their unwanted friends had tracked them to La Malva-Rosa, the beach neighbourhood just north of the port of Valencia. Ben cast a nervous glance around the street where they'd parked the car, facing away from the hotel for a quick getaway. Dead ends were the last thing he wanted right now.

"The key word in dead ends is *dead*."

Michelle tried to appease him with the knowledge she'd acquired since they'd been sitting in the car. "We've got the University campus to our back. There is La Malva-Rosa General Hospital by the beach and Vithas Nisa Private Hospital just off the main road. If you end up anything but dead, you'll be in safe hands."

"That's not very comforting."

"No. What's not very comforting is that the men from Hotel Primavera haven't found us yet."

"Yet?"

Michelle kept her eyes on the hotel at the end of the road. "If they follow the line they drew from Laguna Park, Valencia is the next intersection. They don't even need to know that my father's here. We left a trail a blind man could follow."

"Is that why you spent so long at the gas station?"

Michelle glanced at Ben. "I needed to freshen up after last night. Next time you choose a romantic getaway, find somewhere with running water."

Ben was feeling increasingly out of his depth with this female Jason Bourne. Kidnap resolution training could only take you so far. The skills Michelle Cordero Belen possessed were a long way from stamping on your attacker's foot and running away.

"And what do you expect to do at your father's hotel?"

Michelle's expression softened. "You're a thief, aren't you? You're going to get me into his room."

* * *

HOTEL BLASCO IBANEZ WAS a three-storey boutique hotel with the most exclusive suites on the top floor. Pablo Cordero Belen had booked the entire top floor, and stood in the main suite looking across the Balearic Sea towards Majorca. Practically the same view in reverse of his view overlooking Badia De Palma. The ferry he was watching come into Valencia might well have been the same one he'd seen docking at Puerto De Palma.

He took a drink of fresh orange juice and slid the balcony door open so he could hear the horn as the ferry sounded its approach. There was something calming about the sea, but it was the sound of boats and seagulls and waves lapping on the shore that cemented that calm. Considering the circumstances he was feeling surprisingly calm. He took another drink, then stepped forward to look over the balcony.

The pool looked small three floors below. The pool *was* small. Boutique hotels never had a big pool. He doubted they would need a lifeguard but knew they employed one anyway. The lifeguard also served as barman and corporate hospitality. He wondered what other duties Benjamin Green performed apart from watching the pool and teaching kids to play tennis.

He knew what one of his duties was. Burgling high-rise buildings for his money-laundering boss at Laguna Park. It was the thugs from the money launderer that had complicated the daughter retrieval, plus the unknown pair from England. He didn't know how they had found his daughter, but he doubted they would be able to track her all the way here, because only his daughter knew what kind of hotels her father liked.

Cordero Belen stood on the balcony and finished his orange juice. He knew it was too late to start living a healthy life, but in deference to his doctor, he was trying to reduce the toxins in his body. Orange juice might be cleansing his insides but it was doing nothing to reduce the stress. He pressed two fingers against his throat and checked his pulse. He didn't need to check his watch to know it was racing. Having a wayward daughter could do that to a father. Having a wayward daughter that was jeopardising your legacy was even worse. Fairly soon, he was going to have to make a decision about that, and it was a decision that would be hard and painful. He doubted his pulse was going to slow anytime soon.

* * *

"YOU WERE GOING TO use them as a diversion?"

"With them bringing a knife to a gunfight, I was going to sacrifice them."

Ben sighed. "Sean Connery said it better."

"That was, 'Just like a wop, brings a knife to a gunfight.' These aren't Italian."

"They aren't good trackers either. Unless they're hiding in the bushes."

They'd been sitting in the car for half an hour with no sign of the men from Benidorm, and no movement from Cordero Belen's entourage. In fact, there was no sign of Cordero Belen's entourage at all, but they were there. Somewhere. Watching for the runaway daughter. Michelle scanned the top floor of the hotel, then checked the tree-lined avenue that ran past the main entrance.

"We'll have to go with Plan B then."

She took the carrier bag she'd bought at the gas station from between her feet, and rummaged past the sandwiches and water. The mobile phones were housed in hard plastic packaging that took some effort to open. They were basic Sim-only phones with limited displays but good battery life. She programmed the numbers of each phone into the other and added an extra number into hers then gave one to Ben. Ben watched in silence until she'd finished.

"Do you want us to synchronise watches as well?"

"I want you to get me into his room."

"Passed a bunch of armed men who are ready and waiting?"

"Think of it as a challenge."

Ben slipped the phone into his pocket. "Here's the thing about being a successful thief. You choose your targets carefully. You go in slow and easy when nobody is looking. Then you get out without them knowing you were there until they find out their shit is missing."

Michelle looked at the thief who had stolen her heart. "I don't want his shit."

"What do you want then?"

"A few minutes of his time."

Ben looked at Michelle and felt her pain, the wanting to claw back some love and affection from a parent who was using her as currency in the furtherance of his criminal enterprise. He could understand it but had never felt it himself. He didn't want to claw anything back from his mother, but maybe Michelle was closer to her father.

"So, it's him, not his room."

"Yes."

Ben looked at the three-storey building. Hotel Blasco Ibanez was old but refurbished, with shiny new windows and shutters, but ageing stone and archways. The red-tiled roof looked like an ancient villa, and the keystones and lintels were carved with faces whose noses had eroded after years of sea air. The gargoyles supporting the gutters were stained and featureless. This was an old building trying to look new.

"Then forget about breaking in. Let's bring him out."

Chapter Forty-Five

THE FIRE ALARM CAUGHT Cordero Belen by surprise. The hotel was carved stone and concrete. He didn't think there was anything to burn. There was the sound of feet drumming on the stairs and voices in the corridor; then there was a knock at the door.

"Come in."

Alejandro opened the door but stayed in the hallway. Esteban Salazar didn't stand on ceremony, pushing his way into the room and looking at the man who had brought him out of retirement.

"She is here."

Cordero Belen nodded. "If she isn't, she soon will be. Let's go."

* * *

BEN WATCHED THE GUESTS file onto the patio that surrounded the pool, and felt a shudder at the sight of the lifeguard chair atop its ladder. It looked more solid than the one at Laguna Park but was just as tall. A long way to fall and a hard place to land, but Eduardo Perez hadn't fallen or landed. The Ninja Bitch responsible wasn't here, but the person who paid her was. For the first time, he felt a touch of doubt about helping the daughter of that man meet the man himself. This was the perfect opportunity to take affirmative action instead of running and hiding.

"There he is."

Michelle dragged him away from his thoughts of revenge. She didn't need to point out the man in charge of the biggest cartel in Mexico because the sense of power came off him in waves. The way he held himself. The way he walked. But mainly the way everyone kept pace with him or got out of his way. The bodyguards didn't need any introduction, either. They were big and strong and focussed.

Two men split off and went to check the bin store next to the laundry around the back. Smoke still poured out of the utility room, even though the fire had been extinguished. Nobody expected the arsonist to still be there, but being focussed meant not leaving anything to chance. The other three men stayed with Cordero Belen next to the lifeguard chair. The rest of the guests gathered at the other side of the pool, and members of staff cleared cars from the turnaround next to the patio for the fire department.

The fire alarm stopped ringing.

Cordero Belen separated from his men.

* * *

"IF SHE ISN'T, SHE soon will be."

Cordero Belen replayed those words in his head as he stood with his men beside the green and yellow ladder. The chair at the top was wide and padded and far too comfortable for serious lifeguard duties. Life at the top was always padded and comfortable, unless your daughter went rogue and threatened the legacy that was going to cement your family name in history.

He scanned the crowd standing at the other side of the pool but didn't expect to see her there. She would come from left field, unexpected and surprising. That's what Esteban Salazar had said, and Cordero Belen had no reason to doubt him. The Silver Fox had taught Michelle everything she knew, and so far, she had been putting that training to good use.

The fire alarm stopped ringing. Soon, the guests would file back into the hotel. Now was the time. He nodded at the team leader, then drifted away from his bodyguards. The bodyguards stayed by the pool. The other two men were still in the bin store. Cordero Belen took out his phone and wandered towards the main road as if wanting some privacy to make a call.

He saw her out of the corner of his eye as he raised the phone. Across the road beneath a palm tree. She had a phone to her ear as well. Then his phone began to ring.

* * *

MICHELLE LOCKED EYES WITH her father and dialled his number, keeping track of the other men in her peripheral vision. Three bodyguards were standing next to the lifeguard chair, and the other two were still around the back of the hotel. The continental ringtone sounded in her ear, then her father's voice came on the line.

"Mi Chiquita."

"Papa."

That was as far as they got because the squeal of tyres drew their attention to a car racing along the street. The men through the windscreen were dark-haired and swarthy and completely focussed on Michelle. She recognised the one who had held a knife to her throat, and his presence answered the question of who won the fight at Hotel Primavera. She was about to shout at her father when a little red car ploughed into the side of the money launderers, and forced them sideways across the hotel turnaround.

Chapter Forty-Six

BEN SAW THE CAR through the back window as he watched Michelle talking on the phone. It was speeding along the tree-lined avenue, flashing between sunshine and shade as it passed the tall, straight palms. He didn't have time to think, and acted on instinct. His instinct was to ram the shit out of the car as it slowed to grab Michelle. He started the engine and put it in reverse.

The car reached the hotel turnaround, which was at the bottom of the cross-street that Ben was parked on. He rested one arm across the passenger seat and twisted to see where he was going. The red car sped backwards and hit the other car right in the middle. He just had time to recognise the men from Hotel Primavera before the car was pushed sideways into the turnaround.

Guests screamed and dived for cover.

Pablo Cordero Belen dropped his phone.

The three bodyguards next to the lifeguard chair stuck their hands in their coats and started moving toward Cordero Belen, but Ben seized his chance and reversed even harder. The crumpled car mounted the patio, flipped sideways, and toppled the lifeguard chair across the poolside. The bodyguards were caught between a rock and a wet place, either stay and get hit or dive into the pool. They chose the pool.

The other two bodyguards came racing from the bin store and scooped their boss off the floor, dragging him towards the hotel entrance like the Secret Service protecting the president. Cordero Belen protested, but momentum and urgency trumped letting him talk to his daughter.

Two gunshots rang out across the patio. Ben didn't know who they were shooting at, so he slammed the car into first gear and sped forward out of the turnaround. Michelle tracked the car as Ben flung the passenger door open. There was no *"Get in if you want to live"* joke. There was only expediency. Right now, expediency dictated that they get the hell out of there.

The red car slewed across the road, then straightened, and Ben proved himself wrong about easy access and transport routes. When the shit hits the fan, you can find your way out of anywhere. He turned up a side street and got the hell out of anywhere.

* * *

CORDERO BELEN PICKED UP his phone and surveyed the wreckage. Smoke from the bin store had died down, but steam hissed from the overturned car, and petrol leaked into the swimming pool. Hotel security guided the guests to the alternate rendezvous point since the designated RV point was the hotel turnaround. Cars don't explode like in the movies, but spilled fuel can easily catch fire.

Esteban Salazar was standing in the lobby when Cordero Belen came through the door. El Zorro Plateado looked less confident than he had before. His trainee had ignored her training and used it against him, second-guessing the man who was never second-guessed. Instead of changing her plan after the incident in Benidorm, she had assumed Salazar would expect that, and come straight towards them anyway.

Cordero Belen checked his phone log but the call had come from a blocked number. He put the phone away and looked at Salazar.

"So, now she's done the thing she wasn't going to do. What does she do now?"

Salazar didn't flinch at the implied criticism. "It's not what she does. It's what we do."

"And that is?"

"Now we trace the car."

"You got the number?"

Salazar waved a hand around the hotel lobby.

"This place might be old, but it still has security cameras. And so do the toll booths on the only road out of here."

* * *

"YOU HAD HIS PHONE number the whole time?"

"He's my father. Of course, I've got his number."

"So why didn't we just call him in the first place?"

"Because I didn't want to talk to him in the first place."

Ben had turned left and right out of La Malva-Rosa then followed the coast road past Playa Puebla de Farnals before having to join the AP-7 again. The Little Mule was still kicking above its weight and was barely rattling, despite being used as a battering ram. The armour plating that Enrico Aguilar had welded into the boot had proved its worth, and it was just the paintwork and the light clusters that were damaged. Speed was of the essence now, and they couldn't worry about tollbooths or traffic cameras. Getting new passports and general ID papers was even more important now, because after today, Pablo Cordero Belen was never going to stop looking for them.

Ben glanced at Michelle. She was sitting quietly, rubbing her hands, eyes straight ahead. He thought her chin was trembling, but that could have been the car vibrating at high speed. The look on her face was defiant, but he thought he detected something else. He wanted to pull off the Autopista and give her a hug, but didn't think she'd accept the comfort just yet. Her emotions were still raw. Coming so close to her father hadn't helped. Ben gave her a bottle of water from the cup holder, and their fingers touched briefly on the handover. He kept to the speed limit and eased into the flow of traffic.

"How long since you talked to him last?"

Michelle took a ragged breath that accentuated the trembling. "Long."

Ben didn't press. She would talk when she was ready. They drove in silence for the next five miles, then she let out a sigh and turned towards him.

"I haven't spoken to papa for six months."

Her eyes held a world of pain. "When he told me he was dying of cancer."

III

DEATH IN THE SUN

"Down is still down, if I'm looking or not."
— Benjamin J Green

Chapter Forty-Seven

MICHELLE DIDN'T KNOW WHY she was so angry with her father for deciding to die of cancer. She supposed that might be part of the reason, him deciding to die, because it seemed to her that he was in control of everything. So, if he was going to leave her it was his choice. Of course, she had plenty of other reasons to be angry with him, and having twelve months to live was only the latest.

People were always leaving her, that was the bottom line, and most of them left because of her father. That was the true bottom. From her first boyfriend to the last, it had been her father's meddling that drove them away. Forced them away under pain of death, especially after her friend had been kidnapped and the training began. Her father controlled everything. Including the other death she never talked about.

Her mother hadn't died because of her father, but she certainly left because of him. Abandoned her daughter and headed to America. Michelle hadn't been as close to her mother as she was to her father, but it was still a stinging blow to know the woman who birthed her could simply leave her behind. As she grew older, she understood; her mother could no more have taken her daughter than she could have taken on the drug cartel. It was survival instinct, something she'd passed on to Michelle. Unfortunately, she didn't survive long, being killed in a car crash in California three weeks after she left.

Her father showed no emotion. Another reason to be angry with him.

So, there was a through line of people leaving her. Boyfriends one to ten. Her best friend. Her mother. And now her father, with less than six months to live. She was determined that that list would not include Benjamin Green.

* * *

PABLO CORDERO BELEN CAME out of the en suite bathroom after coughing blood into a Kleenex one more time. He was old school, preferring a nice silk handkerchief to all those throwaway tissues, but coughing up blood could ruin your favourite panuelo and did nothing for keeping your illness secret. So far, only his doctor and his daughter knew about the cancer, and neither of them knew about him coughing up blood.

The cartel boss took a deep breath and crossed the room to his balcony. Fresh air was the best prescription. Fresh air with a sea view was even better. He rested both hands on the balcony rail and looked down at the aftermath of his daughter's visit. His daughter's visits always produced fireworks, and the last time they'd talked had been no exception. He couldn't understand what she was so mad about; he was the one dying of cancer.

But of course, he did know what she was mad about, and in that regard, he couldn't really blame her. He had been a terrible father and a not much better husband. The only thing he excelled at was being the head of the Cordero Belen cartel and a shaper of the future. Right now, shaping the future involved merging with the Martinez family and legitimizing his fortune so that he could pass it on to his daughter.

The trouble was, his daughter was the stumbling block to that future as well as being the beneficiary of it. It was a dilemma he hadn't got his head around yet. The only things he knew how to do were coerce and intimidate. The only way that worked was if everyone feared him. It was hard to be feared when you couldn't even control your daughter. So, stumbling block or future? He had difficult choices to make. Painful choices. If things didn't improve, one of those choices was going to break his heart.

* * *

BARCELONA LOOMED LARGE in the future like an unstoppable force meeting an immovable object. Ben wasn't sure which one *they* were, but did know that forward momentum was only good if you knew where you were going. Where they were going was into the unknown.

Ben said, "We don't want to rush into this."

He was still driving as they approached the second most populous city in Spain. They weren't planning on visiting Number One, since Madrid didn't feature in their future. It was getting late, though, and the thing he didn't want to rush into was a rendezvous with the forger that Eduardo Perez had introduced him to.

Michelle agreed. "No, we don't."

Michelle had regained her composure, and was keeping track of their progress since they'd resumed their initial plan, stick to the coast road. The C-32 had been hugging the coast ever since Sitges, and would soon split to go either side of Aeroport de Barcelona-El Prat. They didn't want to hit the outskirts of Barcelona this late in the evening so it was time to get off the beaten track and rest up before the busy day that lay ahead.

Michelle saw their chance. "Come off here."

The sky was a deepening blue as they came out of the mile-long tunnel beneath the rolling coastal hills. There was only a brief stretch of open air before the next tunnel. The exit sign was for Garraf but it wasn't the fishing port she was interested in, it was the unmade road up into the hills to the left. The decorative arrow for the B&B and restaurant was pockmarked and faded and suggested somewhere off the beaten track. The junction didn't even have an exit ramp, just a deceleration lane and a gentle curve. There were newer signs for the Yacht Club and a Mediterranean Restaurant, but it was Campdasens they were headed for.

Michelle patted the back of her seat. "Can you afford another night in hired accommodation?"

Ben focussed on the winding road. "If you don't knock the money out of your seat."

"I'll be careful."

Yes, her composure was back. Ben thought they'd have to be a lot more than careful if they were going to survive tomorrow, but he didn't mention that. The little red car trailed dust as it climbed the hill.

* * *

THE FAMILIAR VOICE ON the phone wasn't the one Cordero Belen wanted to hear. He let out a resigned sigh and tried not to sound impatient. "What do you want?"

"It's not I want, it's what I can give you."

Consuela Mendoza sounded confident over the phone, but Cordero Belen expected nothing less, even though he had effectively withdrawn her from the field after she lost his daughter at Laguna Park.

"And what is that?"

Of course, he didn't really need to ask. There was only one thing he wanted right now, and it sounded like his only female Sicario was confident in providing it. He looked at the evening shadows as they crept across Malva-Rosa Beach and waited for Mendoza to state her case.

"I hear you missed her in Benidorm, and she got away in Valencia."

This time Cordero Belen didn't hide his impatience. "I don't need to know what didn't happen, only what can happen."

He turned his back on the beach and saw his own reflection in the balcony door. He ignored the reflection and nodded at the two faces obscured by the sunset through the glass. Alejandro came over to the sliding door. Esteban Salazar could hear just fine where he was.

Mendoza gave her boss a few moments to let his impatience build. An impatient man is more amenable to suggestion, if that suggestion brings the thing he is impatient to obtain. "I know where she is going."

She paused again. Cordero Belen didn't speak.

"And I know who she is going to see."

Cordero Belen asked the only thing that mattered. "Can you get there before her?"

And got the answer he wanted. "I am there already."

Chapter Forty-Eight

FIVE DAYS AFTER HE met her. Eighteen hours before the life was sucked out of him. Their last night of relative peace together, so it only seemed fitting that they spend it in church, although strictly speaking, Campdasens Bed & Breakfast was one of a cluster of adobe buildings built around the sides of the empty church. Even so, after coming up the dirt road that skirted Serra de Coma Roja Quarry and Cement Works, reaching the top was almost a religious experience. A sign painted on the white stucco wall said, ALTITUD 242m.

"Wow. This really is The Alamo."

"You seem to have a thing about The Alamo."

"John Wayne and a bunch of Mexicans. What's not to like?"

"Your last Alamo analogy. That's what not to like."

Ben thought back to Malaguenas Autos in El Puche and gave a gentle nod. "That was a kneejerk reaction." He waved at the bell tower that didn't have any bells. "This is the mission that became a fortress."

Michelle looked at the shuttered church that had dining tables outside and a bike rack made from an old wooden pallet. "It's a church that became a café. Not the same thing."

Ben parked the car in a gravel clearing next to the bike rack. The engine ticked as it cooled in the clean mountain air. He turned and stroked Michelle's cheek.

"It's a sanctuary. Let's make the most of it."

* * *

THE B&B ONLY HAD three rooms and was run by two old ladies who smiled a lot and didn't ask for ID. They were also the entire staff of the adjoining café, which catered mainly for hikers and cyclists and any other weary travellers. Campdasens was so far off the beaten track that there was hardly a track. The car park was for deliveries more than guests. As the evening moved toward twilight, Ben and Michelle were the only signs of either.

They took a room at the back with a low-sloping roof and a shared bathroom. There was no one to share it with, so they showered and changed. Changing meant Ben putting his travel clothes back on, but for Michelle, it meant the dress from Zara's. She looked beautiful as they sat at an outside table and ordered from a spartan menu. Ben took a deep breath and leaned back in his chair. The sky was still blue, but stars were beginning to prick the darkening palette. Beyond the hills leading down to Garraf the sea stretched all the way to the horizon. It was that kind of view.

"Beautiful."

Michelle followed Ben's gaze. "It is, isn't it?"

Ben leaned across the table and kissed her on the cheek. "Not the view. The dress. Well, and you. Um, so I guess it is the view."

"Do you always stumble around when you're giving compliments?"

"I don't normally give compliments."

"Well, I'm glad you're starting now."

The older of the two women brought a tray of meat and cheese and three different types of bread. There was a bowl of thick soup with earthenware dishes and a bottle of red wine. Ben wasn't much of a wine drinker but felt it was more romantic. The old woman refused his help when he offered to take the tray. The chipped wooden server looked as old as the woman. It gave the meal a homely feel that reminded Ben of the old man in Abla. He wondered what Enrico Aguilar was eating tonight? Probably chilli and rice.

Michelle poured the wine, and Ben broke the bread. After the stress of the last few days this felt like the perfect antidote, but they both knew there was no avoiding talking about what tomorrow might bring.

Ben held a finger up as if silencing the thought. "Let's make a rule about tonight."

Michelle gave a crooked smile that was almost a smirk. "We're making rules now?"

Ben ignored the mild rebuke. "Let's only talk about good things. Happy memories. Things that make us smile. No more frowning. Tonight is a stress-free zone."

Michelle pushed a glass of wine across the table, then picked up her own. "I know what makes you smile."

Ben's smile was less lopsided. "And that as well."

With that, they clinked glasses, took a drink, then set about the food. Ben had forgotten how hungry he was. It was nice to eat in such good company. He couldn't remember the last time he'd felt this comfortable. He was determined to make it last as long as he could.

* * *

"I DID A MORNING paper round when I was a kid."

"This is, things that make you smile, is it?"

"Not the paper round. Can't imagine getting up that early now. No, there was a field near the last house on my round. Had this scraggy horse in it. Used to come over when I passed, so I gave it an apple I was eating for breakfast. Its eyes were so trusting. Non-judgemental. So, I started taking an apple every morning. Felt like I'd made a friend."

"Yes, animals can do that to you."

They had finished their meal and had pulled their chairs together so they could sit arm-in-arm. There was still some wine left, even though the woman had taken the plates and dishes. The other woman had pulled a red canopy over the table and lit a lantern on the wall. The yellow glow dimmed the star field and attracted bugs that kept bumping into the glass. Michelle poured the last of the wine.

"We had a burro near us."

She clinked glasses again. "My best friend. The one I told you about. We would take fruit they were throwing away at the market. End of the day stuff. The donkey loved it, but it had sad eyes. I think it was a pack animal but had been put out to pasture. It should have been happy. We gave it fruit every day, hoping to make it smile."

She took a sip of her wine. "Then I thought, when do you ever see a donkey smile? Their mouths don't move that way. So maybe it was smiling at us all the time, and we just didn't recognise it. That's how I always remember the burro. A smiling mule."

Ben rested an arm across Michelle's shoulder. "I saw a donkey once, had a dong that hung halfway to the ground. That would have put a smile on Mrs Donkey's face."

Michelle leaned her head against his arm. "It would put a smile on my face."

Ben gave her a gentle slap across the side of her head. "Naughty girl. You're the one who turned down the gigolo."

She kissed the hand that slapped her. "I prefer to be wooed first."

A persistent moth kept battering itself against the lantern. The noise was loud in the quiet outside Campdasens. Ben took a deep breath of clean night air, then let it out slowly.

"Local cinema used to have courting seats at the end of each row along the side walls. Double seats for courting couples."

"That's progressive thinking for England. I thought the English were more reserved."

Ben squeezed her shoulder. "Do I seem reserved to you?"

She turned her face to his and looked him in the eye. "You're the most reserved gigolo I've ever met."

"That doesn't narrow it down much."

She smiled, and he kissed the smile. "But this picture house, the Cottage Road Cinema. Me and my mate used to go to the Saturday matinee, and we'd take it in turns to buy a ticket. The toilets were down a passage to the fire exit, and whoever went in would go to the toilet and open the fire doors. All our mates would come flooding in; then we'd shut the door. After a few weeks, the manager started wondering how the cinema was so full when he'd only sold a dozen tickets. Following week, he had the ice cream lady standing at the fire exit selling Choc Ices and Cornettos. Ruined our Saturday afternoons."

Michelle snuggled up against him. "You like your movies, don't you?"

"*Die Hard* came later."

She smiled again. "*When Harry Met Sally*, too."

She let out a sigh.

"After all that stuff with my friend. The thing we won't talk about on smiley night. Well, after that, we weren't allowed to go to the movies, so Papa built a home cinema in the house. It had eight seats and curtains across the screen. Everything was automated. The curtains, the lights, everything. He rented movies on 16mm, then later on video. Before DVD and Blu-ray. It was cool having my friend around. But it wasn't the same as going out. We didn't have an ice cream lady."

Ben finished his wine and put the glass on the table. "What's your favourite movie?"

"You know what my favourite movie is. You were at the hen party quiz."

Ben shifted in his seat so he could hold her in both arms. "And you know mine. We're a match made in heaven."

Michelle finished her wine as well, and kissed him with wet lips. "So, we've swapped apple stories and movies. How about we put a smile on Mrs Donkey's face?"

"Hee-haw."

They both knew that meant yes. Ben bumped his head on the lantern in his haste, and they both laughed. The moth had given up and moved on by the time they went inside.

* * *

THIS TIME THEY MADE love slowly and smoothly. There was no haste, and there was no aggression. This wasn't sex it was love. It took Ben a while to realise that, but by the time he did, he was well and truly smitten. This was the woman he wanted to spend the rest of his life with. After the third time, they lay in each other's arms under the low-sloping roof.

"Michelle?"

"That's me."

"How much did they pay?"

Michelle turned in his arms, and they lay face to face, their bodies entwined from head to toe. "For what?"

"The hen party. How much did they pay for your gigolo?"

She tilted her head up to his. "You worried I didn't get my money's worth?"

"You didn't get any money's worth."

"You think?"

"Not then."

"I'll ask next time I see them."

That darkened the tone somewhat, because they both knew that the way things were shaping up, she wasn't going to see the hen party again. Ben tried to salvage the mood.

"It's just that, since we've both been feeding donkeys. Our Little Mule has enough money to pay them back."

Michelle kept the mood light as well. "In apples?"

"In whatever you like. For the rest of your life."

Michelle turned her head to get a better look at his eyes. "Are you proposing?"

"I think I am. Yes."

She buried her face in his chest and held him tight. "Ask me tomorrow."

Chapter Forty-Nine

THE MORNING AFTER the night before. If yesterday was all about happy thoughts and smiley faces, today was all about business and whether or not they could survive it. When Michelle said, "Ask me tomorrow," what she really meant was, "Ask me, if we survive tomorrow." The first part of that was discussing the plan over breakfast, but Ben couldn't resist asking one wedding question.

"Why Italy?"

* * *

BREAKFAST WAS ACCOMPANIED by a spectacular sunrise, or it would have been if the lovers had got up early enough to see it. As it was, they ate fruit and croissants in the full glare of the morning sun at quarter past nine. The same outside table. The same old lady. Fresh orange juice, and marmalade for the croissants.

Ben still didn't understand why Cordero Belen had chosen Pisa for his daughter's wedding, not fully accepting the neutral ground theory that the bride was from Mexico and the groom was from Spain, so have the wedding in Italy. If he were serious about forging a tie between the two families, surely using the Martinezs' home country would be a good starting point.

All that was brushed aside after breakfast, though. Once the plates had been cleared, Michelle spread the map of Barcelona across the table. The map she had bought at the gas station when she bought the sandwiches and the mobile phones. She smoothed the folds and tapped the street index down one side.

"What was the address again?"

* * *

THE ADDRESS WAS AT the top end of La Rambla, the famous shopping street in the heart of Barcelona, and the Ninja Bitch was looking at it right now. Consuela Mendoza had been watching it for two days, but after hearing about the debacle at La Malva-Rosa yesterday, she had a feeling this was going to be her lucky day. She looked out of the third-floor window she had rented at an exorbitant fee and scanned the street below.

La Rambla was actually three streets in one, a wide central walkway between parallel roads on either side, one going up and the other going down. The pedestrian area was tree-lined along its entire length, giving it the appearance of a Parisian boulevard instead of a Spanish city. Mendoza's viewpoint was opposite the Font de Canaletes, the landmark fountain that looked more like an ornate lamppost with four drinking fountains around its base. Just down the street, below the fountain, the Hotel Lloret was hidden behind a giant canvas banner that advertised future attractions by Andorra La Vella, from the ground floor up.

The address Mendoza was watching was further up from the fountain, between H&M and Burger King. Not very Spanish. Neither was the premises she was staking out, but she wasn't surprised. The street number that Eduardo Perez had given her was on a small plaque beside the door. The shop name was more prominently displayed, 24 HR HOLIDAY PHOTO SERVICE feeling completely appropriate for someone forging passports and fake IDs.

She looked at the ornate windows above the shop and wondered which one was the forger's. She doubted the illegal work was done in the public face of the business and assumed it was completed upstairs. The basement would be too difficult to secure from prying eyes and waste collection. The width of the shop supported three windows side by side up all six floors to the roof. Each window had an ornate iron railing, giving the impression of a balcony they did not have. Everything was for show, like the photo lab that was a front for the best forger in Barcelona.

The choice of location was ideal. The busy pedestrian walkway provided cover all day and most of the night, and the vehicular strips on either side were too narrow for a frontal assault. If the police wanted to raid the shop, they would have to do it on foot since there was no access to the rear, the delivery area being seconded by Zara and C&A Modas.

No, when the bride and the lifeguard came to get their passports changed, they'd have to come in the front door, and when they did, the Sicario had carte blanche. That was the thing she was thinking about as she waited for the lovers to surface.

The conversation had surprised her, and she wasn't easily surprised. Cordero Belen had sounded calm but sombre over the phone. Once, she'd told him she knew where his daughter was going.

"Can you get there before her?"

"I am there already."

That's when his tone changed, and a hint of sadness entered his voice. "Do you need any assistance?"

She refrained from telling him that the assistance on offer had so far lost the daughter in Benidorm, and got its ass kicked in Valencia. "No."

Cordero Belen had paused, then spoken in a slow, grave tone. "I want you to retrieve my daughter and kill her companion."

It was his next words that surprised her. "This has gone beyond a wedding now. Either bring her in or take her out."

And that was it. A kidnap or kill order. She rested the silenced rifle on the windowsill and watched the street, knowing which it would be.

Chapter Fifty

"I SHOULD GO ALONE. Just in case."

"Can't photograph my face without my face."

"It's your face I'm worried about, you being the person they want back."

In the end, they came to a compromise: Ben would go into the shop first while Michelle waited around the corner. It was the getting to, around the corner, that was the problem. Driving through the middle of Barcelona was like driving in any major city, slow, terrible. and borderline impossible. The main roads were clogged with traffic and One-Way signs, and the back streets were narrow with sharp angles and dead ends. Ben had already expressed his aversion to dead ends.

Ben did the driving so Michelle was free to scout the area for ambush points and familiar faces. The familiar face she was looking for was Number Fourteen on the hen party list. The only thing they both agreed on was that Eduardo had most likely given up the address before he was killed, so the Ninja Bitch would already be here. They didn't come in from the top end of La Rambla, finding a side street one block down instead that led to Placa de Vicenc Martorell, a small park surrounded by six floors of apartments. There was a No Entry sign that read,

EXCEPTE AUTORITZATS

They didn't have authorization, but Ben parked there anyway. He sat for a moment, watching children on the swings in the play area. Their innocent laughter belied the danger that lay ahead. He didn't think he'd ever been that innocent, even as a child. That was the legacy of growing up in the

Green household. He wondered how innocent Michelle felt, being part of the Cordero Belen family. Not many people got kidnap evasion training at eight years old. Ben let out a sigh, then looked at the woman he had fallen in love with.

"I'm sorry for getting you into this."

"You didn't get me into this. I was born into this."

Ben shook his head. "You looked happier by the pool during quiz time."

Michelle leaned over and kissed him gently on the lips. "Looks can be deceptive."

Ben placed a hand behind her head and kissed her back. Once. Then he let go and got out of the car. He took a deep breath to compose himself and let it out slowly. La Rambla was a short walk through a narrow pedestrian street. It was who might be waiting there that worried him.

"Okay, Jason Bourne, you're on Overwatch."

He spoke with a confidence he didn't entirely feel. "I'll do the shop. You check the windows opposite."

Michelle stood beside him as he locked the little red car. Their hands interlaced, and he gave it a little squeeze, then they walked through a shortcut and joined the other shoppers.

* * *

THE NINJA BITCH TRACKED left and right from her position overlooking La Rambla, but didn't see anything out of the ordinary. The forger had chosen a good location, because there were so many shoppers and tourists that it was easy to blend in. The good news was she only had to concentrate on one door, but experience told her to keep an eye on the approaches to give her a few seconds' notice before the runaway bride and the lifeguard entered the shop.

A couple walking hand in hand went into H&M, keeping their backs to the street. Mendoza swung the rifle towards the clothing store and checked through the scope. The female stood in the doorway and looked towards the Font de Canaletes. She didn't look as if she wanted a drink from the fountain and took a photograph instead. A tourist, not a runaway bride.

Mendoza lowered the rifle onto the cushion she'd placed on the windowsill. There were young lovers everywhere. She scanned the three windows directly above 24 HR HOLIDAY PHOTO SERVICE, but there was no sign of any activity. After a few moments, she turned her gaze to the street again. She had been on stakeouts before. She knew how to wait.

* * *

BEN WALKED ALONG Carrer dels Tallers, still holding Michelle's hand. They passed Revolver Records and a cannabis shop that looked as if it mainly sold t-shirts, not cannabis itself. The street was narrow and oppressive, with balconies and ornate windows all the way to the sky. It was the epitome of a bottleneck and the worst place to be caught in the open. Unfortunately, it was also the only approach to La Rambla that didn't involve walking in plain sight along La Rambla, and was just around the corner from the premises they were looking for.

They strolled past the staff entrance to Hotel Lloret, then stopped at the end of the street. A bus rumbled past, heading towards the port. A beggar rattled a tin cup at a family who were crossing from the central walkway. They ignored the beggar and almost walked into a motorbike buzzing along behind the bus.

Ben glanced left and right, not sure what he was looking for. He doubted the Ninja Bitch would be standing on a street corner watching the target premises, so he looked at the windows above the shops on the other side of La Rambla. There were a lot of windows. This was Michelle's field of expertise.

"You see anything?"

"I see that a moving target is harder than somebody standing still."

"You saying I should get a move on?"

"I'm saying it's shit or bust time."

"They teach you that in Mexico?"

Michelle smiled. "We get English TV."

Ben squeezed her hand and kissed her one more time. "Give me five minutes. If the shit doesn't hit the fan, come on in."

He winked at her. "See if they have that on English TV."

* * *

THE WOMAN BEHIND the counter looked up when the bell tinkled above the front door. Sunlight streamed through the big shop window, making silhouettes of the artwork and prices painted on the glass. Ben put the crumpled piece of paper he'd torn out of the *Star Wars* colouring book back in his pocket and glanced at the staff door into the back room. The woman came around the counter and looked at the man, who looked like he needed a change of clothes.

"Can I help you?"

Ben toyed with the note in his pocket. "Eduardo sent me."

"Ah, yes."

"I need to speak with Julio."

The woman held out her hands. "You're speaking to her."

"Her?"

"I know. My father wanted a boy."

Julio Sagrada waved a hand at the equipment and workstation. "And it helps keep me anonymous. Policia Local doesn't think a female does this kind of work."

She glanced at the door. "Where is the woman?"

Ben glanced at the door as well. "Coming."

Sagrada folded her arms across her chest. "You were supposed to be coming two days ago."

"There were complications."

The woman's tone turned serious. "Is that what you call it?"

Ben saw the look in her eyes. "You know about that?"

"I watch the news."

"Oh."

"Dead people. That changes everything."

"I know."

"Dead people by accident is one thing. But we both know Eduardo didn't fall out of the lifeguard chair."

The bell tinkled again, and Michelle came in. Ben ignored her for now and concentrated on the woman Policia Local didn't think did this kind of work.

"It makes this even more important."

"It makes this even more dangerous."

"We can pay you extra."

"I can't spend extra if I'm dead."

"You won't get dead."

Sagrada went to the window. "That's not what the rifle across the street says."

Ben jerked and looked out of the window. Michelle stood beside him and pointed at a third-floor window half a block further up La Rambla.

"Four buildings along. Eduardo did good. Ninja Bitch is watching the Photo Service not the Tattoo Parlour."

Chapter Fifty-One

JS TATTOO & PIERCING was two doors down from Hotel Lloret. It was a narrow frontage with a single shop window and a chipped wooden door with glass panels. Number 109 instead of 129, which was the 24 HR HOLIDAY PHOTO SERVICE. An Andorra La Vella advertising banner, that covered the hotel and neighbouring businesses, shaded the upstairs windows. Upstairs was where Julio Sagrada had her photo studio and dark room.

"Let us begin."

She locked the front door and pulled down the blinds, giving one last glance at the window across the street. She thought the rifle barrel twitched, but that could have been her imagination. Being a creative person, she had a very good imagination.

"Give me your passports."

Ben took them out of his pocket and handed them over.

Michelle looked doubtful. "Why do you need our passports?"

Sagrada wasn't offended. "The best way to keep track of a false identity is for it to resemble your own. I will change the name and birthplace but keep the same dates. That way, you will have less to remember."

She turned away from the door and led them to the back of the shop. "But first, your photographs."

* * *

MENDOZA HAD THE FEELING she was being watched. She rubbed

the back of her neck, the place where telltale signs always manifested themselves, and scanned the street again. There were no upturned faces. No eyes were looking in her direction. Not now, but somebody had been looking at her.

She turned her attention back to 24 HR HOLIDAY PHOTO SERVICE. A couple she had seen going in came out holding a cardboard photo wallet, the man flicking through the prints while the woman giggled and clung to his arm. The door swung closed behind them. There was nobody else inside. She raised her eyes to the windows above the shop, the most likely place for illegal activity. There *was* no activity. In fact, there didn't look to be anything at all through the plain, unshaded windows. There were no curtains or blinds. There were no cabinets or posters or pictures on the walls. There weren't even any storage boxes or supplies. It was an empty room.

The sense of being watched dissipated, but a feeling of unease began to creep over her. Something was wrong. She returned her gaze to the ground floor level, the shop door, and the doorways on either side of it.

Burger King had a steady trickle of customers to the right. H&M had a few less but plenty of window shoppers on the left. Next to that was Aromas De Istanbul, then Musical Emporium. Neither looked busy. Then, there was the front door of the Hotel Lloret, with the big stretch banner sponsored by Andorra La Vella covering the upper floors. A little girl in a bright red coat was knocking on the door of JS TATTOO & PIERCING next door.

Mendoza swung the sniper scope towards the girl. She looked far too young to be getting a tattoo or a piercing. There was no parent or adult with her. She was banging on the window now, trying to look through a gap at the side of the blind. The sign on the door said OPEN in three languages but the shop was obviously closed.

It hadn't been closed ten minutes ago.

Mendoza thought back over the last few minutes, like replaying a security video. She had been looking for couples or lovers. A man had gone in alone, maybe ten minutes ago. She remembered seeing the back of his head and dismissing him as not fitting the profile. She had then scanned the hotel and almost missed the door closing for a second time, still only one person. Not a couple.

The girl had stopped banging on the window and moved to the door. It opened briefly, and a hand dragged the girl inside. The OPEN sign swayed as the door slammed shut. So, the TATTOO parlour was closed but not empty. Snatching the child had looked urgent, as if she were disturbing important business, despite the shop being shut. Mid-morning. Busy time of day. Not lunchtime or siesta. Nobody closes mid-morning in the tourist season.

Mendoza swung the rifle to the first-floor windows, but the stretch banner covered them. Perfect cover if you wanted to work in private, unlike the empty windows of 24 HR PHOTO SERVICE.

Then she saw the number next to the door, 109, not 129, and realised that Eduardo Perez had more guts than she'd given him credit for.

* * *

"I AM SORRY. My niece is off school today."

Julio Sagrada came back upstairs with a little girl in a bright red coat. She sat her in the outer office, then finished the last of the photographs. Michelle. Ben was looking out of the window, the street turned red through the big stretch banner. He could still see people walking the street, but they were indistinct and ghostlike. Red shadows wandering La Rambla.

The studio lights flashed for the last portrait.

"That's it. I can use these for the passports and other photo IDs."

Ben turned back from the window. "How long?"

"Tomorrow."

"We need them tonight." He jerked his head towards the street. "Especially if you're right about being watched."

Sagrada turned the background lights off. "Just because I don't use a darkroom and negatives anymore doesn't mean I can rush the process. Quality takes time. Lose yourself until tomorrow."

"We have been losing ourselves. It isn't working."

Sagrada glanced at her niece through the office window, then looked at the couple standing close together. There was something about them that spoke volumes, a closeness that was in danger of being torn apart.

"That means me staying closed and working through."

Ben took out a wedge of banknotes. "I know."

Sagrada gave him a business card with her mobile number on it. "But not here. Call me after five, and I will tell you where."

Ben nodded his thanks and guided Michelle towards the door. He didn't hear the gunshots, but three holes punched through the nearest window, and two more shattered the middle glass.

Chapter Fifty-Two

IT WAS THE FLASH that confirmed Mendoza's suspicions, dull and red through the stretched banner, but a flash nevertheless. Roughly where the windows would be if they were visible. First floor above the tattoo parlour. A photo studio for illegal passports.

She had to make a quick decision based on the research she'd done before setting up opposite 24 HR HOLIDAY PHOTO SERVICE, the recce she carried out before every surveillance and stakeout. The entire block from 109 to 133 was an unbroken row of buildings with no spaces or alleyways in between them. There was no access to the rear, apart from a delivery bay at the back of Zara around the corner. There was a fire escape behind Hotel Lloret, but that was from the roof and not accessible from the small shops wedged between the bigger premises. H&M and Burger King had their own exits.

JS TATTOO & PIERCING was an afterthought. If there was a fire, you'd have to come out the front door or climb out of the first-floor windows onto the scaffolding that held the stretch banner. There wasn't going to be a fire, but she decided to take the windows out of the equation.

Six shots in quick succession. If she got half of them on target, they would put the fear of God into the couple having their passport photos taken. There was only one way for them to go, down the stairs and into the street. Mendoza fired two more shots as incentive, then lined up on the front door. Kidnap or kill order. She wasn't planning on kidnapping anyone.

* * *

EVERYONE HIT THE FLOOR in unison, and Ben dived on top of Michelle. He knew she was more experienced at this than he was, but instinct took over: protect the ones you love. Ben protected Michelle.

"Get the fuck off me."

Michelle didn't need protecting.

Two more shots hit the middle window, then Ben helped Julio Sagrada through the office door, both at a crouch and crunching glass underfoot. Michelle stood up and moved faster and straighter. There's no point trying to duck and dive, you're just as likely to move into the path of a bullet as miss it. Same applies to crouching. It doesn't make the target smaller target, just a different shape. Michelle went for speed over shape-changing.

Sagrada comforted her niece, who was crying on a visitor's chair. Michelle ignored the crying and guided them both into the stairwell, out of the line of fire. Ben followed and stood at the top of the stairs. Structural alterations had been made to squeeze extra space out of the original building, creating the single commercial premises that was JS TATTOO & PIERCING. The stairs only went down. There was no access to the back of the building. There were no windows. The only concession to fire regulations was a hosepipe and a fireman's axe behind safety glass.

Ben took one step down the stairs, but Michelle grabbed his arm.

* * *

MENDOZA COUNTED THE SECONDS from the last two shots through the window. Her mind's eye traced the potential route from the first-floor photo studio to the tattoo parlour below. She didn't expect them to come out straight away, but there should be some movement behind the front door. The roller blind would flutter when the staff door was opened, and there should be a change in the light through the shop window. She allowed a few more seconds for the little girl slowing them down, then stopped counting. They should be downstairs by now.

She glanced at the holes ripped in the stretch banner, a tight grouping on the first three shots, then a bit more straggly on the rest. One had hit between the windows as she'd changed her aim, but the rest were in two groups of two. The ragged holes flapped in the breeze, bigger than the resulting holes in the windows. She swung the rifle back up and used the scope to look through the three-shot grouping where the hole was bigger.

There was nobody in the studio, and they weren't downstairs. That could only mean one thing.

* * *

KIDNAP RESOLUTION TRAINING had taught Michelle one main thing. Never do the obvious. If the only way was down, then the Ninja Bitch would know the only way was down. Michelle started tapping the plasterboard wall where the stairs should have continued. Once she heard the hollow sound, she turned and smashed the safety glass with her elbow and grabbed the axe.

The fake wall was easy. Three good swings of the axe and all that was left was to pull the broken pieces away. The stairs through the hole were dark and dusty with another plasterboard partition on the next landing. Michelle handed Ben the axe, then knelt beside Julio Sagrada and her niece.

"Wait in the stairwell. They're not after you."

"They shot through my windows."

"To get us moving. Not to hit anyone."

Sagrada had other things to worry about. "I can't have the police searching the studio."

"There won't be any police. There were no gunshots."

Sagrada waved a hand at the broken glass on the floor. "What do you call that then?"

Michelle nodded. "I know. What I meant was, there was no sound. And the windows are hidden behind the banner. Nothing to see. No police. She wants us out the front, but we're not going out the front."

"Won't she come in then?"

"She'll go where we're going. Over the top and out the back." She patted the niece on the shoulder. "I'm sorry about this."

The sound of banging upstairs turned their heads. Ben was already attacking the second partition wall. Michelle looked at Sagrada one last time and made the universal telephone sign with the thumb and forefinger of one hand.

"Tonight."

Then she went through the hole to join Ben.

* * *

THE ROOF WAS WIDE and flat with utility outbuildings and cluttered work areas. Each building had its own unique layout, but the overall theme was, what the eye doesn't see the heart doesn't grieve over. The rooftop was a mess.

"Stay down."

Ben looked at Michelle as if she thought he was stupid. Then, two shots blasted chunks of plaster off the stairway exit, and Ben stayed down. He scampered towards the front of the hotel and crouched behind the retaining wall. The third-floor window opposite was only halfway up the height of the building, so either the sniper was firing from an angle, or she had climbed to the roof. She obviously wasn't waiting for them to come out the front door anymore. It wouldn't take long for her to realise that their only way down was the fire escape, and the only way out was the delivery bays behind Zara. He couldn't let her get there before them. He had to slow her down.

"You take the fire escape. I'll be there in a minute."

"What?"

Ben didn't wait for Michelle to argue and crossed the roof at a crouch. He'd learned from Michelle's fast and straight movement in the studio but couldn't help keeping a low profile. The low profile wasn't enough.

He reached the corner of the building and pulled out a wedge of banknotes, almost 200,000 euros. He fanned them out in his hand, then stood up to throw them into the street. The money separated and became a shower of 100-euro notes. They fluttered like falling leaves, getting the attention of pedestrians almost immediately. There was a surge of humanity at the top end of La Rambla.

Ben turned and started towards the fire escape. Two more shots kicked dust off the retaining wall, then he followed Michelle down the iron stairs. One more shot pinged the metal framework, then they were gone.

* * *

MENDOZA SAW THE SHOWER of money and knew she had lost. Running down the stairs and out onto La Rambla she was already late, without having to struggle through the crowd of people clutching at the falling banknotes. The only thing in her favour was the enclosed delivery area behind Zara. There was only one way in and one way out. The fire escape was a narrow rusty staircase, while Mendoza's stairs were wide and solid. She could gain time and catch them coming out onto the main road.

She came around the corner and barged her way through the crowd. A delivery truck came out of the side entrance and joined the traffic crawling past Placa de Catalunya. She knew who she was looking for now: the hair and clothing. There was nobody fitting the description along the street. She went into the delivery area and saw the fire escape in the far corner. The stairs were empty.

* * *

MICHELLE FOLLOWED THE hallway to the main stairs once they'd climbed back inside Hotel Lloret on the second floor. They went down two more flights of stairs, then turned away from the lobby towards the side of the building. Two minutes later, she pushed open the staff door, and they mingled with the shoppers along Carrer dels Tallers. They were past the cannabis shop that seemed to sell t-shirts and not cannabis before she noticed Ben was struggling to keep up.

"Come on. We can't slow down."

Ben nodded but didn't speak. He looked pale and sweaty. It wasn't until they took the shortcut back to the car that she noticed the blood soaking through his shirt.

Chapter Fifty-Three

A MEMORY RESURFACED AMID the pain. Not a memory from the dark place that was his childhood but of happier times. Ben clung onto it and tried to bring it into focus. It wasn't easy because the darkness always wanted to drag him down. It was trying to drag him down now. His eyes flickered behind closed lids, searching for the nugget of brightness hidden in the dark. His older brother held out a hand to help him up, and the memory popped out fully formed.

* * *

"I'M GOING TO FALL."

"You'll only fall if you look down. The only way is up. So, look up."

"That's the stupidest thing I ever heard. Down is still down, if I'm looking or not."

The brothers were climbing the verandas up the outside of the block of flats they grew up in, the fifth floor for them, ten floors from ground to roof. They were currently on the second floor, and Ben was convinced he was going to die. Christian had other ideas.

"Look on the bright side. If there's a fire, you'll be able to climb down."

"We're not climbing down."

"Same difference."

"And falling down is a lot different to climbing up."

Christian held out a hand. "I won't let you fall."

Ben believed him. Believing his brother wasn't the problem, he always believed him. That's what older brothers were for, making sure their kid brothers didn't fall. No, the problem wasn't the falling, it was him beginning to enjoy the climb. Ben reached up for the third-floor veranda and pulled himself up. Then, the fourth. And the fifth. He didn't stop at their veranda but kept on climbing. When the fall came, it wasn't his, it was his brother's. And it wasn't from the fifth floor; it was from much higher.

* * *

"YOU DID WHAT?"

"I put it back."

"You dipstick. It'll have my fingerprints all over it."

"Then you shouldn't have taken it in the first place."

"We're thieves. Taking things is kind of the point."

They were older now, no longer living in the flats but a semi-detached house on the edge of the council estate. Christian was the family breadwinner but Ben was rapidly becoming the master thief. From his brother's perspective, Ben was also an imbecile, breaking into houses Christian had already burgled and returning the stolen goods.

Ben shrugged. "Weren't you wearing gloves?"

"When I screwed the place, yes. Not back at home."

They were in the kitchen, two weeks after the burglary and ten days since Ben returned the stolen DVD player. Christian had been looking for it because he'd left a copy of *Die Hard* in the disc tray.

"What about the Die Hard DVD?"

Ben said, "It was my copy."

"So?"

"So, you don't steal from family. Or poor people."

"We are poor people. I'm just redistributing the poorness."

"That makes as much sense as not falling if you're looking up."

"You didn't fall, did you?"

Ben couldn't argue with that, but he didn't have to like it. The trouble was he was beginning to do more than like it; he loved climbing and breaking in and, more importantly, getting away with it. His brother had taught him well, but now Ben was close to outstripping him.

"What are you two arguing about now?"

The voice was deep and hard and rough as a bear's arse. Mrs Green didn't suffer fools gladly, and she wouldn't stand dissent among her sons.

"Nothing, Ma." As usual, Christian wouldn't let Ben fall. "Just looking for that Die Hard DVD."

Ben played along. "*My* Die Hard DVD."

Mrs Green stood in the kitchen doorway and scratched the bear's arse. "There ain't no his or yours, just ours."

Ben said, "He stole my DVD."

She folded her arms. "And you stole it from Blockbuster, so shut your yap."

Nobody heard the car pull up outside until there was a knock at the door. They all recognised the knock. Mrs Green nodded for Ben to open the door. The copper was big and hard and flanked by two more on the path to the police van. Christian had climbed too high and was about to fall. The police arrested him for a burglary two streets away thanks to his fingerprints being found on a stolen DVD player that somebody had returned ten days ago.

Six months later, Ben's brother was dead, but Christian still spoke to him despite the pain. And the heat. Ben felt like he was burning up. His eyes stopped flickering behind lids that felt like they were glued shut.

"Don't look down." The voice sounded different, but the advice remained the same. "Keep looking up."

Something cool soothed his brow, and he felt water run into his eyes. The voice wasn't his brother's anymore, even though it was Christian's hand that reached down for him.

"Up."

Then Michelle took hold of his hand and pulled him into the light.

Chapter Fifty-Four

"I DIDN'T KNOW YOU were a Christian."

"Lapsed."

"It must come back in times of need then. You were talking in your sleep."

Ben didn't explain, still getting over the feeling of disorientation at waking up from whatever the hell he was waking up from. He looked at the bare plaster walls, and the cracked window with its slatted shutter half closed against a grey day. At least, he assumed it was grey; it was hard to tell through all the dirt on the glass. There was a chipped wooden chest of drawers against the wall and a faded bedside table that complimented the sagging metal-framed bed he was lying on. Time fought its way to the top of his list of priorities.

"How long?"

Michelle nodded at his midriff. "Not long enough."

Ben looked at the bandages that were wrapped tightly around his waist. The good news was that there wasn't much blood seeping through the dressings. The bad news was that there were a lot of dressings. Pain was down to a dull throbbing ache, but he felt lightheaded and a little nauseous. When he looked up, the room began to spin. Michelle reached out a hand to stop him falling out of bed.

"Take it easy."

The room began to settle and he noticed the state of the room. "This isn't a hospital."

A slow train screeched and crawled its way past the window, rattling an empty vase on the chest of drawers. Michelle moved closer and sat at the foot of the bed, the springs creaking as the mattress sagged under her weight.

"Julio had some contacts."

Another thought crossed Ben's mind. "Passports?"

Michelle took a stack of identity documents out of her pocket. "Yesterday."

"It's not yesterday now?"

Michelle held a finger in front of Ben's eyes and moved it from left to right. It didn't look like he was focussing, physically or mentally. "It's the day after yesterday. Today. After that, it will be tomorrow."

Ben felt too woozy to argue about being talked to like a child. He examined the bandages again. There was a slight stain just above the right hip and another around the back. Michelle explained.

"Single gunshot. Through and through. It took a bunch of skin but nothing important."

"My skin is important."

"Nothing life-threatening."

Ben's head was beginning to clear. He checked the room again.

"Disgraced doctor?"

"Disgraced vet."

That made Ben's head spin again, then the room faded out.

* * *

THE THIRD-FLOOR APARTMENT was in a rundown tenement between Estacion de Francia and the Parc Zoologic de Barcelona, the railway station, and the zoo. Most of the windows were boarded up, and those that weren't had weathered shutters that didn't entirely close. The windows hadn't been cleaned for months, giving the otherwise sunny day a grey and cloudy appearance through the glass.

Rafael Fiveller, the disgraced vet, used to work in the animal enclosure at the zoo until a dependence on painkillers made him unreliable. Now, he scraped a living working in Barcelona's criminal underbelly. He visited the apartment again while Ben was sleeping. The woman was sitting at the foot of the bed, holding his hand.

"Will he be alright?"

"He will survive. Alright depends on how much he wants to bend."

The woman gave him a hard stare that reminded him he wasn't working in the zoo anymore. The look in her eyes told him that she was familiar with the criminal underbelly, too.

"I have cleaned and stitched the wound. There is no infection, but he will need to rest and keep it clean. Over time, he should regain full movement."

He pointed to the bottle of tablets on the bedside table. "The painkillers might make him..." He made a swirling movement around his head.

"But rest. Any exertion could pull his stitches."

The woman looked sad. "There won't be any exertion."

She was still looking sad when Fiveller left.

* * *

THE NEXT TIME BEN woke up, the room was steadier, and the sun was out. He could tell the sun was out because there was a shadow on the floor, but the day was no less grey. The vet really needed to clean the windows. Michelle was standing looking out through the slats. Ben flexed his mouth to check it was working before he spoke.

"You planning on washing those?"

She turned to look at him. "Those?"

"The window."

"There is only one."

"So, are you planning on washing *IT?*"

They were back to arguing again. It was amazing how easy it was to slip into old habits. Sometimes, that was easier than saying what you really thought, which was a whole lot darker than arguing about the window. Michelle moved away from the shutter.

"You're feeling better then."

"The room's stopped spinning. I wouldn't call it better."

"Not as bad."

"No, not as bad."

"And if something is not as bad. That is better. Yes?"

"I'm sorry. Did I do something to piss you off?"

"Yes, you stood in front of a sniper throwing money from the roof."

"It was me that got shot."

"Yes, it was. You fucking asshole."

Then the façade crumbled, and Michelle sat on the bed. Ben shifted his position, using his arms to take the strain, and sat beside her. He took her head and rested it against his shoulder and his façade crumbled as well.

"I'm sorry. I'm sorry. You're right, I'm an arsehole." He kissed the top of her head. "You're Jason Bourne. I should have let you get shot."

Michelle snorted a laugh, and it was only then that he realised she was crying. He kissed her again because he was crying too. It was amazing how far they had come, from hating each other to taking a bullet for her. He hadn't seen that in his future when he was teaching kids to play tennis and letting Eduardo Perez service their mothers. Thinking of Eduardo did nothing to brighten his mood, so he kissed one more time.

Michelle shivered and squeezed him tight.

"Ouch."

"Sorry."

They held each other more gently, and Ben let out a sigh. "I guess we're both sorry."

Michelle gave him a sad little smile. "Love means never having to say you're sorry."

Ben's smile was almost as sad. "Yippee-ki-yay, motherfucker."

This time, Michelle's laugh was more of a chuckle, but it was no less sad. "Who said a man and a woman can't be friends without sex getting in the way?"

"Sex did get in the way."

It was Michelle's turn to kiss Ben. "No, it didn't."

Ben looked her in the eye. "Friends?"

She didn't blink. "Friends."

Even though her smile looked more genuine, he couldn't help feeling there was still some sadness in reserve. He shifted on the bed to ease the pressure on his dressings and tried to lighten the mood. "Did you see the names on the passports?"

Michelle hadn't checked the passports yet. She disentangled herself from Ben and looked at the documents now, then she laughed. "Harry and Sally."

Chapter Fifty-Five

DARKNESS FELL ON THE disgraced vet's apartment, and Ben didn't even notice. He had been slipping in and out of sleep for most of the afternoon, not really what you'd call unconsciousness, but just tired after all the painkillers and the stress. At least his head had cleared, and he felt a lot stronger. Even so, he wasn't going to be jumping off rooftops anytime soon. He turned over, keeping his back to the bedside lamp, and that's when he realised it was evening.

"Hey, we should think about getting out of here."

He shuffled up on his pillow and turned around. The woman sitting in the corner of the room wasn't Michelle. Ben had to look twice before he realised it was Julio Sagrada. The forger kept to the shadows and let Ben figure it out for himself. The note on the bedside table didn't bode well.

* * *

Harry,

I waited until you were sleeping because I do not think I could say this in person. I cannot let you take the risks anymore. It has been a wonderful adventure, but this was never going to work. It is too dangerous, and too many people have been hurt already. If the wedding does not go ahead, hurting you is the least my father will do. And you were right; there are plenty of arranged marriages that succeed. This will succeed because it will keep you alive. Now, take the little mule and disappear. You have no need to steal anymore. Adios mi amor, and yippee-ki-yay.

Love, Sally

* * *

BEN READ THE LETTER twice, then slumped against his pillow. The car keys were on the bedside table, next to the envelope. A streetlamp outside threw irregular shadows across the wall and ceiling, all angles and lines as it shone through the slats. Julio Sagrada sat with her hands folded in her lap and didn't speak. Her face couldn't hide what she was thinking, though, and that gave him encouragement.

"When did she leave?"

"The last time you fell asleep."

"When was that?"

"When it began to get dark."

"And you knew."

Sagrada shifted in her chair. She looked uncomfortable but defiant. "I am a woman. Of course, I knew."

"Then you know I'm not going to let her go."

"I suspected."

Ben swung his legs out of bed and tested his balance. The room didn't spin. His head didn't feel woozy. He was still wearing the same clothes he'd been wearing since their ill-fated visit to Zara. Michelle really had looked beautiful in that dress. Ben wasn't bothered about looking beautiful, just clean.

"Where can I get some—"

Sagrada kicked a sturdy bag across the floor. Ben opened it and took out a new pair of jeans, a sweatshirt, and fresh underwear and socks. He looked at the woman sitting opposite. She shrugged.

"I am good with sizes."

Ben was already in her debt and didn't know what to say. He thought back to the photo studio above JS TATTOO & PIERCING and the mad scramble onto the roof. He didn't even know how the woman got out.

"I'm sorry about scaring your niece."

"You didn't scare my niece. It was the people your woman is going to meet."

Ben put the bag down. "You know who she's going to meet?"

"I know lots of things. And what I don't know, I listen to or find out. I listened to your woman when she called her father."

Ben was running various scenarios through his head; Michelle going to her father's hotel, Michelle arranging a location of her choosing, Michelle having to meet at a place of her father's choosing. If she was planning on going through with the wedding, Ben reckoned she'd do whatever her father told her.

"And she repeated the address, didn't she?"

Sagrada nodded. "I assume to make sure she got it right."

Ben didn't believe that any more than she did, but why write a farewell note if you were going to leave a trail of breadcrumbs? He didn't try to figure it out. So far, he didn't understand anything going on in Michelle's head. Maybe it was a subliminal message, or maybe she didn't know she was being overheard. Whichever it was, there was one piece missing.

"When are they meeting?"

"In an hour."

Ben stood up and dropped his trousers. There was no time to be shy. He tore the labels off and put the new jeans on. The sweatshirt covered the bandages. He didn't bother changing his underwear but he did change his socks.

"It's a good job I woke up when I did, then."

Sagrada put the dirty clothes in the bag. "Who do you think woke you up?"

Chapter Fifty-Six

THE TARGET BUILDING WAS a multi-storey car park that was still under construction at Placa de les Glories Catalanes. The entire street was just one huge building site, three concrete structures being built alongside the roadworks that were redirecting the 207 where it merged with the C-31 out of Barcelona. One of the buildings was still in the early stages, but the other two were almost complete, an office building and the multi-storey car park. The interiors were stripped concrete and dangling wires, but all the floors were in place, including the rooftop parking level with construction lights and painted lines.

The roadworks looked like a sandstone quarry, the centre of the wide flat roundabout resembling sand dunes and rocky outcrops with pieces of heavy machinery abandoned for the night. Security lights stood tall and bright, throwing shadows across the dunes like a scary moonscape.

Sagrada had said the meeting was in an hour. Ben got there in thirty minutes. The thing about breaking into a building was to give yourself plenty of time. Breaking into a building with no walls didn't need time, but he wanted to be on that roof before Michelle walked into the shitstorm that her father would no doubt unleash.

He parked the little red car between an excavator and a dumper truck and left the door unlocked for a quick getaway. He waited to make sure there was no movement on the building site, then crossed the dunes to the unmade road. Carrer de los Castillejos was dark and desolate, the buildings standing out against the darkening sky. He found the one he wanted and stood next to an advertising hoarding that also doubled as the staff entrance.

He pulled the board away from the fence and slipped through the gap. The name he'd been told to look out for at the top of the sign read,

MARTINEZ CONCRETE

* * *

A MANICURED HAND OPENED the compound gate, then got back in the expensive car and drove into the ground floor of the multi-storey car park. Pablo Cordero Belen didn't bother closing the gate behind him, following the concrete ramp on the right instead. There was space for an electronic barrier and a payment booth, but neither had been installed yet. They would be the finishing touches to the latest expansion of the Martinez Empire. Being able to put your name on the front of your building was certainly an inducement, but going legitimate wasn't the endgame, it was making a lot of money and cleaning the fortune Cordero Belen already had.

A short-circuiting security light sparked somewhere in the upper floors. Dangling wires, coiled and tied in loops, brushed the paintwork as the car eased up the first level with a low rumble and dipped headlights. Making a lot of money was only part of what the driver was thinking about, because for any of this to work, there was first the small matter of a wedding. If that didn't go ahead, there would be ramifications, and Cordero Belen would be the man meting them out.

* * *

MICHELLE HEARD THE RUMBLE of the exhaust and stepped back into the shadows. One of the security lights was arcing, sparks dancing across the concrete. Parking bays had been crudely marked out with a spray can, waiting for the final coat of paint once the building was finished. She didn't understand the reasoning behind that, unless it was to make sure they'd got the size right before they sealed the rooftop level.

Three other lamps stood tall and bright in the corners of the parking apron. The multi-storey car park was the building nearest to completion, and the scaffolding had been removed from the outside, but there was still a heavy chain-link fence to stop workers falling off the roof. Or being thrown off the roof, knowing the kind of people her father usually associated with. She didn't plan on being thrown off the roof.

There were two pallets of building materials and a forklift truck near the top of the ramp. Somebody had left a magazine and a food container on one of the pallets. The magazine caught the wind and fluttered across the concrete, making her jump. She never used to be this nervous meeting her father, but then again, the stakes had never been this high before.

* * *

BEN WAS OUT OF breath by the time he climbed the last flight of stairs. The concrete stairwell was dizzying in its regularity, not just because it meant climbing in a circle but also because there were no outside walls yet. The stairs resembled that endless staircase drawing by M. C. Escher or something by Salvador Dali. By the time he reached the top, his pulse was thumping so loud in his ears that it drowned everything except the sound of his own breath.

He paused in the final stairwell, looking over the edge into the bowels of the building. The stairs were obviously for pedestrian access, and probably the fire escape too. The dual lift shafts ran up the central core next to the M. C. Escher staircase, but he couldn't see the vehicle ramps that would circle the structure leading from one parking level to the next. Some internal walls had been tagged with plasterboard panels, but there were no windows, just gaping holes where the frames should be.

Once he'd got his breath back, he went up three steps, then stopped and listened. Nothing louder than his raging blood. He took a deep breath, then let it out slowly, trying to calm the pulse throbbing in his ears. He thought he heard electrics sparking somewhere in the distance and a low rumble, but there was no sense of distance or direction.

He went up three more steps, his head drawing level with the rooftop. The concrete was scattered with pallets and utility outbuildings, a square block for the elevator winches, and something that might have housed the air conditioning. A low wall ran all the way around the edge, with a temporary fence to stop workers falling off the roof. The entire level was in darkness.

Ben listened one more time, then climbed the last few steps and stood in the shadow of the elevator housing. Something felt wrong. He'd never been on the roof of a building under construction before, but this didn't feel like a rooftop parking level. Where was the ramp? Where were the parking bays? And why was this rooftop in darkness when there were security lights on the building next door.

He edged towards the retaining wall and looked through the chain link fence. The other building was two floors shorter than this one, with three security lights on poles in the corners. The fourth lamp was blinking on and off, sending sparks dancing across the concrete. Temporary parking bays had been marked out, awaiting the final coat of paint.

A figure stepped back into the shadows, and Ben leaned over to look at the bottom of the building. A battered sign hung from the open compound gate, and Ben let out a sigh. Martinez Concrete was constructing both buildings. Ben was on the wrong roof.

Chapter Fifty-Seven

PABLO CORDERO BELEN drove up the final ramp and stopped next to a splintered pallet and a forklift truck. He left the engine running, the low throaty rumble giving comfort in the otherwise quiet night. Sparks bounced off a second pallet, stacked with building materials and a discarded food container. He flicked the headlights to full beam, and the length of the rooftop parking level came into focus. The full length, but not the sides. There were still areas of shadow he couldn't see.

His daughter had learned her lessons well. It broke his heart to know it would be to no avail. He turned the headlights off but left the engine running and got out of the car. The door closed with a solid clunk. After the glare of the headlamps, the rooftop settled into the more yellow glow of the security lights. The short-circuiting lamp went out altogether, and the sparks stopped dancing.

"Mi Chiquita."

After several moments Michelle stepped out of the shadows to the right.

"Papa."

They stood looking for a long time, then walked towards each other. Neither spoke. Michelle stood proud and erect. Then her father folded her in his arms and let out the faintest sob.

* * *

BEN WATCHED FROM the other roof. He thought about shouting a warning, but a warning about what? Maybe a shout of encouragement, but again, encouragement to do what? Michelle was there because she was going to agree to her father's terms, and in doing so, release Ben from his obligations. What more could he say from all the way across here?

Cordero Belen got out of the car, and Michelle came out of the shadows, both stepping out of the cocoon of safety that their environments provided. They stood facing each other; then her father gave her a hug. Ben stood transfixed, unable to move or speak. He doubted if his mother would give him a hug in similar circumstances, and he supposed that was the problem, a hint of jealousy that there was still affection in the Cordero Belen household, while the Green family was all burnt bridges and acid tongues.

Michelle hugged her father in return and they stood like that for a long time. Her father gave her one last squeeze, then they separated. After a few more moments, he gave a little nod, and they started to talk. Ben looked for any signs of tension or anger, but that's all he could do, watch.

* * *

CORDERO BELEN GAVE HIS daughter one last hug, then stepped back. It was good to hold her again, and he wished he'd done it more when she was growing up. There is no instruction manual for being a single father, and the manual was completely absent when that father was the head of the biggest drug cartel in Mexico. He'd made mistakes, he knew, but he had built an empire and reckoned he deserved some credit for that. If bringing up a daughter had slipped through the cracks, then so be it. He felt sad but not repentant.

"You have been busy in Spain."

"Nothing that I planned."

"You planned your hen party."

"No, *you* planned my hen party. Including a chaperone."

Cordero Belen shrugged. "For protection."

"Against the gigolo?"

"The gigolo was not my idea."

"It wasn't mine either."

Cordero Belen stood firm. "And yet here we are."

"No thanks to the chaperone."

This was straying into a delicate area. Cordero Belen performed a slow pirouette, spinning on one foot and holding his arms out for balance. He had always been a good dancer, but the pirouette was to buy him time. When he stood facing her again, he gave Michelle a sad little look.

"She exceeded her instructions."

Not explaining what her instructions were.

Michelle ignored the sad face and gave him a hard stare in return. "And when she killed the lifeguard?"

They exchanged hard looks, but Cordero Belen was secretly proud of the stance his daughter was taking. The training had done more than give her tactical awareness, it had made her face hard questions and come up with answers. One of the answers was, there is always collateral damage.

"You involved the lifeguard. When you ran off with his friend."

"It had nothing to do with him."

Her father kept his tone light, but there was steal behind his words. "You cannot have Don Quixote without Sancho Panza."

Michelle insisted. "It had nothing to do with him."

Her father wasn't swayed. "Or have Harry without Sally."

Michelle blinked as if slapped. Her shoulders didn't slump, but she stood less erect, and her jawline softened. Her father's tone became more reflective as he took a step or two towards the car, like a man taking an evening stroll with his daughter. Michelle followed but didn't speak, letting her father do the talking.

"He used to ride a donkey, you know?"

"Harry?"

Her father smiled. "Sancho Panza."

He stopped his little stroll around the car and stood next to the pallet with the discarded food container. The smell of dead sparks hung in the air like cordite after a gun battle. He turned to face his daughter and let out a sigh. When he looked into her eyes, he saw the little girl she used to be, before the kidnapping and the training and the loss of innocence.

"Do you remember the burro you used to feed after school?"

* * *

BEN MOVED ALONG THE retaining wall to try and get a better angle on the scene being played out on the neighbouring roof, but no matter how far he went, the view was the same. Cordero Belen stood with his daughter, then he did a strange little pirouette and walked in a slow circle around the car. When he stood with Michelle again, he rested one hand on a pallet of building materials and appeared to settle into a conversation that looked calm and friendly.

But something felt off, the calmness looking forced and unnatural. Ben couldn't put his finger on what it was but he trusted his senses, they had stood him in good stead over many years as a master thief. Or Robin Hood. He knew that if a job felt hinky, then it was a job he shouldn't do. Michelle talking to her father, was a job he felt she shouldn't do.

All of which was absolutely no use from all the way over here. He doubted he could shout loud enough to get his message across, and he didn't have a torch to flash in her eyes. He looked around to see if there was anything he could throw onto the other roof, but the fence was too high and the distance too great. He considered running down the stairs but knew that would be a fool's errand, going all the way down the M. C. Escher staircase, then all the way up the car park ramps. Whatever was going to happen would happen long before he came to the rescue.

He slapped the chain link fence in frustration. He had never felt so helpless.

* * *

MICHELLE FOLLOWED HER father around the car and stopped when he stopped. She stood facing the car and watched him rest an arm on the pallet of building materials. He looked relaxed but a little sad. She could understand that, she felt a little sad too.

"Do you remember the burro you used to feed after school?"

The question didn't just take her back to her childhood; it took her back to Campdasens Bed & Breakfast with Ben. Thinking about the well-hung donkey putting a smile on Mrs Donkey's face brought a smile to her own.

"The smiling mule. Yes."

Her father seemed to notice the food container for the first time, and the untidiness clashed with his need to keep everything in order. He picked up the plastic box and walked to an oil drum that was being used for industrial waste. Michelle watched him but didn't follow. Now, it was her turn to rest an arm on the pallet while she listened, standing with her back to the entrance ramp. Her father dropped the container in the bin and came back.

"Do you remember what happened to it?"

Michelle didn't need to hear what happened to the donkey. "I'm here to get married. The rest doesn't matter."

Her father tilted his head. "Doesn't matter? You have dragged me halfway across Spain, got two people killed and a bunch more injured, and you say the rest doesn't matter?"

Michelle stopped leaning on the pallet and stood up straight. "You wanted a wedding. I'm here for the wedding. Just leave Ben out of it."

"You didn't leave the burro out of it."

"This isn't about the burro."

"It isn't about the wedding either. It's about the marriage. From this day forth, etcetera, etcetera."

"That's what I'm here for."

Cordero Belen looked at his daughter. "You should not have fed the burro. Because of who you are, the market owner gave you whatever you wanted. More food than a burro can eat. Every day. For many days. The burro began to like you. It depended on you. Soon it would not obey its master and grew fat and lazy."

He gave a little shake of the head. "Every action has consequences. Fallout has collateral damage. Collateral damage meant the glue factory. Your love for the burro signed its death warrant."

"Leave Ben out of this."

"There is no, out of this. You made sure of that."

Michelle couldn't take her eyes off her father. This man had been ruining her life since before the kidnap resolution training. Since before she had a life. Her mother had left when she was too young to remember, and her best friend was dead. It was all part of the poisonous world her father lived in. It was poisoning her life now. There were no more rebuttals. She was listening so intently that she didn't notice the tiniest nod of the head as he spoke.

"Distraction technique only works if your subject believes the distraction." He let out a sigh of resignation. "You were never here for the wedding."

* * *

BEN COULD SENSE THE change in atmosphere despite not being able to hear what was being said. It was written all over the body language on display on the opposite rooftop. He saw Michelle stand firm and her father look resigned. To the uninitiated that might have looked like Michelle had won, but Pablo Cordero Belen wasn't the kind of man to give in that easily. The conversation might have slowed, and the facial expressions become graver, but there was electricity in the air that belied the calm exterior.

The words stopped coming. The pair faced each other in stony silence, whatever had been discussed completely unresolved. Michelle stood beside the pallet of building materials. Her father stood facing the car and the entrance ramp. It was movement on the entrance ramp that caught Ben's attention.

A tall, dark figure with grey hair and a slight stoop walked quickly towards the pallet. His left arm swung as he walked, but he kept his right hand down by his side. It wasn't until he came up behind Michelle that Ben realised what he was carrying. The long, fat barrel of the silenced pistol came up in one smooth motion, and the man shot Michelle at point-blank range.

Chapter Fifty-Eight

TEN MINUTES AFTER MICHELLE came out of the shadows. Almost three-quarters of an hour after Ben climbed the M. C. Escher staircase. Six days after the runaway bride nearly knocked him over with a taxi in Cabopino and Ben made the biggest decision of his life. After all of that, all of those strands, they all came together in one single point in time. Right now.

The ending that sucked the life right out of him.

Ben dropped to his knees and clamped both hands over his mouth. He let out a silent scream that almost shredded his throat. Tears formed in his eyes, but wouldn't fall. He used the chain link fence to claw himself back up and saw the grey-haired man bundle Michelle's body into the boot of the car. Her father stood doubled over as if he'd been sick, a man coping with the terrible thing he had just ordered to be done.

Ben had no sympathy for the father who had just lost his daughter. Ben had nothing much of anything. He watched Cordero Belen straighten up and get in the car. The other man closed the boot, then got in the front passenger side. The solid clunk of the doors sounded muffled by distance but felt like a slap in the face. In the blink of an eye Ben's mission had changed from evade and rescue to something much more serious. Vengeance. Payback. And the person he was going to make pay was over there on the other roof.

* * *

IT WAS FUTILE. Ben knew that before he started, but he had to try. He took the stairs two at a time all the way down, feeling dizzy and lightheaded by the time he reached the bottom. He jumped in the little red car and hit the entrance ramp, doing forty. He had to trade speed for control on the corners and came out on the rooftop parking level feeling dizzier than at the bottom of the M. C. Escher staircase.

The rooftop was empty, of course, it was, but he got out of the car and checked anyway. He could see the big wide tyre marks of the heavy sedan but nothing else. There were no shell casings. There was no blood. Either they had cleaned the floor, or the hitman had used a small calibre weapon. Ben had read about that in some book he couldn't remember, the entrance wound being small and then the .22 bullet rattling around the skull and mashing brains. He felt sick even thinking about it. He felt sick anyway.

And helpless. There was that feeling again. He'd pretty much been a spare wheel on this entire trip, Michelle being the expert on kidnap resolution, driving, and evasion techniques. All Ben had done was steal the money.

He stood in the middle of the parking level and felt the shock begin to take a grip. His breath came in shallow gasps, his lungs unable to take the oxygen they needed. He began to shiver, the warmth of the evening doing nothing to negate the cold that was settling into his bones. He felt nauseous, but his stomach wouldn't let him be sick. He doubled over as a stomach cramp clenched his muscles, and he dry heaved.

The night was crisp and clear, stars pricking the dark blue sky as it descended into blackness. Ben was descending into a blackness of his own as he scoured the floor one last time. There was nothing to indicate Michelle had ever been there, and that thought tugged at his heart. Apart from the Zara dress in the back of the car and the forged passports, he had nothing to remember her by. The seat backs were full of money, but that didn't count. He'd stolen the money to fund their getaway, but now the getaway was history.

He thought about the argument on the night of the gigolo and their discussion at La Despensa in Cabopino. Some decisions move your life forward, and some choices change your future forever. He hadn't intended to fall in love, deciding to run off with the bride being as much a fuck you to Max Overend as Michelle's father, but after five days on the road, falling in love is exactly what he had done. And now he had nothing. The woman who had rescued him from Malaguenas Autos and jumped out of a window with him at Hotel Primavera, wasn't even a bloodstain on the concrete.

The dress. His mind kept going back to that. How beautiful she had looked in the changing room at Zara, and even better at Campdasens. It was folded up on the backseat of the Little Mule, the only thing of value, apart from two and a half million euros in the lining of the seats.

He shook his head. There *was* something else of value, but not to him. To the man, he had stolen it from in a tenth-floor hotel room in Leeds. That man would give anything to keep it out of the wrong hands and the police would give anything to know what was in it.

The germ of an idea began to grow in the back of Ben's mind. He glanced at the floor again, and was surprised to see a spot of blood he hadn't seen before. Then another. He opened his coat and noticed the spreading stain on his shirt. Another drop splashed on the concrete. The floor tilted, and his head began to spin. He turned to lean on the car door, but he was too late. His legs gave way, and he slid down the side of the car. When the floor came up to meet him, he wasn't bothered at all.

IV

YIPPEE-KI-YAY

"Getting it done is the only thing. Getting away isn't an option."
— Benjamin J Green

Chapter Fifty-Nine

A TRAIN RATTLED PAST the window, and there was a muffled announcement from the station. A police siren sounded somewhere in the distance, the familiar hee-haw, hee-haw of the Policia Local. The station announcement was in Spanish, and in the end, that was what brought Ben around. Not the noise, but the fact that he was in Spain, more specifically, Barcelona. As soon as he crawled out of the darkness, he tried to close himself down again. The reality he was waking into was too painful.

Michelle is gone. That thought was bad enough, but his next thought was even worse. *And it was all my fault.*

The darkness refused to reclaim him, and noises from Estacion de Francia kept him awake. His eyes felt gummed shut, but he didn't want to open them anyway. He turned over in bed, and the pain shot him awake. His eyes flew open.

"Slowly. Slowly. Take your time."

Julio Sagrada stood up from the chair beside the bed and placed a calming hand on his shoulder. The room stopped spinning, and Ben saw the familiar bare plaster walls and cracked window. The slatted shutter let in dirty light that still didn't show if it was sunny or grey, but it was definitely day, not night. That realisation turned him over more slowly. He couldn't remember anything after sinking to the floor of the multi-storey car park.

Sagrada saw the confusion on his face. "You crashed the car into the front door."

The confusion didn't go away, so she sat next to the bed. "This is what happened."

* * *

BEN HAD MANAGED TO get in the car and drive back to the disgraced vet's apartment. It was still dark, so thankfully, there weren't any pedestrians, because he was on the pavement as much as the road. When he finally swung into the unlit road between the station and the zoo, he lost control and ploughed into the concrete pillar that protected the door.

Sagrada was still in the apartment waiting for news about the rooftop meeting. Seeing the condition Ben was in told her everything she needed to know. The meeting had gone badly, but she didn't find out that Michelle had been killed until Ben blurted it out while the vet attended to his wounds.

The vet hadn't been happy about being called out again in the middle of the night, explaining that if Ben didn't rest this time, the consequences could be much more serious. He reinforced the stitches with gauze and sticking plasters and wrapped the whole thing in bandages after disinfecting the wounds. Painkillers and antibiotics were the end of his involvement. The rest was up to Sagrada and her patient.

That was twelve hours ago. Sagrada had parked and secured the car in an alley round the back of the apartment block so the police wouldn't get suspicious about the front-end damage. The bodywork was surprisingly robust and the concrete pillar had survived with barely a scratch. The door was old and flaking. It was still old and flaking, and didn't look any different.

When Ben had been brought up to date, he looked at the dirty window and heard voices in his head. *"You planning on washing those?" "Those?" "The window." "There is only one."* He closed his eyes as he tried to savour the memory, the sound of her voice, and the smile on her face. He began to cry, because she was right. Where they had been a pair, now there was only one. The tears came in rasping sobs, and there was nothing Sagrada could do to help.

Chapter Sixty

ONCE THE GRIEF BURNED itself out, there was rage. Grief was something Ben had felt before, when his brother died, but rage was a new emotion for him. He had always gone through life with a whistle and a smile, treading lightly and leaving zero footprint. He'd never had to face the consequences of his actions, because his actions were simply stealing things. Now, zero footprint had become a body-shaped print, and theft was about to become vengeance.

Where Julio Sagrada hadn't been able to help him with the grief, she was more than able to help him with her contacts. Working amid Barcelona's criminal underbelly had its fair share of downsides, but lots of benefits. One of those benefits was, she knew lots of criminals. Her intelligence-gathering network was second to none, and gathering intelligence was the first part of Ben's plan.

* * *

BEN'S GRIEF HAD BURNED itself out by early evening. By the time the streetlights came on, he had the basic outline of a plan. The first thing he had to ask himself was, how do you punish a man who only has six months to live? The answer was, for any normal man, you can't, but for a man trying to cement the family legacy, you attack the legacy.

The second thing he needed to do was relocate, because Julio Sagrada wasn't the only person with contacts in Barcelona's criminal underbelly. Pablo Cordero Belen might well have killed his daughter, but that wouldn't be enough for him. He would want to cauterize the wound, and that meant burning the man she had run away with. Benjamin J Green.

The disgraced vet would be easy to trace, knowing that Ben would need treatment after Consuela Mendoza had shot him on the Hotel Lloret rooftop. Rafael Fiveller's apartment was no great loss, but finding somewhere safe required Sagrada's expertise. In the end, the safest place was the place you'd already been. Gunshot victims never go back to the place they've been shot, so Ben booked a top-floor suite at Hotel Lloret. He was going back to La Rambla.

* * *

"YOU HAVE ACCESS TO the lift and stairs from your living room door."

Sagrada pulled back the bedroom curtain. "And the fire escape through the window."

Ben stood in the narrow hallway between the bedroom, the bathroom, and the lounge, and surveyed the penthouse suite.

"You sure we couldn't have got something bigger?"

Sagrada closed the curtain against the security light out back. "*He* is staying at the something bigger."

Ben didn't mention that it was a rhetorical question. He let out a sigh. His usual whistle and a smile approach didn't fit with the change of circumstances. He doubted he'd ever have a whistle and a smile again. This was serious. It was time to treat it as such.

"Good. The bigger, the better. Because big is more difficult to defend."

"You're going to attack?"

"I'm going to sneak in and stab him where it hurts."

"With the right knife, stabbing hurts everywhere."

Ben nodded, not a hint of a smile on his face. "Everywhere is what I'm aiming for."

Sagrada came out of the bedroom and joined Ben in the hallway. She looked doubtful that this tall, slim man was tough enough to take on the Mexican colossus. His skills didn't lie in that direction; he stole things. That didn't bode well for a positive outcome.

"You are going to be Ronnie Biggs and take his property?"

Ben wondered why the Great Train Robber was always the first English criminal they thought about in Spain. Half the British underworld had relocated to Spain in the sixties and seventies.

He shook his head. "Robin Hood. I'm going to give him something back."

* * *

FINDING OUT WHERE Pablo Cordero Belen was staying wasn't the problem; Julio Sagrada had provided that before Ben even moved into the Hotel Lloret. The problem was that for the plan to work, Ben would have to draw together several parties who had no interest in working together. Breaking into the penthouse suite of the Mandarin Oriental Hotel was the easy part. Bringing the others together at the right time would need a little help.

Sagrada could only provide some of that. The rest was down to the telephone book and one number he knew off by heart. Ben gave Sagrada the basic outline of his plan, and she nodded where she understood and asked questions where she wasn't sure. She checked that his wound was okay and left him the two bottles of tablets the vet had given her.

Once she'd left, Ben took out the mobile phone that Michelle had bought at the gas station between Alfaz del Pi and Valencia. He held it gently in his hand, feeling the touch of her fingers when she'd programmed the phone. The number he wanted wasn't in the contacts; it was in his head. He dialled it from memory and checked his watch. Yes, he should be there.

The phone rang three times, then just kept ringing. It didn't go to voicemail or cut off after another three rings. Ben sat beside the table lamp in the lounge and was about to hang up when Max Overend answered. Ben got right to the point.

"Max. Do you want to get out from under this?"

Chapter Sixty-One

THE MANDARIN ORIENTAL was a five-star hotel on the busy Passeig de Gracia. It boasted six floors of luxury rooms and a rooftop pool and restaurant. It was among the most expensive hotels in Barcelona, charging almost £400 per person per night. Ben wasn't sure how many people Cordero Belen was paying for, but once again, he'd taken the entire top floor, comprising of the honeymoon suite and two penthouse apartments. Cordero Belen was in the honeymoon suite, a touch of irony there, or maybe just Cordero Belen rubbing Ben's nose in it.

It was also less than half a mile from the Hotel Lloret. That would be Ben rubbing Cordero Belen's nose in it, if the cartel boss had known where Ben was staying. Ben intended to be the one doing the nose rubbing, but in a much bigger way, and that was largely dependent on being able to break into the honeymoon suite.

Ben could break into anywhere. It would just take time.

As with all burglaries, it started with casing the joint, getting the plans for each floor, and assessing the hotel security. Ben needed a good night's sleep. Casing the joint would start in the morning.

* * *

BEN SAT AT A street café on the tree-lined Carrer d' Arago, one block up from the Mandarin Oriental on the opposite side of the street. There were lots of trees and umbrellas around the pavement tables, giving Ben enough cover while still being able to see the hotel. He didn't really need to see the hotel, but line of sight meant nobody could sneak up on him without taking a major detour.

The sun was high enough that it had cleared the rooftops along Passeig de Gracia and was blazing down on Casa Bonet and the Nike Sporting Goods Shop on either side of the café. The trees and umbrellas meant the tables were in shade. Ben took a drink of iced Coke while he considered what he'd learned from his recce.

The Mandarin Oriental was just one business on a block that was built in a square, like the rest of Passeig de Gracia. Ben had walked all the way around the block until he came back out front. The hotel didn't have a car park, but there was an underground parking garage for the entire block. There was a park and garden with a concrete basketball court in the middle of the square behind the English Language School. There was only one way in and one way out of the square.

The hotel reception nestled between Tiffany & Co. on the right and Brioni on the left, with several other shops along the ground floor frontage, but Mandarin Oriental took up the next six floors along half the block. The smoked glass doors were twenty feet tall, with figures carved into the concrete pillars and gold lettering across the top. There were no balconies. This wasn't the Don Carlos Leisure Club; there would be no climbing to the honeymoon suite. There was also no bin storage around the back so there would be no fire alarm diversion either.

That meant this would have to be a uniform disguise or a delivery job. Or a break-in from the roof. The roof was Ben's preferred option. He loved clambering over rooftops. Once he'd made his mind up, the choice of rooftop decided itself. The roof to the right was two floors lower than the hotel, but the corner building on the left was the same height. That gave him a choice of IKKS, the Soler + Farmacia, or Pilar Oporto. He should be able to access the roof through any one of them.

That was the how taken care of. The next thing was what to do once he was in there. He'd been toying with an idea that would bring several groups together but wasn't been sure to what end. Until Julio Sagrada gave him the result of her background research on the wedding that would no longer take place.

* * *

"HE'S NOT INTO drugs, then?"

"He's into concrete."

"That's not the powder I was thinking about."

Sagrada expanded. "Martinez Construction is the largest contractor in Spain. Including the Balearics and the Canary Isles. It also has partners in France, Italy, and Greece."

Ben joined the dots. "Including Martinez Concrete."

Sagrada nodded. "The rooftop meeting."

Ben didn't. "That motherfucker."

Sagrada's tone hardened. "Yes, he fucks mothers. Drugs fuck everyone."

Ben was intrigued. "Anyone in particular?"

Sagrada considered whether to tell him or not, then gave an almost imperceptible nod. "The reason my niece called at the shop the other day. That's the anyone in particular."

"Her mother?"

"My sister."

Ben didn't pursue it. Some things are best kept to yourself. Ben hadn't talked about his brother until he'd met the one person he could unburden himself to, and now that one person was dead. Sagrada obviously had her own reasons for throwing in with the Yorkshire thief. Ben brought the conversation back to the person they were talking about.

"And the groom is the heir to the drugs empire."

"Concrete. Martinez isn't a drugs empire."

"But Cordero Belen is a drug cartel."

Neither of them spoke for a moment, both considering what that meant. Ben thought about the money he'd stolen from Laguna Park. After a few minutes, the plan in his head took a different shape, and he gave a cold, hard smile.

"He isn't expanding his drugs empire; he's laundering it. He wants a legitimate face for his millions." He turned the smile off. "But I'm going to Robin Hood his arse, and give him something a legitimate face can't live with."

Chapter Sixty-Two

BEN FINISHED HIS COKE and waved for the bill. He left a generous tip, then went shopping in the Nike Sporting Goods Shop next door. He bought a bright pink baseball cap and a neon yellow windcheater, putting the dark hat and coat he'd worn during his recce in the carrier bag. Crossing the street, he looked like an LGBT Belisha Beacon. He always felt a little sad that they'd replaced the Belisha Beacon pedestrian crossings with traffic lights in the UK.

It was time to do some window-shopping at IKKS and Pilar Oporto, using the next best thing to the pizza delivery jacket. Nobody ever remembered a man wearing a pink hat and a yellow coat; they just remembered the pink hat and yellow coat. He entered the first store around the corner from the Mandarin Oriental and started planning how to get to the roof.

* * *

IN THE END, HE didn't need to check out Pilar Oporto, because he got to the roof on the first try through IKKS. The busy clothing store had four floors of designer collections, including a MIU MIU ladies store and menswear and children's departments. The relevant word there was busy. There were too many customers and not enough staff spread across four shopping floors. Storage and warehousing took up the fifth floor to the roof and could be accessed through a staff door on each shopping floor. There was also a customer toilet on the second and the fourth. Ben waited until all the staff were engaged, then headed towards the fourth-floor toilet. When he took off the pink hat and yellow coat, he all but disappeared. Nobody saw him deviate through the staff door.

Half an hour later Ben sat in the lea of the elevator housing and looked down into the landscaped gardens of the inner square. He had seen enough to know how he was going to get into the honeymoon suite and how he was going to avoid any bodyguards that might be covering the doors. Getting out wasn't a problem either, having several options, depending on whether he was seen or not. There was the tastefully designed fire escape behind the Mandarin Oriental, the less tasteful ironwork behind IKKS, or the same way he had come up through the storage rooms and cargo elevator.

The sun felt warm on his back as he rested against the elevator housing, but he couldn't shake the cold feeling that was settling into his bones. Despite the exhilaration of sitting on the edge of the precipice, it was the emotional precipice that worried him. The feeling that this was the end no matter how well it went. That felt appropriate, considering why he was here.

He drew his knees up to his chest and watched a group of children playing basketball behind the English Language School. The sounds of laughter drifted up from the central square but did nothing to lighten his mood. Despite having lined all his ducks in a row, this was still a risky proposition, and not just because timing was the most perilous aspect.

He hugged his knees and turned from the basketball court below to the solar panels atop the Mandarin Oriental. There were several tables at the rooftop restaurant and a handful of sun loungers beside the half-length pool. The elevator housing was flanked by a pair of giant fans for the hotel air conditioning, and there were two half-landings/balconies with tables and umbrellas for private functions. Ben's private function was dependent on the recruits he had acquired after a couple of telephone calls.

Max Overend had been eager to help, not because he liked Ben, but because it was the only way for him to survive. There was no way the money launderers were going to keep him on as manager after losing their last shipment. To that end, Max had agreed to tell the money retrieval team from Benidorm and the Leeds gangster's hit squad where they could find the money/incriminating diary. Ben gave him the name of the hotel and the honeymoon suite.

Julio Sagrada provided the final piece of the puzzle. Gathering intelligence was only part of her involvement, providing the hammer was her most important contribution. There was no point in Ben planting the diary in Cordero Belen's hotel room safe if the police didn't arrive to find it. Ben wasn't on good terms with the police, since they didn't know he existed apart from being the brother of a Yorkshire thief who died in prison. In any case, West Yorkshire Police weren't going to send a unit to Spain on a promise from the thief's brother.

It was Sagrada who was going to provide the police intervention, Policia Local in the first instance, with international cooperation as a follow-up. She would also provide the leak that would plaster Cordero Belen's name all over the news. She was mildly impressed with Ben's plan but completely scornful of his exit strategy.

"Just because Cordero Belen has six months to live doesn't mean he will take this lying down."

"In six months, he can take it any way he likes."

Sagrada tried to stress the seriousness of Ben's situation. "This isn't one of those, cut the head off the snake situations. There will be more snakes."

"I'm only interested in one snake."

She looked worried at his lack of concern. "Getting this done is one thing. Getting away clean is another thing entirely. The snakes will hunt you down."

"Getting it done is the only thing. Getting away isn't an option."

Which accounted for the cold feeling settling into his bones as he watched the children play basketball, and the sun reflect off the solar panels. The bottom line was, he had nobody to get away for, anyway.

Chapter Sixty-Three

TIMING WAS THE KEY, coordinating all the elements of Ben's plan so they came together at the same time and place. The place had been set, the honeymoon suite of the Mandarin Oriental Hotel. The time would take a little organising. Julio Sagrada needed a while to reach her friendly Policia and finesse him towards an international raid. She called Ben in his room at the Hotel Lloret as the sun was setting over Barcelona.

"Policia Local is liaising with Policia overseas. They can be ready tomorrow."

That prompted Ben's second call to Max Overend.

"Can they make the deadline?"

"Just tell me when."

"Tomorrow. Two p.m. Don't be late." Then he hung up.

* * *

THERE IS A SAYING in the military that no plan ever survives first contact with the enemy. When Ben was a kid taking boxing lessons in Yorkshire, that manifested itself when his technique didn't survive the first punch on the nose. At that point, he saw red and would beat the shit out of whoever bloodied his nasal passage. When it came to crime, the military saying could be translated into, no plan ever survives first contact with other criminals. Ben's first contact with other criminals wasn't really contact at all, it was stealing from the money-laundering organisation at Laguna Park. Second contact was meeting Bad Breath and Broken Nose, then jumping out of the hotel window in Benidorm.

It was Bad Breath and Broken Nose who put a spike in Ben's plans. Because they didn't wait until two p.m. They got there early.

"Hey. You see who I see?"

"Where?"

Bad Breath pointed across La Rambla. "Pink hat and yellow coat."

Broken Nose snorted a laugh that hurt his nose. "He came back."

Bad Breath shook his head in disbelief. "Am I lucky or what?"

* * *

BEN PAUSED AT THE Font de Canaletes as he shifted the diary in his inside pocket. It was mid-morning, and he'd waited until after breakfast before going to the car to retrieve the incriminating evidence, leaving the money stuffed in the back of the seats. He was deciding what to do with the two and a half million euros as he crossed La Rambla back to the Hotel Lloret. If the plan went wrong, he intended to leave the keys for Julio Sagrada with a cryptic note. In fact, even if the plan went okay, there was no future for him, Sagrada was right about that. The snakes would come after him; there was no point in them finding the money as well.

He scratched the back of his neck and looked around. The pedestrian walkway was busy with tourists and shoppers, but he didn't see anything untoward. He glanced up at the window across the street where the sniper's rifle had been poking out four days ago. Maybe it was that that was making him feel uneasy.

With one last look along La Rambla he tucked the diary into the yellow jacket and zipped it up. He splashed water from the fountain over his face, then headed to the hotel.

* * *

BAD BREATH WAS WRONG, Artengo and Garcia weren't particularly lucky. That was their names, both of them only being known by their surnames. Artengo was the one with bad breath, while Garcia had the broken nose. He'd got that being beaten up by a couple of Yorkshire thugs at Hotel Primavera in Benidorm. Artengo had always had bad breath. They both had sore ribs though, from being rammed off the road in Valencia. By the man they were looking at right now.

Finding Benjamin J Green outside Hotel Lloret was their only piece of luck. Up until then, they were simply trying to get back in their boss's good books, after losing the money in Benidorm and the woman in Valencia. Having been told that the money would be in the honeymoon suite at the Mandarin Oriental they had got here early so they could get first crack at recovering it. Getting here early meant they had time to kill, and decided to spend it looking at the place where the annoying little thief had been shot. On the roof of the Hotel Lloret. It was a bit like people going to see the Dakota Building where John Lennon was shot, only more satisfying.

The man in the pink hat and yellow coat stopped beside the fountain and scratched his neck. He looked around, and Artengo thought they'd been spotted, but then the thief zipped up his coat and went into the hotel. Garcia nodded for them to follow. Artengo checked the gun tucked into his belt, then crossed the street. He wasn't taking any chances this time. If there was any more shooting, he didn't want to be the one getting shot.

* * *

BEN WENT STRAIGHT to his room and slipped the diary under the mattress. He didn't know why he hid the battered leather book, but it just felt like something that shouldn't be out in the open until it was time to be out in the open. When that time came it wasn't going to be out in the open, it was going to be in the safe at the bottom of the wardrobe. The same as every hotel in Spain. The same as Laguna Park and the Don Carlos Leisure Club.

He left the bedroom door open, then went into the lounge. The front windows overlooked La Rambla but were still hidden behind the Andorra

La Vella advertising banner. Ben looked down at a street that was red, blue, or yellow, depending on which part of the banner you were looking through. Blue tourists wandered up and down the pedestrian area. Red shoppers came out of H&M and Burger King. There was some kind of disturbance out front of the hotel, but Ben couldn't see what it was.

He turned away from the windows and crossed to the minibar. He wasn't thirsty but needed something to keep his mind off the job ahead. He looked at his hands. They were shaking. He flexed his fingers, then squeezed the hands into fists. The shaking didn't stop, but it eased to a mild tremble. He couldn't remember the last time he'd been this nervous ahead of a break-in. Maybe the first time, when he was returning a stolen television. Not the time he returned the DVD player with *Die Hard* in the disc tray; he had been much more assured by then.

He snapped the ring pull on a can of Coke, and the pffft hiss calmed him down. He ignored the glasses on the tray and drank straight from the can. On any other day, he would have crushed the empty can and made an internal quip, but he didn't feel like quoting *Jaws* today. There would be no "Yippee-ki-yay motherfucker," either. Today was all business, and the business wasn't burglary it was revenge. Bearing that in mind stopped him being flippant.

He took another drink and looked out of the window again. The commotion at the front of the hotel had stopped, but there was still a crowd staring at the lobby entrance. The itch on the back of his neck started again, and he heard feet pounding on the stairs outside his door. He was halfway there to put the deadbolt on when the door opened, not with a kick and splintering of wood but with a passkey. The key card was still on a chain with the concierge's name badge.

Chapter Sixty-Four

"JUMP OUT OF THE window. Go on. I dare you."

Ben backed off from the gun, pointing at his face, but didn't speak. The man with the gun followed Ben into the lounge, and the one with medical tape over his nose closed the door. The gun waved a threat.

"That's the thing with penthouse suites. Long way down."

Ben looked at the name badge swinging from the chain. "You're not Cesar Martinell."

The gunman waved at himself and then Broken Nose. "Artengo and Garcia."

As if they were a double act. Ben gestured at the medical tape. "You didn't bring the Yorkshiremen with you then?"

Artengo jabbed the gun at Ben like a man who thought guns made you tough. "No. I brought hellfire. And I am going to rain it down upon you."

Ben moved to the middle of the room, keeping away from the furniture. Artengo and Garcia were hemmed in by a glass-topped coffee table and an ornate dresser, with their backs to the door. That didn't help Ben at the moment, his only option being the windows behind the Andorra La Vella banner. Like Artengo said, a long way down, but not far to the roof if Ben used the scaffolding. Not while he had a gun stuck in his face, though.

"If I get rained on, you won't get the two and a half million."

"In the safe at Mandarin Oriental? You think we're stupid?"

Ben didn't offer an opinion, just waited to see what their plan was.

"You haven't broken in yet to put it there." Artengo tapped his watch. "We're early. And the early bird catches the worm."

Ben edged away from the coffee table, drawing them into the gap. "They have that saying in Spain?"

The gun steadied. "I'm practicing my English. See if you understand this." He drew the hammer back with a click. "Show me the bedroom."

* * *

JULIO SAGRADA HEARD VOICES through the door and lowered her hand without knocking. She'd seen the door closing as she came out of the elevator and listened as the voices moved into the lounge. The voices didn't sound angry, so that was good, but they were voices, which meant someone was in there with Ben. That was bad. The only person who knew where Ben was staying was Sagrada, so anyone else was a threat. Sagrada took threats seriously.

She listened for a few more seconds to make sure the voices were still in the lounge, then dashed across the hallway to the fire escape. She slipped her shoes off so they wouldn't clang on the metal staircase, then climbed out of the window.

* * *

"WHAT DO YOU WANT in the bedroom? You tired?"

Artengo backed out of the bottleneck and waved Ben through. "You're a safe cracker. Crack the safe."

"What safe?"

Artengo stepped forward and hit Ben across the nose with the gun. "The safe where you're keeping the money. In the bottom of the wardrobe." He raised his eyebrows. "I live in Spain. You don't think I know about Spanish hotels?"

Ben pulled three tissues out of a box on the dresser and dabbed his nose. It was bloodied but not broken. He had to force himself not to follow his boxing training and exchange technique for rage. He indicated the gun.

"Those things can go off by accident. You've made your point."

Artengo didn't lower the gun. Ben tried a different approach.

"Look. You shoot me in the head, and you don't get the money. Plus, headshot is a small target. You're more likely to shoot somebody across the street."

Artengo lowered the gun halfway and stepped aside. Ben walked through the bottleneck that wasn't a bottleneck anymore and entered the bedroom. Artengo followed, and Garcia stood guard in the doorway. A gentle breeze wafted the curtains as Ben opened the wardrobe.

Artengo barked an order. "Crack it."

Ben sat on the bed and nodded at the wardrobe. "Cracked."

The small safe in the bottom of the wardrobe was in default mode, which meant it was open. The digital reader showed 0000, the standby code. The safe was empty. Artengo kicked the wardrobe door closed, and it bounced back, hitting him in the face. The gun came up, angrier this time, as he jabbed it at Ben.

"Where is it?"

Ben shifted his position on the edge of the bed. "It was never in there." He indicated the size of the safe by making a small shape between his hands. "Two and a half million? This is a chain hotel. Package that size would have to go in the hotel safe."

Artengo wasn't falling for that this time. "You tried that at the last hotel."

Ben shrugged. "It's not there this time either. So don't shoot me by accident."

The gun was trembling as Artengo's knuckles turned white. "When I shoot you, it won't be by accident." He seemed to notice Ben's position on the bed for the first time. "What are you hiding?"

Ben held his hands out. "Where?"

"Under the mattress. Stand up."

Now Ben was worried. He settled himself heavier on the bed. "Do you know how much space two and a half million takes? It's not like some little old lady keeping her pension under the mattress."

The knuckles were so white it was amazing the gun hadn't gone off already.

"Stand up."

Ben stood up.

"Over there."

He went over to stand in the doorway with Garcia.

"Now, let's see."

Artengo tucked the gun in his belt and used both hands to grip the edge of the mattress. He flexed his knees, kept his back straight, then stood up, yanking the mattress up and over against the fluttering curtains. Ben winced and couldn't look. Garcia let out a gasp of breath.

Artengo let out more. "Fuck."

Ben craned his neck to look past the gunman. The divan was smooth and clean and completely empty. The hotel room door closed with a bang, and Julio Sagrada shouted, "Honey, I'm home."

Chapter Sixty-Five

BEN SNAPPED HIS HEAD around, and for a moment, it was as if he'd moved back in time. Michelle Cordero Belen stood in the hallway between the bathroom and the lounge and flicked the hair out of her eyes. The friendly tone. The twinkle in the eyes. The sarcastic smile playing across her lips. It was all Michelle. He felt his heart break all over again when the face morphed into Julio Sagrada, and the voice became more Spanish.

"Did I come at a bad time?"

Then she saw the gun as Artengo pulled it out of his belt. "Ben. What's going on?"

Ben waved at the overturned bed. "These two think I'm keeping two and a half million under the mattress."

* * *

EVERYONE REPAIRED TO THE lounge, Garcia leading the way while scratching an itch on his broken nose, and Artengo corralling Ben and Julio, waving his gun again. The bottleneck was now an obstacle with the gunman standing guard. Garcia blocked the windows as a potential escape route. If Ben had to assess his situation, he'd have to say, he was fucked.

A through breeze from the bedroom to the front windows fluttered tissues on the dresser, and Ben let the cool fresh air wash over him. Then his eyes widened. He could hear a bus rumble past on the street six floors below and a distinctive police siren somewhere across the city. The sounds combined with the breeze to remind him of something, the window was closed when he went into the bedroom. He glanced at Sagrada, and she rolled her eyes in an arc from the bedroom fire escape over the roof to the lounge window. She clicked her heels to draw his attention to her shoes. They were scuffed from climbing down the scaffolding after she'd put them back on. Stocking feet aren't good with scaffolding.

Artengo noticed the shoes. "Who are you, Mary Poppins, now?"

Ben was the movie buff. "Mary Poppins didn't click her heels. It was that short lesbian in *From Russia with Love*. The shoe with a poisoned knife in the toe."

Sagrada feigned offence. "Are you calling me a lesbian?"

Artengo's attention moved up from the shoes. "Changing your hair won't hide who you are. We almost snatched you outside the Blasco Ibanez in Valencia. Then this would have been a different story."

Ben saw his chance to play the Cordero Belen card. "It would have been a different story if her father had caught you instead of me."

"You didn't catch me."

"I rammed you off the road. Right into the hotel turnaround. And the old guy on the phone, he got a good look at you."

"So?"

Ben gave Artengo a sad little smile, as if he felt sorry for the gunman with bad breath. "You don't know much about Mexican drug cartels, do you?"

"I live in Spain. Why would I know about Mexican drug cartels?"

Ben went out on a limb. "Because your boss launders money for the Spanish drug cartels, and they are doing business with Cordero Belen. The man who got a good look at you."

Ben indicated Sagrada. "And this is his daughter. The woman you're pointing a gun at."

"I'm pointing the gun at you."

"You think he'll make that distinction?"

Garcia looked nervous. Artengo adjusted his grip on the gun and wiped sweat from his brow. He kept his position across the coffee table, keeping the bottleneck closed. Ben still had nowhere to go, despite the window being open to the scaffolding. The bus rumbled off, but the siren was growing louder.

Artengo seemed to notice it as well, and he glanced at the window.

Garcia stopped scratching his nose.

Ben saw the gun waver as indecision played across Artengo's face.

There would never be a better time than this. Ben stepped in front of Sagrada and planted his foot on the edge of the coffee table. Artengo saw the movement and brought the gun up, too late. Ben shoved the coffee table hard against Artengo's shins, and the gunman's legs buckled. His eyes blazed with anger and confusion. How could this shit keep happening? With a gun this time as well?

He went down to his knees, raising the gun as he fell. His hands stopped shaking, and his knuckles tightened. Tension and anger were released at the same time. The gun went off three times, drowning the police siren outside. Ben threw himself at Sagrada, knocking her sideways, and the headshot became an even smaller target. Artengo didn't shoot somebody across the street he shot Garcia. The man with the broken nose proved how unlucky he really was. He not only got shot in the chest, but he fell out of the window, bouncing off the scaffolding all the way down.

Chapter Sixty-Six

BEN ATE A HAM and cheese baguette with his Coke this time. Same table at the same café on the same street. Ninety minutes after Garcia hit the pavement and two hours before Ben was due to burgle the honeymoon suite of the Mandarin Oriental. Time seemed to have taken a different turn, either speeding up after the shooting or slowing down as he waited for his last big job.

The sun blazed through dappled leaves and turned red through the roadside umbrellas. The baseball cap was still pink, but the yellow coat looked even brighter. He felt surprisingly calm as he took the first bite of his sandwich. That might have been because he had finally stepped up to the plate and taken a swing for the team. He didn't know why he was thinking in American sporting terms. Probably to do with the movies again. He took another bite and replayed the movie in his head.

* * *

BEN FELT ANYTHING BUT calm as the man with the broken nose went out the window, and the gunshots rang in his ears. He'd never been shot at from close range before, and the adrenaline dump was messing with his fine motor functions. He needed his fingers to work, or grabbing the gun would to be a problem.

In the end, he didn't need to grab the gun because Artengo let out a gasp of shock and began to cry. The gun slipped out of his hand and bounced off the coffee table onto the floor. Artengo looked at the open window as if he couldn't believe what he had just done. All the anger drained out of him. Instead of wrestling him to the ground, Ben found himself patting him on the back and giving soothing platitudes. Artengo and Garcia were obviously more than a double act.

The police siren turned into the top end of La Rambla. Ben sat on the coffee table. It was time to act. "Okay. You can't stay here."

Artengo turned dazed eyes on Ben but didn't speak.

Ben nodded at the door. "The police are here because you snatched the concierge's pass key and came charging up the stairs. Now, one of you is out there on the street."

Artengo let out a quivering sigh.

Ben held up a hand. "Sorry. But they've got you on CCTV, last thing you need is for them to find you here with a smoking gun. It's time to leave."

Car doors slammed downstairs, and the siren stopped. Raised voices drifted up from the street, and another siren started further away. Calling for backup. Shots fired and gunman still on scene. A third siren joined the second. There was no time to be polite.

"You need to get the fuck out of here. Now." Ben indicated the bedroom where the mattress was still upended against the curtains. "Fire escape. It comes out round the back of Zara. Exit the loading docks into the next street."

Artengo nodded and got up. He didn't ask about the money. He didn't threaten retribution. He had just shot his friend and was sinking into shock. Ben ushered him towards the bedroom and raised his eyebrows to Sagrada. She pointed at the fire escape.

"Us too?"

Ben shook his head. "We're checking out. Through the lobby."

Sagrada glanced around the hotel suite. "Have you got time to pack?"

Ben looked Sagrada in the eye. "I don't have anything to pack. Except..." He pointed at the upended mattress. "And that isn't there."

"Ah, yes." She took the diary out of her pocket. "This."

"So, you didn't come in the door."

"You're the thief. I can't open locked doors."

"But you can climb over the roof."

She handed him the book. "I mix with criminals. Sometimes I have to move."

Ben felt the adrenaline dump begin to calm down. His hands stopped shaking, and he slipped the diary into the yellow windcheater. The zip made a crisp rasping noise; then he nodded at the bed.

"How did you know?"

Sagrada opened the door and listened for footsteps coming up the stairs. All she could hear was distant voices and the crackling of radio traffic. She waved towards the elevator. "The Policia don't know which room, so they will have to evacuate the hotel. We don't have time for this."

Ben didn't move. "How?"

Sagrada pressed the call button and the floor indicator showed the lift coming up from the fourth floor. She looked at the Yorkshire thief standing in the doorway and let out a sad little sigh.

"It's where you hid the passports. When you were sick."

* * *

BEN FINISHED THE SANDWICH and swilled it down with the last of his Coke. It was that last thought that gave him pause, remembering being treated by the disgraced vet in the apartment around the back of Estacion de Francia. Not the apartment or the dirty windows, but who had been there with him during his recovery. Julio Sagrada may well have noticed that he hid the passports under the mattress, but it was the person he shared those passports with that really stuck in his mind. Probably would for the rest of his life.

He brushed the thought aside. He needed to focus. So far, this last big job had gone anything but smoothly, and he was beginning to doubt the wisdom of bringing so many disparate groups together at one time. The theory behind it was sound; make as big a disturbance as possible to give the police a reason to be in the honeymoon suite. Once they were in, anything they found would be admissible in evidence. The thing they were going to find was links between a Yorkshire gangster and a Mexican drug lord and a shit load of bad people. Enough to drag Cordero Belen's name through the mud and ruin the plan to legitimise his business.

But now they were missing Artengo and Garcia and any connections with the money laundering gang. There was no guarantee that the Yorkshire hitmen would be any more punctual than the Spaniards, and without the conflagration, there would be no emergency response. Ben pushed back from the table. Maybe he should just go in and shoot Cordero Belen. It's what they'd done to Michelle. He wished he'd kept the gun instead of dropping it down the toilet at Hotel Lloret.

He called for the bill and left another generous tip. Ben didn't expect to live long enough to spend two and a half million. He patted his inside pocket to reassure himself that the diary was still there, then crossed the road. There had been enough obstacles; it was time for the burglary to go smoothly. He walked along the shady side of Passeig de Gracia and angled towards IKKS. He saw his reflection in the shop window, the bright yellow windcheater standing out against the dark interior.

It was the dark interior that alerted him. The department store was closed.

Chapter Sixty-Seven

THE SIGN ON THE door was in Spanish, but Ben got the gist of it. The store was closed for refurbishment or repair, or some other reason that IKKS needed to keep customers out while the work was being carried out. The display lights were out, but there were people in overalls at the back of the shop. None of that helped Ben.

He ignored the pharmacy next door and went to Pilar Oporto instead. The ladies' clothing store looked like it only had two floors, but the main problem was there were no customers. Three women chatted at the cash register and threw occasional glances at the street. There was no way a man in a pink hat and yellow coat would get past them unnoticed. The bright disguise was now working against him.

He continued along the street until the first entrance that wasn't a shop. The heavy wooden door had half a dozen letterboxes and a panel of doorbells. The buttons corresponded to name plates and apartment numbers. Ben pressed them all.

Nobody replied. He checked his watch. The delay was getting serious. He pressed the doorbells again. After a few moments, a crackly voice came through the speaker.

Ben spoke into the grill. "Entrega de paquete."

A stream of Spanish came over the speaker. Ben wasn't fluent, so he repeated his message. "Entrega de paquete por favor." Parcel delivery was usually enough to open most doors. The Spanish voice sounded exasperated, but the lock buzzed, and Ben was in.

He went up the stairs two at a time until he was above the shops, then took it more slowly past the apartment doors. Nobody came out to greet him, the little-old-whoever-it-was preferring to wait for the knock on the door. He followed the Salida de Incendio signs towards the back of the building from the second landing, careful to avoid the heavy footsteps that generate panic and calls to the police. The Fire Exit door opened onto the metal stairs of the fire escape, two buildings along from the Mandarin Oriental.

Ten minutes later, he was on the roof and realised there were only two landings of apartments. Add those to Pilar Oporto's shopping floors, and that meant the building was only four storeys high. That was two floors lower than IKKS and the Mandarin Oriental. He wasn't high enough.

* * *

BACK WHEN HE WAS a kid following in his brother's footsteps, Ben used to love climbing. The burglaries he enjoyed reversing the most were the ones where his brother had broken into somewhere high up. It was the thrill of climbing, not the buzz of breaking and entering, that he found such a turn-on. That, plus returning stolen goods like Santa in black. That kid would have loved the challenge of climbing two extra floors on a building with no handholds, but that kid wasn't on a deadline, having lost his girlfriend and been shot at in a Spanish hotel. The thirty-five-year-old Ben Green was just pissed off.

He leaned out around the wall of the next building to see if there was another way up. There wasn't. The neighbouring fire escape was between the pharmacy and IKKS, and covered three buildings in one. To get to it he would have to climb past the windows of the storerooms and hope nobody was looking. Somebody once told him to hold his hands out and shit in one, then hope in the other, and see which one filled up first. Right now, he had come up with a handful of shit.

He stepped back and looked up at the wall. Gargoyles supported waterspouts at either end, and some of the plaster three feet beneath them was eroded due to water damage. There were cracks in the plaster in several other places, but nothing deep enough to offer a foothold without something else to support him. He turned and looked around the flat roof. Several of the residents must have used it as a sundeck because there were a handful of sun loungers and a glass-topped garden table. A pile of industrial waste was covered by a tarpaulin and tied down in case of wind.

Ben tested the sun loungers and picked the strongest. It was a solid plastic affair, not the tubular metal and canvas type they sold in England. Leaning it against the wall would give him a six-foot ladder, and reaching up from there gave him fifteen feet. Five feet short.

He went to the tarpaulin and unthreaded the rope from the loops. It was strong, thin nylon, maybe ten feet long. Rummaging through the rubbish, he found a pair of rusty garden shears. Putting the two together gave him a grappling hook and line. He looped it around one shoulder, then crossed to the sun lounger. Six feet was an optimistic estimate if the lounger stood straight up, but angling it against the wall for stability lowered it by a foot. Using both hands to search for handholds, he climbed the cross struts until he was standing on the very top. He slipped the rope off his shoulder and looked up. Whatever his brother had told him about not looking down, it was looking up that almost overbalanced him. He had to crane his neck backwards to look straight up and see how solid the gargoyles were. Leaning back shifted his weight, and the lounger slipped.

Ben threw the rope in a swinging arc as the sun lounger's legs bit into the roof. The ladder stabilised, but not for long. The grappling hook flew over the gargoyle and dangled down the other side. Ben pulled back on the rope, slow and even, until the garden shears were just below the waterspout. He let out some slack, then whipped the rope in a loop. It took three attempts to flick the rope over the gargoyle's head and lock it against the shears. He tested its strength. If he was quick, it just might hold.

He was quick. Using the cracks in the plaster as footholds, he pulled himself up the five feet he needed and grabbed the retaining wall. The sun lounger tumbled over the edge and dropped into the garden. Ben rolled over the wall and flopped on the higher roof. He pulled the rope over with him, then lay on his back, gasping for air. There were no protests from the courtyard. Nobody came charging up the fire escape from the apartments.

He hugged the coiled rope across his chest until his hands stopped shaking.

* * *

BEN CHECKED HIS WATCH again and puffed out his cheeks. He reckoned he'd been lying there for five minutes or so. He still had time. Sitting up, he surveyed the new rooftop. It was one building across from IKKS, and his perch from the other day. Walking carefully so nobody in the room below would hear footsteps on the roof, he clambered over the low walls and skylights until he was up against the elevator housing and stairwell access for the department store.

This time, when he sat down, he let out more than a sigh of relief. He let out an unintentional fart and started laughing. Burping and farting had been good childhood entertainment. When you'd just nearly fallen off a roof, it was a great stress reliever. Ben stopped laughing and took a deep breath. In the great shit-or-hope weigh-in, he reckoned his hands were evenly balanced.

He sat in blessed silence and listened for the children playing basketball, but the English Language School was quiet. The kids must be in class. He was about to get up when his phone began to ring. The noise sounded loud in the silence, and he fumbled in his pockets. He'd forgotten he still had the phone Michelle had bought from the gas station between Alfaz del Pi and Valencia.

Ben clicked answer and was surprised to hear Julio Sagrada's voice.

"Are you there yet?"

He settled against the wall again. "Let me guess. You got my number the same time you found out about the mattress."

"Never mind. Get out of there."

Ben got serious in a hurry. "Why?"

"They're checking out."

For a moment, Ben was nonplussed. "Who?"

"Who do you think? Cordero Belen."

"All of them?"

"He doesn't go anywhere without all of them."

Ben looked over at the hotel roof but couldn't see any movement in the honeymoon suite. He couldn't see any movement anywhere. Even the rooftop restaurant was empty. His mind began to settle and he understood the import of what she was saying. The target was moving. The mission was fucked.

"Where's he going?"

"I don't know."

Ben felt the tension return. Apart from needing to know where Cordero Belen was going, there was also the question of why he was leaving. Did he know that Ben was here? Was he changing locations so the police raid would come up negative?

Sagrada restated her point. "Get out."

That was easier said than done. At least getting down to the apartment roof was less dangerous than climbing up.

"Okay." He hung up and tied the rope to the gargoyle. He was about to lower himself over the side when his phone pinged, Sagrada confirming her point by text, no doubt. He glanced at the screen and felt his heart climb into his mouth. The text was short and to the point.

"Harry. *Die Hard* meets *The Italian Job*. Love, Sally."

Chapter Sixty-Eight

THEY BUNDLED MICHELLE out of the honeymoon suite in a laundry basket and took her down to the car in the service elevator. She wasn't bound and gagged because she knew that if she caused trouble El Zorro Plateado would shoot her for real this time, not with a tranquiliser dart.

The Mandarin Oriental didn't know she was here and would most certainly have objected to having a kidnap victim stashed in one of their rooms, even if that victim was the daughter of the main guest. Anyone who took up the entire top floor would be afforded certain privileges, but kidnapping wasn't one of them. It was up to Michelle to put her kidnap resolution training into practice.

Just not quite yet.

Finding her phone had been a good start. Sending the text was even better.

* * *

MICHELLE HAD SENSED movement behind her, but was so focussed on her father that she missed her mentor coming up on the blind side. She should have known better, because the Silver Fox had trained her well, but as he was fond of saying, "I taught you everything you know, just not everything I know." That had certainly been true on the rooftop car park at Placa de les Glories Catalanes.

She had been there to get Ben off the hook by agreeing to the wedding, but her father knew her better than that. As soon as Ben was safe, she would have deployed her evade and escape technique to jilt Martinez at the altar, and the wedding would be off. With no wedding, there was no merger, and it was the family legacy he was concerned about at the moment. It was more important than he was, since he only had six months to live, and because of that it was more important than his daughter too. She should have realised that and had a contingency plan, but there was only ever one plan: lie, then escape.

The figure coming out of the shadows was like her past catching up with her. She should have known that as well. You can't live the life she had lived without consequences. The consequence was getting shot in the back. The tranquiliser dart had stung, and the next thing she remembered was sitting with her father in a fancy hotel room.

"Mi Chiquita."

Michelle was groggy but managed to respond. "Papa."

Then the room began to spin, and she fell asleep again. But it was far from a peaceful sleep. The dreams weren't dreams; they were the tormented emotions of a damaged child who had never grown up. Her mind was full guilt and recriminations. Mainly about falling in love with Ben, only to let him down. Then there was sadness and anger. That was all aimed at her father. Sadness at not being a better daughter to her father or mother. Sadness also, for a father betraying his own flesh and blood. That particular sadness quickly turned to anger over the same thing: a father betraying his own flesh and blood.

She didn't know how long she was asleep, but it was daylight when she finally woke up. The first thing she did was vomit in a bucket next to the bed. The second was slap her father across the face.

* * *

WAS THAT TWO DAYS ago? Was it yesterday? What day was today? Her father bringing breakfast in bed didn't help clarify the timeline, and what he told her only muddied the waters.

"You will make a beautiful bride. We leave for Italy tomorrow."

"Tomorrow? I thought we had a week."

"You *had* a week. Until you decided to go running around Spain."

Michelle dropped croissant crumbs all over the bed and guzzled scrambled egg and bacon like an Englishman. That thought brought her up short, and she took a mouthful of fresh orange juice to clear her throat.

"Ben?"

Her father sat on the edge of the bed. "He's going to have less than a week. When I find him."

Michelle let out a sigh of relief. Ben was still safe. "I came for the wedding, so you wouldn't need to find him."

"And that might give him more than a week."

"Forever, not a week."

Her father's eyes softened. "You like him that much?"

"I like him enough for him not to do a high dive from the lifeguard chair."

"That wasn't me."

"It was on your orders."

"She exceeded my orders."

"Which were?"

Her father took a deep breath and looked his daughter in the eye. "To keep you safe. That's all I ever wanted."

"How about, keep me happy?"

"If I was good at keeping people happy, your mother would never have left."

"She didn't leave, she was killed."

"Car wreck isn't the same as being killed."

"She's dead."

"Not because of me."

"Did somebody exceed their orders then as well?"

Her father's shoulders slumped, and Michelle saw that she'd hit a nerve. For a moment, she felt sorry for him but didn't let him off the hook. He was responsible for too much pain in her life. She stared at him and waited for an answer. When it came, she was surprised how intuitive he was.

"It wasn't your fault, your mother leaving."

Michelle crumbled but tried not to show it. For all her adult life and most of her childhood, she'd been blaming herself for her mother running off. She thought she must have been a bad daughter, or not good enough for her mother to stay. Over the years, she had channelled that into anger and directed it at her father. He was an easy target, being as hard and ruthless as he was. Now, it looked like he was carrying his own share of the guilt.

"She left because of me. And she died before she could let you know."

Michelle still didn't speak.

"When you are head of the family, there are no easy choices."

Michelle found her voice. "Especially when it's a family that kills people."

"Defends against people."

"But chooses family legacy over the family itself."

"Your mother *was* the legacy."

"But I'm not. The merger is."

Her father stood up, his face showing that he'd had enough of playing the grieving father. When he turned to face her, he was once again the head of the Cordero Belen cartel. A shiver ran down her spine. His voice hadn't changed, but his tone was cold and business-like.

"Italy. Tomorrow."

The door didn't slam on his way out, but the quiet click made her jump. The following day, she got dressed for the first time since being shot on the rooftop car park. Fresh clothes, but the same jacket. When she shrugged into the coat, something bumped against her hip. The seam of the pocket was split, and she had to rummage about in the lining. When she pulled her hand out, she smiled. There wasn't much time, so she kept it brief. Her fingers typed the message and pressed send.

"Harry. *Die Hard* meets *The Italian Job*. Love, Sally."

When the laundry basket was wheeled into her room, the phone was back in her pocket. Just keeping Ben safe wasn't an option anymore. She vowed to explain that when she met him in Pisa.

Chapter Sixty-Nine

BEN MET JULIO SAGRADA on a park bench in Placa de Catalunya. The tree-lined square was adorned with sculptures and monuments and was a short walk from the Mandarin Oriental at the top end of La Rambla. It wasn't the trees or the sculptures that made it an ideal place to meet though; it was the people. El Corte Ingles department store spewed customers onto the street, and there were three subway entrances if they had to make a fast getaway. He might be being paranoid, but with all the reversals and quick changes lately, he was playing it safe, back in dark clothing now, having dumped the pink cap and yellow windcheater.

He circled the square twice before sitting next to her.

She turned to face him. "You look nervous."

"My plan just went to rat shit, of course, I'm nervous."

"I am nervous, too."

Ben nodded. "Nervous is good. It sharpens the senses."

"Sharp is what we need."

Ben scanned the crowd, between talking to the forger, who was so much more than a forger. He drummed his fingers on the bench. "My plan had too many moving parts."

Michelle didn't nod. "The parts were motivated, but difficult to coordinate."

A bus pulled up at the stop outside the subway entrance, blocking the view of El Corte Ingles and half the road. People got on, and people got off, then the bus circled the square before heading north. Ben checked to see if anything had changed, but the crowds were in constant flux.

"We just lost two more parts at the Mandarin Oriental."

"The Englishmen. Yes, I heard."

Ben reflected on the bullish nature of the Yorkshire mentality, charging in where angels feared to tread. The two men from Leeds that Max Overend had contacted, were the epitome of charging in. They had been arrested, forcing their way into the honeymoon suite, only to find that the safe was empty and the guests had left. At least they'd got the timing right, unlike the money launderers who had arrived early and fucked things up at Hotel Lloret. Now, they were down four pieces on the chessboard, and the chessboard had checked out of the hotel.

No, he needed a simpler plan with fewer pieces. Just him and Cordero Belen and the police. And something else. With Michelle back in play his exit strategy had drastically altered. Before, he hadn't been concerned about what to do afterwards, because he didn't have an afterwards. Now, he not only had to take down Cordero Belen, but get away clean. The way things were shaping up, he didn't think getting away clean was an option, so he'd settle for getting away dirty.

Sagrada broke Ben's chain of thought. "I am reluctant to check with my sources. Cordero Belen has the same contacts through the Martinez connection."

"Paper trail leading back to you."

"I am already exposed. After the shooting at my studio."

Ben let out a sigh. "Yes. I'm sorry about that. But they're leaving Barcelona now. You should be safe."

Sagrada turned weary eyes on him. "In my line of work, life is never safe."

"With the criminal underbelly."

"Yes."

Ben thought about what he was going to ask next and paused while he weighed up his options. He didn't have any. Julio Sagrada was his only hope, so he asked her anyway.

"This criminal underbelly, is it just local, or do you have reach?"

Sagrada tried to read his expression. "This is the European Union."

Ben gave her his most innocent smile. “Who do you know in Pisa?”

Chapter Seventy

ACCORDING TO BEN'S SATNAV, Pisa was a ten-hour drive from Barcelona. If you took the main roads and kept to the fastest available speed limit. The little red car wasn't going to reach the fastest available speed limit, so Ben had eighteen hours drive time, with an overnight layover in Montpellier and an early start the following day. He went from Spain, to France to Italy, in one long drive that gave him plenty of time to think about the worst-case scenario and the optimum outcome. He reckoned the optimum outcome had a fifty-fifty chance at best.

He hoped Michelle wasn't working from the same set of statistics.

* * *

CUTTING THE FAT FROM his original plan meant there were fewer moving parts and not so many players to coordinate, but it also put Ben front and centre when it came to executing the plan. That increased the danger by sixty-six per cent, since the money launderers were either dead or scattered, and the Yorkshire hit squad had been arrested. Two-thirds of Ben's distraction team were off the board, leaving Ben to do the heavy lifting and take all the risks.

That's where Julio Sagrada came in, providing alternate manpower and essential equipment. You can't blow up the top floor of a hotel with hope and good intentions, and you can't just snatch the bride and jump on a bus. Dustin Hoffman might have had the right idea, but Simon and Garfunkel weren't going to sing the end credits for the Sexy Bitch and the Good

Looking Man. It was going to take a lot more than that.

Essentially, the plan was still the same: plant the evidence, give the police a legal excuse to find it, and get away clean. Getting away clean hadn't seemed that important before, but now that Michelle was back in the equation, the future felt a lot more important. Pulling the *Die Hard* trick of blowing the roof so Hans Gruber could sit on a beach growing fat off the interest was going to be more difficult. Surviving the explosion was only part of the problem.

Ben thought about that on the long drive through Spain, France, and Italy. The overnight stay in Montpellier had been the most difficult, because he remembered the last overnight stay on the runaway bride road trip. One of three. It felt like a lifetime ago that the arguing couple had stayed at the adobe house around the back of Estacion de Servico Cepsa, Enrico Aguilar donating the Little Mule and giving sound advice. The next had been the abandoned villa at Alfaz del Pi, but it was spending the night at Campdasens B&B that really stuck in his mind.

That was when they had first made love. It was where Ben had told Michelle about his paper round, and she had mentioned the donkey near her villa. It was where they had first opened up to each other and begun to feel there was a future if they survived the situation they were in. That future had been squashed on the rooftop car park in Barcelona, but it had been revived at the Mandarin Oriental. Now, all he had to do was follow the trail of breadcrumbs and save the princess. And live to tell the tale. It was that last part that was causing him sleepless nights.

Or one sleepless night. In Montpellier, on the way to meet his destiny. He just hoped Michelle had managed to keep the mobile phone she'd bought at the gas station and that the Find My Phone App was as accurate as advertised. After that, it was back to what he did best: case the joint, find the best way in, and plan his exit strategy. Then it would be a case of happily ever after. If there was an after.

Chapter Seventy-One

CASING THE JOINT WAS made more difficult because there were two joints. Julio Sagrada had come up trumps with the first part of his request, finding out where the Cordero Belen circus was staying in Pisa. The answer was not in Pisa. At least not for their entire stay. The main location was a boutique hotel at Palazzo Gambacorti overlooking the Ponte di Mezzo across the Arno. The river snaked its way through Pisa on its way to the sea and was surprisingly underdeveloped. Most European cities embraced their river culture, building hotels, restaurants, and riverside cafés along the banks. The Arno was just a stone and brick channel with a concrete walkway on either side at water level. No cafés. No umbrellas.

Hotel Pietro was traditional but expensive, with only a handful of rooms and a view across the red-tiled rooftops of the old town. There was minimal parking and no escape from the constant hubbub of tourists along the pedestrian shopping street below. In short it was the very opposite of Cordero Belen's preferred location, so he had also booked a more secluded hotel at Marina di Pisa on the coast. Hotel Pietro's main claim to fame was a view of the cathedral and the Torre di Pisa, the leaning tower showing above the rooftops to the north. It was also where the wedding party was going to be held, after the ceremony at a small private church.

Ben sat at a street café in Piazza Garibaldi across the bridge and checked the Find My Phone App. There was no location. Michelle's phone must be turned off. Ben had Coca-Cola with a slice of pizza and looked at the upper floors of Hotel Pietro across the river. Sagrada had given him the address on the final stretch of his drive from the north.

"He's booked in for the three days until the wedding."

"In the middle of Pisa?"

"In the middle of tourist hell."

"That doesn't sound like him."

"He didn't make the reservation. It was the Martinez family."

"Doesn't sound like them either."

"It's traditional. The church isn't far away."

Ben scanned the penthouse suites, checking for suitable handholds and climbing surfaces. The lobby entrance was in the square with limited reserved parking on Lungarno Gambacorti. He didn't know what they would be driving, but assumed it would be a convoy of executive cars. There was no convoy of anything parked outside the hotel.

"What about the other stuff?"

"You can pick it up at the Post Office."

"Post Office? You're kidding."

"The old one that's now the CPT Uterservici. The public transport office. Around the back next to the city walls."

He finished his pizza, swilled it down with the last of the coke, and checked his watch. It was time to collect the "other stuff." He brought up the Find My Phone App again in case Michelle had turned her phone on. It was still blank. Staying on the northern riverbank, he walked to the next bridge and crossed Ponte Solferino, heading south towards the Post Office.

* * *

THE MAN WAS SWARTHY, old, and grizzled, and didn't look anything like the organised crime man Ben was expecting. He also had a smile and a twinkle in the eye that creased his leathery skin whenever he broke into a grin. He broke into a grin a lot, even when there was nothing to smile about.

"Welcome, welcome." He gave Ben a hug and a squeeze that almost popped his lungs. "To the shadow of Pisa." Then, a mock serious face that was at odds with the laugh lines and twinkling eyes. "Did you know the engineers have been working to straighten the angle?" Now, an expansive throw of the arms. "What will tourists come to see when the leaning tower is no longer leaning?"

Ben wasn't sure what to make of the Italian. "You *are* from Julio Sagrada?"

The man puffed out his chest. "I don't look like an Italian hitman?"

"Not really."

A conspiratorial wink. "You did not think Julio Sagrada looked like a forger either, did you?"

"She told you about that, huh?"

"This is a network. In a network, we know everything."

"Then you know why I'm here."

Giuseppe Battisti nodded. "But not where you are going. That you do not know yourself, I think."

"Fifty/fifty. I'm edging towards the second fifty."

"Then we must be ready for when you find out which fifty."

Ben nodded at the sports bag next to the big man's leg. "Did you get what I asked for?"

Battisti held the bag up. "Do you know how to use it?"

Ben told him what he wanted to do, and Battisti told him how to use it.

* * *

SEA AIR AND SCREECHING gulls made Michelle feel at home. Not the home where she'd grown up, in the desert landscape of Mexico, but the sea views and hotels that her father favoured when travelling. Top floor overlooking the sea. Masts and rigging and fluttering flags swaying in the marina. Subject normal.

The door clicked shut as her father stepped into the hallway to talk with El Zorro Plateado. Esteban Salazar hadn't been more than a few feet away ever since he'd shot her with the tranquiliser dart. If he wasn't in the room, he was always just outside. They weren't leaving anything to chance. He'd trained her too well.

Leaving her alone while he spoke to her father was a mistake, though. Michelle reached into her pocket and turned the phone on, checked that there was a signal, then turned it on silent.

* * *

BATTISTI PUT THE EXPLOSIVES back in the sports bag, then held the top open so Ben could see the cling-filmed block of white powder and a dozen dealer baggies. They were all in a clear plastic bag.

"Dealer weight. But not enough to break the bank. Even with what you're paying me, you can't afford that much."

"Just so long as he can't claim it's for personal use. I want him to go down for dealing, not using."

"He won't go down for anything. We both know that. But the scandal will stop him taking over Martinez Concrete."

Ben looked at the Italian. "She told you about that as well?"

Battisti's face creased into a knowing wink. "Network."

Ben took the offered bag. "Police and the news are ready?"

"Polizia di Narcotici are waiting for the signal. The press are waiting for *them*. Your forger has a lot of contacts, my friend."

Ben nodded. "Network."

Battisti pointed at the sports bag. "You know how to program the numbers into your phone?"

Ben remembered Michelle adding her number to the phonebook. "Yes."

"Don't get them mixed up."

Ben thought about the five mobile phones and the five detonators. He didn't want to be phoning one of them instead of calling the police, or it was going to be a very short day. The sun had moved across the sky, throwing the ancient city walls into sharp relief and making the ex-Post Office look like a military bunker. Buses droned past on the other side of the wall where the coach park augmented the bus station. A low-flying passenger jet skirted the city as it came into land at Aeroporto Internazionale Galileo to the south.

Battisti's face turned serious. "Remember. This might be a network, but we are all criminals. Don't trust anyone until it is just you and your bride."

"She isn't my bride."

Battisti smiled. "She will be."

Ben looked at the Italian. "Julio noticed a lot, didn't she?"

Battisti tapped the side of his nose and was about to speak.

Ben stopped him. "Network. I know."

The two men stood facing each other, and for some reason, Ben felt like giving him a hug. He settled for a handshake, and the bear of a man almost crushed Ben's hand. He hefted the sports bag in the other hand and was about to leave when his phone pinged. The Find My Phone App flashed a notification on the screen.

"We're on. It's the second fifty."

Chapter Seventy-Two

BEN DROVE TO Marina di Pisa alongside the Arno on the SP224, a fairly straight road that only deviated to follow the curve of the river. The afternoon sun had drifted west and was coming through the side window of the little red car. The bag of explosives was in the passenger footwell, away from the sun. He didn't know much about plastic explosives but assumed it was similar to ice cream; it didn't like being melted by hot sun through glass.

The road ahead was clean and bright, the lush green hedgerows standing out against the clear blue sky. Private jetties and yacht clubs dotted the roadside along the river, getting bigger and more expansive the nearer Ben got to the sea. It only took twenty minutes for the suburbs to replace the countryside. Marina di Pisa was only a small conurbation, mainly traditional buildings with red-tiled roofs, but one building stood out.

Ben pulled over to the side of the road and scanned the horizon. He was surprised that Martinez Construction had been given planning permission, but he supposed that if you were in bed with the drug cartels, you could build anything you wanted. What the groom's father had built was a concrete replica of the Leaning Tower of Pisa, only bigger and not leaning.

* * *

"ARE YOU COMING down for lunch?"

"I prefer it up here. It's what you want, isn't it? Keep the princess locked away at the top of the tower."

"You think you're a princess?"

"I'm your princess. That's all that counts."

Pablo Cordero Belen nodded. His daughter was as headstrong as ever, but she was right, she had always been his little princess. He wanted to sit her down and tell her how much he loved her, but knew that would be a hard concept to sell when he was forcing her into an arranged marriage. Even so, he wanted to make sure this was a mink-lined prison. His little princess deserved nothing less.

"The hotel isn't finished yet, but I'm sure I can get room service to bring something up."

Michelle gave her father a sideways glance and raised an eyebrow. "I'm sure you can. Maybe they can get rid of the paint smell while they're at it."

It wasn't so much the paint as the paint thinners that were contaminating the fresh sea air. Several of the floors below were still being decorated, and the penthouse suite on the landward side was getting its final coat of paint. Cordero Belen's suite wasn't on the landward side it was overlooking the sea. As always. The cartel boss might well duck and weave in business, but when it came to travel, he was as predictable as the weather. Hot and sunny with the chance of thunder.

"So? Lunch?"

Michelle looked at the masts swaying in the marina and a lone white cloud drifting across the sky. She shook her head. "I've lost my appetite."

* * *

AFTER A BRIEF DETOUR, Ben parked on a piece of spare land that had been cleared for building, but where construction hadn't yet started. On the edge of town, away from the visitors' car parks and tourist shops. The next parcel of land was in a better location, adjacent to the marina between two roundabouts on the main access road. Construction on that piece of land was not only underway but was almost complete. The bespoke hotel that looked like the Leaning Tower had all the bells and whistles of a luxury apartment building. Ben had a good view through the chain link fence, so he stood beside the car and scanned the area.

Casing the joint. The thing he did best.

The first thing he checked was the car park around the back. A convoy of executive cars was parked close together against the rear of the hotel. The only other vehicles looked like builders' vans or staff cars. There was a skip for waste materials in the far corner near the bin store. Ben ticked that off his list; it would take more than a fire in the bin store to cause a distraction this time. The fire alarm wasn't going to evacuate the building or alert the police. It would have to be something bigger.

He glanced at the sports bag in the footwell, then looked away.

Next, he checked for suitable handholds and climbing surfaces. Unlike the Don Carlos, the balconies were carved stone, not mirrored glass, but the principle was the same. Keep your head up and pull with your arms and push with your legs. The main secret was not to be seen. The other secret was, if you are seen then blend in. He already had a plan for blending in, and it didn't involve wearing a pizza delivery coat or a pink cap and yellow jacket.

An air horn sounded beyond the marina, calling the powerboat racers to the starting line for the warm-up race. A bit like qualifying at a Grand Prix to see who would be in pole position. Ben wasn't sure if there was a pole position on an ocean race. Outboard motors started up. The throbbing beat of the bigger boats gurgled and popped like the pleasure cruisers at Cabopino.

Ben ignored the boats preparing for their first race and checked his watch. There was plenty of time. The noise from the races was due to last all afternoon. He turned his attention back to the builders' van in the car park. A workman came out of the staff entrance near the bin store and opened the back of the van. No key. The van wasn't locked. Good. There were tins of paint and various tools, but more importantly, there was a box of drop cloths and coveralls. The man collected two tins of paint and closed the van. Still no key. Still not locked. Still good. He carried the paint to a makeshift freight elevator that ran up a track on the outside wall. It was little more than a dumbwaiter with a rope and pulley all the way to the top floor. The man pulled on the rope, and another workman collected the tins on the tenth-floor balcony, then the first workman went back in through the staff entrance.

The air horn sounded again, and the gurgle and pop burst into an explosive roar as the first heat got underway. The powerboats drowned out all other sounds, something else that was good. The sun beat down, and the sky stayed blue, only broken by a lone white cloud drifting from the west. Seagulls screeched soundlessly, unable to breach the wall of sound along the coast.

Ben got back in the car and checked the contents of the sports bag. Everything was there. All the phones were turned on and fully charged. Signal strength was four out of five bars. He took out his own phone and called each one to make sure he'd programmed them correctly. Each one rang on cue. He checked that the permanent marker hadn't wiped off, labelling the phones 1 to 5. Once he was satisfied, he turned them on silent and put them back in the bag. He took a deep breath, closed the bag, then got out of the little red car for the last time.

Chapter Seventy-Three

BEN WAS HALFWAY up the ten balconies when déjà vu set in. Twice. If that was possible. Maybe three times. He didn't think it was the best job in the world this time, but he did still feel like Tom Cruise in that *Mission: Impossible* film, clinging to the side of the Burj Khalifa. That was the first piece of déjà vu, which led directly to the second, climbing the balconies of the Don Carlos Leisure Club. That one brought to mind the reason he'd been hiding at Laguna Park in the first place, burgling room 1042 from the eleventh floor in Leeds. Déjà vu times three.

He paused on the fifth-floor balcony to shake off the memories and concentrated on the job in hand. The balconies were head height with a bit more for comfort. Standing on the carved balustrade gave him the reach to grab the next balcony and pull himself up; then it was just a case of repetition.

Reach.

Pull.

Stabilize.

Reach.

Pull.

Stabilize.

Even the repetition took him back to the Don Carlos. This feeling of déjà vu just wouldn't let him go. He forcefully blanked the memory of his brother, telling him, "You'll only fall if you look down. The only way is up. So, look up," but the act of blanking it meant he was thinking about the memory. He still thought it was the stupidest thing he'd ever heard, and his mind retorted with, "Down is still down, if I'm looking or not."

Ben looked down. The three executive cars were still parked close together against the back of the hotel, and the builders' van was still parked near the bin store. He looked up. The block and tackle that secured the pulley was five storeys up, the rope swaying in the sea breeze. Apart from the top floor, there were two more balconies with decorating supplies covered by blue tarpaulins, four and six. He'd already attended to the fourth floor. It was time to go on. He followed his brother's advice and looked up.

Reach.

Pull.

Stabilize.

Keeping one eye on the balcony door, he climbed over the balustrade and did what Giuseppe Battisti had taught him. Five minutes. He was getting better at this. After making sure that the tarpaulin covered his work, he climbed back over the balcony rail and reached up.

Reach.

Pull.

Stabilize.

Reach.

Pull.

Stabilize.

Tom Cruise continued up the Burj Khalifa, and *Mission Impossibl*e became Mission Almost Complete. Just one more charge to set, then all he had to do was plant the evidence and sound the alarm. Not necessarily in that order.

* * *

MICHELLE STOOD ON the balcony and watched the second heat of the powerboat race. Out beyond the Yacht Club and past the sea wall that surrounded the marina. The air horn was deafening, and she covered her ears until the roar of the boats took over. The clear blue sky wasn't so clear anymore. Two more clouds joined the lone white cloud from the west. Not exactly an approaching storm. The storm was coming from the other direction. She glanced through the patio door. Her father sat with her mentor in the spacious apartment. She felt no desire to sit with either of them.

The phone buzzed in her pocket, and she went to the far end of the balcony, out of sight of the two men who had shaped her life. The message was from the third man. She smiled at the brevity of Ben's text.

"Yippee-ki-yay. Five minutes."

* * *

GIUSEPPE BATTISTI WALKED along the sea wall as the second wave of sound battered the marina. Masts bobbed and swayed in the more genteel surroundings of the yacht club, while the real energy was expended on the open water. The Italian ignored the yachts *and* the powerboats. His point of interest was going to be the narrow mouth of the entry and exit channel.

Half a dozen anglers dotted the walkway and park benches along the marina wall, their rods and lines trailing the Arno as the river spilled into the sea. Battisti shrugged the fishing tackle holdall where it had slipped from his shoulder and hefted the bait bucket in his other hand. The holdall felt heavier than the ultra-light fishing rods on display along the walkway, but his broad shoulders and muscular frame made it look effortless.

He wished the Englishman had taken his advice about not trusting anyone, because the boy had made an impression on the grizzled hitman. Putting your life on the line for love wasn't something Battisti had come across too often, and it warmed his heart to think that the boy might actually have a chance of pulling this off. If he hadn't placed his trust in the wrong person.

He stopped at the end of the walkway. The public area was fenced off, and access to the end of the seawall was restricted. He stood against the low railing and scanned the channel. The red painted light tower stood out against the blue sky, not exactly a lighthouse but more of a concrete light fixture. There was a green painted fixture on the other arm of the sea wall. The bulbs were coloured as well, giving sailors a positive sighting when approaching after dark. Red on the left and green on the right. Battisti would be firing from red.

He checked his watch. There wasn't much time. The Polizia di Narcotici were waiting at the second roundabout on the access road to Marina di Pisa, Julio Sagrada's contact having managed to get an assault team and a search dog. They were waiting for the evidence to be planted and the incident that would give them permission to enter. Police forces the world over used the same code; police can force entry without a warrant to protect life. The signal would make it clear they needed to protect life. Any evidence they found would, therefore, be admissible in court.

The news crew was also waiting, but not on the access road. That might look too much like a setup. They were two streets away on Via Francesco Barbolani. Cameras at the ready. News feeds hooked up and waiting to transmit.

All of those things were on the landward side of the replica Leaning Tower that wasn't leaning. Nobody was looking at Benjamin Green's getaway route. Nobody except Giuseppe Battisti. He felt the weight of the sniper's rifle on his shoulder and tried to ignore the bad taste in his mouth.

Chapter Seventy-Four

THE ROPE SWAYED at the end of the balcony as Ben climbed over the final rail. He looked down at the three tins of paint he'd fastened to one end of the rope. He'd considered just putting them on the dumbwaiter but wanted them to be more secure. After testing the weight he'd decided that three was the perfect weight. Four would have been too heavy, and two wouldn't provide enough of a counterbalance.

He lifted the tarpaulin and found three colours of paint and a selection of partly used paint thinners. There was other building material, as well, but the paint and thinners were the most combustible. He shaped the plastic explosive against the middle tin of paint, then put the thinners on either side of it. The detonator stuck out of the side, attached to the fourth mobile phone. He laid the phone in the gap between the supplies and covered it with cleaning cloths.

Once he was satisfied, he went back over the side.

"You'll only fall if you look down. The only way is up. So, look up." Ben's brother gatecrashed his thoughts, and he found himself talking to Christian as he dangled from the balcony rail. "Down is still down, if I'm looking or not." He didn't look down, focussing instead on the balcony of room 1042. Or the present-day equivalent.

The top floor would be too heavily guarded, so Ben needed to gain entry one floor down. Dressed like all the other workmen. Unlikely to raise suspicions if he was seen outside the ninth-floor hotel rooms. In five minutes, nobody would be looking at the man in the paint-splattered overalls. Checking that the corridor was empty, he entered the empty ocean-view apartment and got ready to climb one last time.

* * *

MICHELLE HEARD A NOISE on the balcony below and checked her watch. It was exactly five minutes since she'd received the warning text. That couldn't possibly be a coincidence, so the noise below had to be Ben. Harry and Sally were about to go Yippee-ki-yay. She moved to the middle of the balcony so she could get an angle through the patio door without being obvious.

In the end, obvious didn't matter. An explosion around the back of the hotel rattled the glass, and the two figures inside dashed into the corridor. Three more explosions followed, shaking the tower that wasn't leaning. Ten seconds later, a hand grabbed the balcony rail.

* * *

BEN SET OFF FOUR explosions in quick succession, making sure he got the sequence right. The executive cars in the car park were followed by the balconies on the fourth, sixth, and tenth floors. The building shook. Pieces of plaster crumbled from the ceiling. He looked over the edge and dropped four mobile phones into the swimming pool. The lifeguard chair looked more expensive than the one at Laguna Park. Eduardo Perez had been right; you cannot avoid the inevitable.

Climbing onto the balustrade, he reached up to the balcony above.

Reach.

Pull.

Stabilize.

He only had to do it once, then he pulled himself over the railing and flopped at Michelle's feet. The runaway bride dropped to her knees and squeezed him tight. They didn't kiss, they just held each other for a long moment, then Ben stood up and looked through the patio door.

"Gone?"

Michelle nodded. "Into the corridor."

"Lock the door."

Ben slid the patio door open and stepped inside. The layout was universal. All hotels used the same template, just with more expensive fixtures and fittings in the high-end establishments. This was a high-end establishment. The other thing all hotels had in common was a guest safe. He quickly crossed to the bedroom and found the wardrobe.

Feet pounded the stairs at the end of the corridor, and raised voices shouted back and forth outside the door. Ben tuned the noises out and concentrated on the keypad. The digital reader showed green in the dark of the wardrobe. He took a deep breath and began to run security codes through his head. Standard codes issued to all guests, so nobody would lock themselves out, plus the staff code in case anyone did. He knelt down and leaned into the cavity, flexing his fingers. Safecracker mode.

He didn't need to crack the safe. The door was open.

Sirens sounded in the distance, and the direction of the footsteps changed, running away from the penthouse suite, not towards it. Ben opened the bag and took out the leather-bound notebook. Lots of names and numbers and transaction details. He'd been holding on to that book for a long time and felt a little sad at letting it go. Brushing the feeling aside, he put the notebook in the safe together with the block of white powder and dealer baggies. He closed the safe but didn't lock it, piling the spare bedding in front of it before shutting the wardrobe. He went into the lounge to join Michelle.

"Done."

"You would think so, wouldn't you?"

Pablo Cordero Belen spoke in a quiet voice, but it was the man with the grey hair who was pointing the gun at him.

"But you are not done yet."

Chapter Seventy-Five

PABLO CORDERO BELEN put the key card back in his pocket and moved to the middle of the lounge. The man with the grey hair and the gun sidestepped to keep a clear line of fire. Michelle backed against the wall, then slumped into a chair beside the chest of drawers. Ben stood in the bedroom doorway like a fox in the hen house; caught, fucked, and likely to get shot.

"Sorry about the cars."

"The cars weren't mine."

"They were somebody's."

"Are you worried about the somebody?"

"Not worried exactly. Just sorry that somebody is always collateral damage."

Cordero Belen looked at the man who had been a thorn in his side for almost two weeks. "Collateral isn't the damage you should be concerned about."

Ben looked at the father of the bride. "Me?"

Cordero Belen nodded. "Not collateral at all."

Police sirens were joined by the distinctive tones of the Provinciale Vigili del Fuoco, the fire brigade deploying along with the ambulance service. A bit further away than the Polizia di Narcotici. The police were going to get here first. There was another muffled explosion along the corridor, more tins of paint bursting into flames.

Ben glanced at the ceiling. "No sprinklers?"

Cordero Belen kept his eyes on the thorn. "This is a concrete building.

Concrete doesn't burn."

"Something's burning."

"Not enough to be worried about."

Cordero Belen moved towards the fireplace, and the man with the gun took centre stage. The father of the bride rested a hand on the mantelpiece and let out a lung-emptying sigh.

"The question is, what were you doing in the bedroom with my daughter?"

* * *

MICHELLE WATCHED HER father play the aggrieved parent, and waited until the time was right. Positions were changing all the time, her father to the side of the lounge while Esteban Salazar moved to the middle. Not far enough forward yet, but getting there. This was a fluid situation. She needed to wait until it flowed in her favour. There were muffled voices in the corridor, but the door had swung shut again. The only person with a key card was her father.

She shifted in the chair to make the bulge in her belt more comfortable and give easier access. When the positions were right. She gave Ben a sharp look, trying to send a message with her eyes, and waited.

* * *

BEN FELT EXPOSED standing in the bedroom doorway, but more importantly, he was drawing attention to the bedroom. He didn't want anyone going near the wardrobe until the police arrived. He came into the lounge and moved towards the patio doors, where one panel had been slid half open on its runners. The man with the gun stepped forward, threatening any further movement. Ben caught Michelle's nod of approval and stopped halfway to the balcony.

"You don't think I'm going to jump off the tenth-floor balcony?"

Cordero Belen pushed off from the fireplace. "There is a pool down there."

"Like in that *Lethal Weapon* film? With Joe Pesci?"

"More like James Bond. When they throw the girl over the balcony."

"And Connery says, 'Nice shot.'"

"But the gangster says he didn't know there was a pool down there."

"Except you do know there's a pool down there." Ben put added steel in his voice. "Like there was a pool at Laguna Park. Where my friend broke his neck being thrown down the lifeguard ladder."

Cordero Belen matched Ben's tone. "Now that is collateral damage."

Ben stood firm, but he couldn't argue against the truth of that statement. Eduardo wouldn't have become collateral damage if Ben hadn't kicked the hornets' nest in the first place. Taking off with the runaway bride had seemed like a good idea at the time, but the cost was too high. Too many people had paid the price for Ben's frivolous act.

"Your deal with Martinez Concrete is going to be collateral damage. When the police find you pointing a gun at me."

"I am not pointing a gun at you."

Ben shuffled another half step towards the balcony door. "Do you know what acting in concert means? The police were always trying to threaten my brother with that. Make him think that because we were brothers, they could get me for acting in concert with his burglaries. Well, when you employ a man, and he does what you tell him to do. When that man points a gun at someone, that's as if you're pointing it yourself. Not a tranquilizer gun either."

The grey-haired man spoke. "I am not pointing a tranquilizer gun."

Ben listened to the sirens stop one by one as the emergency services arrived at the hotel. He moved one more step, then faced his tormentors. His back against the balcony door with both men facing him.

"I know you're not. But she is."

Chapter Seventy-Six

MICHELLE STEPPED UP behind her mentor and shot him point blank in the back. The pffft of the shot sounded quiet against the mayhem outside. A look came over Salazar's face that was both surprise and pride, then he sank to his knees. She leaned over and took the gun from his relaxed fingers.

"Stings, doesn't it?"

Her father lowered his head and closed his eyes. When he looked up again, Michelle could see the pain behind the calm expression. Father and daughter looked at each other, and both knew that their future was lost. There was no going back for either of them. While his face became a mask, his voice couldn't hide the sadness.

"Mi Chiquita."

Michelle's voice wasn't much happier. "Papa."

Ben kept quiet. This was family time. But the chaos outside wouldn't allow for the moment to last too long. In the end it was Cordero Belen who broke the deadlock.

"Are you going to shoot me too?"

* * *

BEN WATCHED MICHELLE'S face crumble. There was a lifetime of hurt, and not enough time to express it. She looked heartbroken that her father would even ask, so Ben stepped in.

"Hell, no. I want you awake when the police come through the door."

He dipped into the bag and brought out a pair of handcuffs. "And I want you to have a front-row seat when Harry and Sally sail off into the sunset."

"Harry and Sally?"

"It's an in-joke."

Ben snapped one cuff on Cordero Belen's wrist and marched him onto the balcony. A flotilla of powerboats was moored just beyond the sea wall, competitors waiting to be called to the line. Inside the sea wall, the marina glistened in the afternoon sun, yachts and pleasure boats bobbing gently in the sheltered waters. Ben pulled up a garden chair and snapped the other cuff on the balcony rail.

"Make yourself comfortable." He pointed out to sea. "We're heading that-a-way."

The noise in the corridor died down as the footsteps headed for the stairs. There was banging and shouting from the lower floors. A lot of shouting. Policemen sound the same in every language. Loud. Forceful. Commanding.

Ben went back inside and crossed the room to Michelle. He took the guns and dropped them on the settee, then put his arms around her. For a moment she stood still with her arms by her sides, then she brought them up and hugged him back. He could feel the tension vibrating through her body. He kissed her on the forehead and held her tight. There were no words to console her, so he didn't try.

The corridor was quiet now. He let her go and stepped back. Still no words, just a look that said, it's time to go. Michelle glanced at her father out on the balcony, then nodded at Ben. It was always going to end this way. There was never going to be a father/daughter reconciliation.

Now, it was time for the exit strategy.

* * *

BEN'S EXIT STRATEGY was a rope and a pulley and a fast drop down ten floors. What he hadn't accounted for was the rope being on the same balcony as he'd set the explosives or just how long three tins of paint would burn. Michelle looked at the smouldering balcony.

"I thought the *Die Hard* plan was to blow the roof, then sit on a beach growing rich on the interest. You only blew up a balcony."

Ben kicked the burning tins of paint to one side and used the tarpaulin to damp down the flames lapping at the rope. "I'm improvising."

Michelle looked over the balcony rail. "That's a long way down."

Ben summoned his brother. "You'll only fall if you look down. So, look up."

Michelle gave him a withering look, then looked down anyway. There were several police cars blocking the car park and a fire engine on the access road. The three executive cars were burned-out wrecks, still steaming from the water that the fire brigade had poured on them. All the firefighting now was on the inside, checking the floors one at a time for smoke and secondary fires. The car park was empty. The rendezvous point for the guests was around the front by the swimming pool. Nobody ever got burned to death in a swimming pool.

Ben held the rope out to Michelle, wrapped it around his wrist, and grabbed it above the loop to show her how. Michelle took it from him and looked a lot more proficient than Ben. She'd been trained to get out of worse situations than this, but dropping ten floors still seemed like a bad idea.

"Really?"

Ben held his hands up. "If you've got any better ideas."

Michelle looked over the side again, noting the three paint tins tied to the end of the rope. She had lots of better ideas, just none she could implement at short notice. She climbed over the balcony and tested the counterbalance. The rope slid through the pulley but with enough weight at the other end that she wouldn't drop too fast. She looked at Ben and took a deep breath. Without another word, she let go of the balcony and walked backwards down the side of the building, giving a little jump at each balcony on the way down. Not quite abseiling, but close enough.

The rope was still smoking just above her handhold. Twists of thread parted and tore open.

Fifth floor.

Fourth floor.

She tried to reach up above the burned rope but her momentum was all down.

Third floor.

Second floor.

So close and yet so far away. If the rope snapped now, she would only break her legs, not kill herself. Looking on the bright side didn't help. The smoke became wispy tendrils, but the rope held.

First floor.

Ground floor.

She untwisted the rope from around her wrist and let the paint tins pull the rope back up for Ben. Fast and loose. She almost got rope burns, but within minutes, Ben was ready to follow. He tugged at the rope. The three tins weren't going to slow his descent as much as Michelle, but there was no time to add ballast. The rope had stopped smoking, but fraying was the enemy now.

"Fuck it."

He swung his legs over the railing and let nature take its course. Not so much abseiling as falling with grace.

Ninth floor.

Eighth floor.

More twists of rope frayed and snapped.

Seventh floor.

Then, the fraying rope became the least of his problems as the man with grey hair leaned over the tenth-floor balcony, and pointed a gun down the length of the rope.

Chapter Seventy-Seven

ESTEBAN SALAZAR LEANED over the balcony and tried to get his eyes in focus. The hotel replica of the Leaning Tower of Pisa felt like it was actually leaning, first one way, then the other. The horizon was doing all sorts of strange movements. The first thing he saw when he looked down was the boyfriend descending on a length of rope. That's when his vision cleared, and his expertise kicked in.

Salazar grabbed a long-handled paintbrush and jammed it into the pulley. The rope slammed to a stop, and Salazar levelled the gun at the figure dangling at the other end. The figure split into two men, then three men, then back to one. He held the gun in two hands to keep it steady, then applied slow pressure to the trigger.

The face looking up at him pleaded for mercy. Not the boyfriend but the girl Salazar had been training since she was eight years old. Michelle Cordero Belen stood at the bottom of the rope, looking up at her mentor, and gave a gentle shake of the head. Salazar stared into her eyes, remembering her feeding the burro on her way home from school. A young girl in Mexico, before her best friend was kidnapped, and her world changed forever. That was when Salazar entered her life, but more importantly, that was when Michelle came into his, the daughter he never had. And here she was now, pleading for him not to shoot her new best friend.

He applied more pressure to the trigger.

Michelle's eyes widened.

Salazar looked at the eight-year-old girl from Mexico. He glanced at the man she was risking her life for, then looked back at Michelle. She looked even smaller and younger from up here. More vulnerable. He hadn't trained her to be vulnerable. That was the deciding factor. He focussed on the target and squeezed the trigger, but his fingers wouldn't work. The world began to sway as the tranquiliser dart kicked in again, and he slid to the floor.

* * *

JERKING TO A STOP at the sixth floor slammed Ben against the balcony rail. He heard Michelle gasp six floors below as he spun out of control. It took three attempts to correct the spin and plant his feet against the wall. Following his brother's advice didn't help this time, because looking up meant he could see the gun pointing down at him from the tenth-floor balcony.

There was a moment when he felt like Hans Gruber in reverse, the *Die Hard* villain dangling out of the window, except this time it was Bruce Willis pointing the gun, not Alan Rickman. Then, the moment passed as the man with the gun swayed to one side and disappeared.

Jerking to a stop did something else apart from slam Ben against the wall. It accelerated the fraying of the rope. More strands snapped in the scorched section above his grip. The rope was now half its original thickness and getting thinner all the time.

Ben scrambled for a grip on the balcony rail. More strands snapped. The rail was too hot from the burning paint. Of all the balconies he had to stop at, it had to be the one where he'd set the explosives. The paint was still burning, augmented by the full-length curtains after the patio door had shattered in the heat. The fire brigade was still working their way up one floor at a time, currently extinguishing the other fire Ben had started on the fourth floor.

The rope dropped six inches, held by only a quarter of the remaining strands. Ben couldn't climb onto the balcony. It was too far to drop, and he couldn't climb up. He committed the cardinal sin and looked down.

Michelle looked up at him. Their eyes met. He let out a sigh but she wasn't shaking her head, she was jerking it towards the dumbwaiter track.

The rope snapped.

Ben stuck one foot in the track and grabbed the cross struts. The paint tins that had been his counterbalance crashed to the floor, and the rope snaked down after them. Using the track as a ladder, he climbed down as fast as he dared. His hands were still shaking, but he was filled with a new lease of life.

The new lease of life ended when he was two floors from the ground. That was when he realised the dumbwaiter wasn't built to carry his weight. With a groan and a creak, the track came away from the wall, and Ben fell backwards.

* * *

MICHELLE LET OUT MORE than a gasp this time, she let out a shriek. Everything felt like it was moving in slow motion, but she knew the end was only seconds away. Ben was falling down the line of the dumbwaiter track. The dumbwaiter itself had been disabled, and the paint tins had impacted in the flower border. Big soft craters in the freshly turned soil.

Ben was too far up to make a big soft crater.

He was going to break his back.

Michelle snatched the discarded tarpaulins next to the coiled rope and yanked them under the track. They formed a big, untidy heap like a deflated bouncy castle. Ben hit the castle and didn't bounce. The trapped air puffed out the sides and took some of the impact. The flower border took the rest.

She wrestled her way through the tarpaulin, trying to uncover the crumpled figure among the thorns. Ben wasn't moving. She wrestled some more until she got him untangled, then his eyes flew open and he puffed out an explosive breath.

"Fucking Jesus fucking Jesus fucking Christ."

The words ran into one another, and he patted himself down. Michelle was still in shock, so she did what her training taught her to do. When in a life-threatening situation, calm your breathing, relax your muscles, and treat it as if it wasn't a life-threatening situation. Her way of doing that was to make light of it.

"That's two hotels and two flower borders."

Ben found his voice once he knew there were no broken bones. "Let's not do that again."

Michelle helped him to his feet. "Now we're down, what's the rest of your plan?"

"Now we make our getaway."

Michelle scanned the car park. "Where's the car?"

Ben stretched the kinks out of his body, and flexed his neck. "We're not using the car."

Chapter Seventy-Eight

THE BOAT THAT Julio Sagrada had hired was in the second berth along on the rental jetty. The pontoon was one of five that stretched into the marina from the northern walkway, and was sheltered by the seawall all the way to the exit channel. The twin lighthouses on either side of the channel were painted red and green, red on the right looking out and green on the left, but the lights weren't turned on during daylight.

Ben fished the keys from his pocket as they came out of the footpath between the two plots of spare land. One plot had the little red car, and the other wasn't spare at all. The hotel was a hive of noise and activity, with emergency lights flashing all along the frontage. Ben ignored the hotel and guided Michelle towards the jetty.

"They aren't going to look for us in the middle of a powerboat race."

The air horn sounded, and the third heat started beyond the sea wall.

Michelle disagreed. "They're going to look for us until the end of time."

Ben counted the berths along the rental pontoon and stopped at number two. The thirty-foot Bayliner 285 was powered by a Mercruiser 350 V8, and had a scuba deck at the stern and a flying bridge above the main cockpit. Ben remembered that from the promotional info, but what stood out was the personalised artwork on the transom. It suggested the boat was used for pleasure over fishing.

Captain 4 PLAY
Live Love Laugh

He pointed at the stern rail. "This is us."

Michelle snorted a laugh. "It's like being back at Laguna Park."

"I was the tennis pro and lifeguard."

"You were a thief and a gigolo."

"Reluctant gigolo."

She squeezed his hand. "That's what I liked about you."

The Bayliner was moored stern in to the jetty. Ben stepped onto the scuba deck and helped Michelle aboard. The boat bounced and swayed under their weight, sending a school of brightly coloured fish dashing for cover. Ben opened the gate in the transom and let Michelle through first. She had to squeeze between four drums of marine fuel strapped to the stern rail. Enough petrol to see them all the way up the coast if they needed to go that far.

Ben tucked the bag between the petrol drums so it wouldn't fall overboard, but kept the phone in his pocket. He'd never driven a motorboat before, so he held the keys out to Michelle. She shook her head.

"It was all sand and cactus in Mexico."

Ben took a deep breath and examined the control panel. "Okay. Let's have a look. How hard can it be?"

* * *

GIUSEPPE BATTISTI LISTENED to the explosions and the sirens and glanced at the hotel. That was the signal. The Polizia di Narcotici would be breaching the penthouse suite soon, but that wasn't his concern. The runaway bride and her thief would be coming this way. It was Battisti's turn now. He took a portable sign out of his bag and stood it at the end of the walkway. It said,

EMERGENCY REPAIRS
WORKS ACCESS ONLY

in English, French, and Italian. He reckoned the Germans and Spanish must have to fend for themselves. He stepped over the barrier and walked to the red lighthouse, slipping the sniper's rifle out of its case as he went. He had already scouted the location and knew the best position to take his shot.

Kneeling behind the lighthouse, he attended to his weapon. Without knowing he was doing it he began to whistle, *Always Look On The Bright Side Of Life*. The tune was the same in Italian and English.

* * *

PABLO CORDERO BELEN watched his daughter climb aboard a motorboat in the marina and felt a wave of sadness, and yes, not a little guilt. If he had been a better father, it might not have come to this. That was a strange thing to be thinking as his world went up in flames, and the merger that was supposed to cement his family's future went down the toilet, but he always knew that, at the point of death, it was his daughter he would be thinking of. This felt like the point of death.

He rattled the handcuff to shift into a better position and sat forward in the garden chair. The boat bounced and swayed as the boyfriend moved under the flying bridge with the keys in his hand. Michelle stood between four drums of marine fuel at the stern rail. In the distance, a figure disappeared behind the red lighthouse at the mouth of the exit channel.

Yes, Cordero Belen felt a twinge of guilt.

Then the police burst in, and he had other things on his mind.

* * *

BEN CHECKED THE controls while Michelle untied the stern line. She coiled the rope and dropped it on the aft deck. The control panel was similar to a car's, but with the buttons and switches in different positions. There was an ignition key, a throttle and a steering wheel. The dials he could ignore, and he wasn't going to be sailing by compass, he was going to follow his nose.

He turned the key and pressed the starter button. The motor roared into life, the deep throaty rumble vibrating through the deck. He remembered the twin-engine cruiser reversing into its berth in Cabopino, just before Michelle nearly ran him over with a taxi. They had come a long way since Cabopino.

He gripped the throttle and eased it forward. The tone of the engine changed, and the boat began to move. Inches at a time, then feet as it edged out of the second berth along the rental jetty. He turned the wheel, and the boat swung slowly to the right. He didn't know which was port and starboard. There was a slight delay from turning the wheel to the boat following instructions. He made a note of that for any other manoeuvres. This wasn't like turning a car; there was no immediate payoff to the controls. He felt a swell of pride as he edged into the channel and turned towards the exit.

Michelle came and stood beside him, and they looked like any other couple setting off on a boat trip. She slipped an arm around his waist and rested her head on his shoulder. Ben kept both hands on the wheel; he wasn't that confident yet. The boat kept to the middle of the channel, and he only moved to the right when he saw another boat coming in the opposite direction. There were obviously protocols about which side of the road to drive on. He was getting the hang of this.

The Bayliner cruised past the third pontoon and then the fourth. After the fifth, it was a straight run until the curve of the seawall created a bend towards the red lighthouse at the mouth of the channel. Ben eased off the throttle and let the boat idle while still keeping steerageway. He put one arm around Michelle's waist and turned to face her.

"Do you believe in happy ever after?"

Michelle put both arms around him, keeping loose control.

"I believe some people's ever afters are shorter than others."

Seagulls screeched in the quiet between races. The sun glinted off the clear blue waters of the marina. Fish darted about beneath the surface, avoiding the anglers that were fishing off the seawall. Masts bobbed and swayed at the yacht club while tourists had cold drinks at the café bar. Ben leaned forward and kissed Michelle on the forehead.

"Well, if my ever after ended right now, I'd take it."

He steered one-handed and followed the channel out between both lighthouses. The boat rose and fell as it took the swell of the open sea. The powerboats were still gathered to the right, waiting for the next race. Michelle leaned in and gave Ben a proper kiss, holding him tight in a final embrace. She stepped back and raised an eyebrow at his questioning look.

"Just in case this all goes wrong."

She kissed him again. Then it all went wrong.

Chapter Seventy-Nine

THE FIRST SHOT splintered the Perspex canopy of the flying bridge. High and wide. Not taking account for the rise and fall of the ocean swell. The second punched a hole in the side of the Bayliner, and Ben felt a spark of excitement and panic. This was actually happening. The end was nigh.

He opened up the throttle, and the boat surged forward, levelling out and taking a straighter line. More power helped the boat cut through the waves. He glanced over his shoulder and saw the figure kneeling beside the red lighthouse. It was the second time he'd had a rifle pointed at him. He didn't want it to be the second time he got shot.

More power and a slight right turn. The Bayliner headed straight out to sea, showing its wide flat arse to the man with the gun.

* * *

BATTISTI STOPPED WHISTLING and squeezed the trigger. Slow and easy. A soft intake of breath, hold it, fire, then breathe out. He did the same again, holding his breath for each shot, to give a steady platform for his aim. The first shot was high and wide, splintering the Perspex on the flying bridge. The second was more of a broadside shot and punched a hole in the hull above the waterline. Tracking the Bayliner as it passed the red lighthouse was like shooting fish in a barrel, or hitting a barn door at five paces. He couldn't miss.

Then, the boat made a course adjustment and throttled up. The Bayliner settled in the water, knifing through the swell, and headed towards the flotilla of powerboats waiting to join the starting line. The most direct route out to sea. Horns blared their warning. The flotilla splintered and boats did crazy loops to avoid a collision. The Bayliner surged ahead, showing its stern to the sniper. Battisti could just make out the signage on the transom.

Captain *4 PLAY*
Live Love Laugh

He smiled at Julio Sagrada's sense of humour, the runaway gigolo, and the love boat, but what he was mainly smiling at was the wide flat arse of the Bayliner. The stern rail glinted in the afternoon sun, underlining the four squat barrels of marine fuel strapped to the transom.

He lined up his shot. The last fish in the barrel.

* * *

HANDS WAVED, AND racers shouted, but all they could do was get out of the way. Engines roared as the powerboats pulled sharp turns to avoid a collision. Ben aimed for the middle of the flotilla, and the flotilla miraculously disappeared. There was only one boat left, riding gently to its sea anchor, so Ben eased left to miss it by twenty feet.

Michelle turned to see where the shots were coming from, one arm firmly around Ben's waist. She gave him one last squeeze, then she froze. Ben glanced over his shoulder to see what she was looking at, then he squeezed her back.

The stern flag whipped and fluttered in the rush of air, lining up perfectly with the firing position beside the red lighthouse. Beneath the flag, he could see the four drums of marine fuel strapped to the transom and nestled between them the sports bag that Giuseppe Battisti had given him behind the old Post Office in Pisa. The Polizia di Narcotici was currently seizing the drugs, but the final block of plastic explosives was still in the bag. The number Ben hadn't called.

* * *

BATTISTI TRAILED THE boat just long enough, then fired. The bullet punched a hole in the second petrol drum from the left but only produced a leak. He fired again. Same result. Marine fuel spilled over the transom and flooded the aft deck. All the powerboats were clear now. The Bayliner kept a straight line for freedom, leaving turmoil in its wake. For a brief moment, the Italian thought he heard the shrill tone of a telephone ringing and nodded.

"Happy never after, English."

He took a deep breath.

Held it.

Then, fired again.

The love boat exploded in a ball of flame that ripped the hull apart. Shrapnel peppered the waves, and the flying bridge was blown skyward. The stern flag came off its moorings and caught the thermals like a wayward parachute. Thousands of banknotes were blasted into the air, burning like fireflies in the afternoon sun. Millions of euros. Getaway money with no getaway.

The fireflies continued to flutter and burn as the Bayliner sank amid a spreading oil slick. Cushions and wreckage dotted the surface. The powerboats circled the wreckage, performing search and rescue, but there was no one to rescue.

V

NEVER AFTER

Chapter Eighty

THE FAMILY WERE wheeling their suitcases from the hotel reception when the father was overcome by a sense of déjà vu; only the déjà vu was him wheeling the suitcases downhill at Laguna Park. His daughter had made a break for it, and he'd reached out to grab her sleeve. "Hold up there, little pony." He always used to call her Little Pony. One of the suitcases broke free and picked up speed down the slope. The father had seen disaster. The son saw "Lightning McQueen."

That was a year ago. This year, there was no slope and no runaway suitcase. His daughter was a year older, and his son had moved on from Lightning McQueen. It was still sunny and it was still hot, but that was all that the south coast of Tenerife had in common with mainland Spain. Costa del Silencio was a quiet, flat urbanization with more retirement facilities than hotels, but Hotel Pedrosa was a new build and had obviously cost the owner a lot of money.

The father considered it money well spent and had no qualms about booking with a first-time hotel owner. To be honest, he had been considering booking a holiday in Marina di Pisa, but all that stuff in the news last year had put him off Italy. Who would have thought that a Mexican drug cartel would have been brought down in a hotel owned by a Spanish cement mogul? Not to mention the money laundering for the drug trade in Spain and the runaway couple who had been killed when their boat exploded at a powerboat race. Gunshots from the harbour? Explosions at the hotel? No, Costa del Silencio sounded like a much quieter proposition.

He paused halfway from the reception and checked his keys. The main hotel had executive suites, but the family rooms were bungalows dotted around the grounds. The central walkway gave access to half a dozen hacienda-style adobe buildings with red-tiled roofs and orange walls. Each bungalow had its own pool and a secluded patio. He found the number, and had to backtrack to the bungalow they had just passed. "Okay, kids. No fighting over the bedrooms."

* * *

THE OWNER WATCHED the family backtrack to Hacienda El Numero Cuatro and couldn't help smiling. It made him feel happy to see the guests enjoying themselves. It made him feel safe. Building Hotel Pedrosa hadn't been so much about financial investment as building a future for him and his wife. Seeing a family that was already a few years down that road gave him hope for his own future. And the woman he loved.

There was a flurry of activity as the father struggled with his keys. Leaving the suitcases unattended, he tried to find the right key for the front door. The gentle slope of the tiled patio was designed to let rain flow into the pool, but it had a similar effect on the modern suitcase. The rolling luggage did what *it* was designed to do. It rolled. Towards the pool.

The owner was about to shout a warning but held himself back. He had promised his wife that he wouldn't get involved with other people's problems anymore. He kept quiet and let the father sort it out for himself.

* * *

LIGHTNING MCQUEEN CAUGHT the suitcase in time, showing a burst of speed that surprised his father. Little Pony giggled. She giggled a lot during stressful situations. Their mother remained calm as always and took the keys from her husband. Once she was inside, she slid open the patio door and helped with the luggage.

"That's my room."

"No, it's mine."

"It's neither of yours until I say so." Proving that mother's law ruled.

She checked the three-bedroom bungalow and allocated rooms, the back right for Lightning McQueen and the back left for Little Pony, leaving the master bedroom with the en-suite bathroom for the parents. Happy ever after, or at least for the duration of the holiday.

While his wife helped the children unpack, the husband threw the flight bag on the settee and unzipped the travel pouch. He took out the clear plastic folder with their passports and travel documents and tore the boarding passes up before dropping them in the waste bin. Then he took out the money.

* * *

THE OWNER STOOD by the pool, intending to offer a helping hand but not wanting to intrude. Taking his wife's advice about not getting involved with other people's problems. He waited to make sure they'd got the luggage in safely, and was about to leave when he had a déjà vu moment of his own.

He saw the husband take a thick envelope out of his flight bag and wedge it under the settee cushions. He recognised the travel money wallet and wondered how much they'd brought with them for the envelope to be so thick. A lot would be his guess. Too much for a week, so they were probably here for two. Even so, that was a lot of money to be carrying around, so the husband was hiding it under the cushion.

The owner couldn't stand by and let that happen. Instead of going back to the walkway, he went to the patio door and pointed at the settee.

"You don't want to keep your money there."

He smiled as he thought about Laguna Park and tapped the sliding door. "Locks aren't very secure."

Then he gave the kind of security advice that Robin Hood might give and left before Michelle could tell him off. Ben was smiling all the way back to reception, thinking about money in hotel safes and the leatherbound notebook he had retrieved at the last moment. You could never have too much insurance.

A Note from the Author

Ideas come from the most random places. This one came from a holiday in Tenerife, where I had to endure a hen party quiz beside the pool. And numerous holidays in Spain, when I walked past the imposing bulk of the Don Carlos hotel and resort. How my mind twisted those holidays into this tale of sex and violence in the sunshine is anybody's guess. Maybe I'm not wired the same as everyone else.

Acknowledgements

There will always be too many people to fit on one page, or in my tiny memory, but here are the few I *can* remember. Shawn Reilly Simmons, the publisher who saw the potential for this book. Donna Bagdasarian, my former agent, who encouraged me to widen my scope from the original UK crime novels. And my dad, for never reading my books because he didn't want to criticize his son. To all of you, a great big hug.

About the Author

Ex Army, retired cop and former Scenes Of Crime Officer.Colin Campbell is the author of British crime novels, *Ruins of Midnight* and *Blue Knight White Cross,* and US thrillers *Jamaica Plain, Final Cut,* and *Shelter Cove*. His Jim Grant thrillers bring a rogue Yorkshire cop to America, and his Vince McNulty novels bring a Yorkshire *ex*-cop to Hollywood. He has also written several children's books about troubled youths seeking redemption. For more info visit www.campbellfiction.com.

AUTHOR WEBSITE:
www.campbellfiction.com

SOCIAL MEDIA HANDLES:
Facebook: https://www.facebook.com/colin.campbell.1336/
Instagram: https://www.instagram.com/campbell.fiction/
YouTube: Colin Campbell Books, Tennis and Cars - https://www.youtube.com/@colincampbellbookstennisca1275

Also by Colin Campbell

Darkwater Towers

Through The Ruins of Midnight

Ballad of the One Legged Man

Gargoyles: Skylights and Roofscapes

Blue Knight White Cross

Jim Grant Series

- *Jamaica Plain*
- *Montecito Heights*
- *Adobe Flats*
- *Snake Pass*
- *Beacon Hill*
- *Shelter Cove*
- *Catawba Point*
- *Permission Granted: Grant and McNulty Stories*
- *Chance Harbour*
- *Operation Snow Queen*

Vince McNulty Series

- *Final Cut*
- *Tracking Shot*
- *Northern Ex*
- *Forced Perspective* (with Jim Grant)
- *Swing Gang*
- *Double Exposure* (with Jim Grant)

YA Books

Silent Flight Holy Night

www.ingramcontent.com/pod-product-compliance
Lightning Source LLC
Chambersburg PA
CBHW020257030826
48979CB00026B/1374/J

* 9 7 8 1 6 8 5 1 2 9 0 1 9 *